ALPHA WOLF
NEED NOT APPLY

TERRY
SPEAR

sourcebooks
casablanca

Published by Sourcebooks Casablanca, an imprint of Sourcebooks, Inc.
P.O. Box 4410, Naperville, Illinois 60567-4410
(630) 961-3900
Fax: (630) 961-2168
www.sourcebooks.com

Printed and bound in Canada.
MBP 10 9 8 7 6 5 4 3 2 1

To the ambassador wolves, Zoerro (timber gray wolf) and Sabine (Arctic wolf), that we were able to pet at Wild Spirit Wolf Sanctuary in New Mexico, and to Rory Zoerb, who brought the wolves to visit, and Leyton Cougar, the sanctuary's director, who help to educate visitors about wolves and wolf-dogs. Thanks for sharing such a truly wondrous experience with us!

Chapter 1

THE FULL SPHERE OF THE MOON AND A SPRINKLING OF STARS lit the sky as Eric Silver ran as a wolf through San Isabel National Forest where he served as a law enforcement park ranger when on duty. The forest was located two hours from Silver Town, Colorado, owned and run by the Silver wolf pack since the town's inception.

He used to don his wolf coat at night when he was off-duty just to enjoy the woods. He found the forest peaceful and rejuvenating as the cool, dry wind whipped the pinyon branches about. Until he'd found ten areas where pot was growing—the scent left by several unknown wolves in each of the areas was too much of a coincidence for him to conclude humans were growing the weed.

Now Eric's nightly wolf excursions had become a dangerous business that could turn deadly in a heartbeat. Pot growers had already murdered a couple of park rangers at other locations. The drug dealers had too much to lose if they got caught at this. But the wolves didn't know a wolf pack was trying to track them down.

Then Eric smelled a whiff of the scent of one of the wolves he was certain was involved in growing the illegal cannabis. His heart pounded as the thrill of the hunt raced through his blood. Finally!

The male wolf loped through the trees dead ahead, unaware that Eric had caught his scent.

Eric and his pack had to catch the bastards running this operation before humans did. This was the first time Eric had been close to one. He couldn't lose the wolf now.

Keeping *lupus garous* secret from humans was paramount.

Neither Eric, nor any of his pack members, had ever expected to be chasing down pot-growing wolves. Humans were no problem. He would just get hold of his human boss, who would contact various law enforcement agencies to take the criminals down.

But Eric couldn't let anyone other than his pack members know about this—*not* when the lawbreakers were wolves. As a wolf, he had no way to call for backup at this point. He'd been out here for six weeks searching for the wolves and not once had he come across any of them. The way things were going with this investigation, it stood to reason tonight would be one of the few nights he hadn't bothered to call for backup because he hadn't needed anyone any of the other times. He'd figured he could manage on his own if he did run across one of the wolves.

The wolf's scent was the same as he'd found at the site of all ten plots of cannabis, and even the scent the wolf gave off now included the smell of cannabis as if he'd brushed up against the plants on a regular basis. Damn the wolf and his partners.

Eric needed to identify who he was. Yet he was in a real quandary.

If the wolf were in human form, Eric could have arrested and incarcerated him in the Silver Town jail. Since the town was wolf-run, they could keep him there safely. But the culprit was in his wolf coat and Eric assumed the wolf wouldn't allow himself to be captured. That was the difficulty. Darien, his cousin and the leader of their pack, would be furious that Eric had gone after the wolf without calling for backup this time, but what could he do now? He couldn't let the wolf get away.

All his senses on high alert, Eric concentrated on the wolf's scent as he continued to run ahead of him. The wolf was confident, not fearful—which meant he didn't yet suspect that anyone was trailing him. Eric glimpsed a tuft of black fur stuck to some of the underbrush, and it smelled like the wolf he was following.

They had reached a goatlike path that led to a secluded patch of marijuana. So far, so good—the wolf still didn't suspect he was being followed. Thankfully, for Eric's well-being, no other wolves seemed to be in the area right now. He knew the only way to take this one in was to injure him in a wolf fight, though he would risk being injured too. And then if Eric wounded him, how would he transport the wolf? He'd have to wing it.

He moved in to take the wolf down but saw movement to his right. Another wolf. Damn. More beige than gray, the wolf had been hiding in the brush. Hell, one gray wolf against two big gray males? Darien would kill Eric for getting himself into this bind—if he lived through it. He didn't have a choice now. Kill or be killed.

Eric whipped around before the wolf hiding in the bush had a chance to attack. He dove for the wolf's right foreleg, hoping to subdue this one before he had to deal with the other wolf. The wolf wasn't prepared for Eric's quick assault, and with two hard chomps in quick succession, Eric brought him down. The wolf yipped and growled, backing away from Eric on three legs, while favoring his injured one.

At that, Eric swung around to face the wolf he'd been following. The wolf had finally seen Eric and had tried to sneak up on him silently, like a wolf on a hunt. Eric was certain he couldn't attack this wolf in the same way and get away with it, so growling ferociously, he feinted going for his foreleg, then swung around and bit into the wolf's hind leg. With a snap, he broke it and the wolf yipped in pain.

Neither wolf was totally disabled, which was the problem with just breaking their legs. Eric knew of a wolf—a real wolf—that had lost a leg in a trap. She continued to have pups, and when she lost her mate, she began attacking sheep to provide for her young. Luckily, the sheep owner humanely caught her and took her to a wolf sanctuary where she and her pups were cared for. But she proved that a wolf could survive on three legs. Which meant these wolves were still dangerous.

Both of the wolves eyed him, growling low, their heads lowered, their tails tucked between their legs, which made him suspect they were beta wolves. One lifted his chin to howl as if he finally realized he'd better do something or be in even worse trouble. Eric knew he was about to call his pack for help. And then Eric would really be a dead wolf. He leaped and tore into the wolf, biting him in the throat just as he felt the black wolf tackle his back. The wolf at his back couldn't get a good hold of Eric because of his broken leg, thank God.

Once Eric had taken out the first wolf, he twisted around to deal with the black wolf. The wolf snapped his jaws at him, lunging forward, yipping in pain. He tried to kill Eric with every ounce of strength he possessed. Eric fought him, biting and growling. Still, the wolf managed a lucky bite to Eric's flank and then lifted his snout to howl.

Hell. His heart racing, furious with the damn wolves for doing something illegal and putting all their kind at risk, Eric tore into the wolf. He only wanted to take him in. He didn't want to have to kill him. But when he heard another wolf coming, Eric finished the injured black wolf off and raced back down the mountain. The newcomer would have to deal with his dead pack members. Eric could have fought this wolf, but not a whole pack if even more of them were in the vicinity.

Even now, he was at risk of running into them. His heart drumming and his flank burning from the bite, he tried to ignore it and ran full out as if a whole pack of wolves was on his tail. With the enhanced healing abilities of the *lupus garou*, he would recover sooner than if he were just human, but the process could still take some time, depending on how bad his injury was.

Eric reached his truck and shifted, the transformation warming his muscles and bones, though his wound burned even more. The shift was instantaneous and he quickly unlocked his door using the code, grabbed his medical bag, and fumbled around inside it for the antiseptic. After wiping the wound down, he bandaged the injury. It wasn't too deep, thankfully. He was hurrying to pull on his clothes when he heard a wolf yip about a half a mile away, in a different direction than where he'd just been.

His need to protect kicked in, yet the new wolf could very well be from the same pack that was growing pot.

What were the odds that members of two *lupus garou* packs besides his were here in the park?

He grabbed his medical pack and headed out at a run, calling CJ, his deputy sheriff brother, at the same time. "Killed two of the wolves involved in the drug operation. Left when a third was on its way. Now I'm investigating a wolf injury." He gave coordinates for the drug site.

"Wait for me to get there. I'm calling it in to Darien and the sheriff, but I'm on my way."

"Can't wait, little brother. I'll be cautious."

"All right. I'll let everyone know what's going on."

Ending the call, Eric approached the area, careful to stay downwind. When he was close enough to see what the problem was without the wolf seeing him, he witnessed five wolves hovering over an injured she-wolf. She was lying on her side near the base of a cliff where evidence of a recent rock slide littered the area. By the way the other wolves were reassuring the injured wolf, Eric assumed they were *lupus garous*, which surprised the hell out of him. He'd never seen any in the park before his run-in with the other wolves earlier today. But considering the size of the national park, that was understandable. Their scents assured him that none of these wolves had been near the cannabis plants he'd already located. Although they could still be members of the same pack and involved with the operation in other ways.

He slowly walked out of the cover of the trees toward the rocky cliff, hands raised to show he wasn't going to shoot them, wanting them to know he was there to help the injured wolf. "I'm a *lupus garou* like you." Since he was off-duty and no longer wearing his uniform, he filled them in on the rest. "I'm a law enforcement park ranger. My name is Eric Silver. I can take the she-wolf in my truck to the clinic in Silver Town, two hours south of here. The town is all wolf-run."

Two of the wolves snarled and growled at him, but they didn't draw closer. He assumed they were betas, trying to figure out what to do. They couldn't take care of the wolf themselves, not as wolves. And running around in the woods as naked humans carrying an injured wolf was going to require a lot of explaining if they ran into anyone else.

The injured wolf was still lying on her side. She tried to sit up and yipped, lying back down.

"Just lie still," Eric said, motioning for her to stay put, his voice gentle and reassuring.

He needed to get closer so he could examine her, but he was cautious about the wolves who were threatening him. Even beta wolves could tear a person apart, so he needed permission to draw closer. Though they probably wouldn't hurt him, he couldn't risk injury by ignoring the threat.

When they wouldn't back down, he tried again to convince them he only wanted to help. "I can carry her to my truck, only a mile from here. Some of you can come with me so you know I'm serious about getting help for her."

They continued to snarl at him, protecting her, but Eric wouldn't back off either. He wasn't leaving until someone took care of her.

Then one of the men shifted. He was maybe in his forties, with black hair and hard amber eyes. "We don't need your help." Even so, the man was obviously in a quandary.

Eric took the wolf's shifting as a good sign. Not of friendship, but the wolf would have remained a wolf if he had felt threatened, especially since he appeared to be in charge. He would have led the wolves to attack Eric then, if he was going to do it.

At that point, Eric slowly drew closer to the injured wolf. Then he crouched to examine her, hoping they would finally let him help.

When he touched her right hind leg, she yipped. "Okay, girl, I'll be gentle. I just need to check to see if it's broken or something else." He carefully ran his hand over her leg, and she pulled it away from his touch.

"Is it broken?" the man asked, sounding worried.

"I don't feel any break, but it's obviously tender. It could be a bruised tendon, torn ligament, or even a hairline fracture of the bone."

"She can't walk on it. We're parked about five miles out."

Eric said again, "I'm parked only a mile from here on one of the official-use-only trails. I can carry her to my—"

"No. We don't need your help. We'll take care of it."

"But—"

"I *said* we'd take care of her."

Eric raised his hands in a sign of truce, but he wasn't leaving until he saw that they could provide her with the care she needed. "How are you going to do it? I'm trained in first aid. I can call others from my pack to help get her out of here, or I'll carry her to your vehicle." As much as Eric hated offering, he'd carry her the five miles to their vehicle if that was the only way they'd go for it.

"All right. You can carry her to our campsite then."

Eric let out his breath in exasperation. Every mile he moved her would cause the poor wolf more pain.

The man in charge had already shifted back into his wolf form. He and the other males were watching for signs of anyone else approaching, while the one female stood by the injured she-wolf, looking concerned. Eric made a makeshift splint, and as soon as he bound the injured she-wolf's leg, she whimpered. He hated that she was in pain and wished he could give her something for it. As gently as he could, he lifted her in his arms. This was going to be the longest hike he'd ever made. He wished the wolf in charge had listened to reason.

As a wolf, this would have been no problem, even though he was feeling some pain of his own. But as a human carrying an injured wolf, the trek was all the more difficult. He stumbled over too many exposed roots to count because he couldn't see the path, making the she-wolf whimper or yip in pain. He fought groaning himself a time or two.

Eric loved the wide open spaces in the park, the seventy-degree temps during the day, and fifty-degree temps during the night—even though in the summer things became rather hectic with all the visitors. He would never have expected to be dealing with this much wolf trouble in one night though, when he'd never seen any other packs in the area before.

When they drew closer to a creek, he heard feminine laughter. Despite how chilly it was, the women were splashing around, which intrigued him, although he was worried they might see him carrying a wolf, surrounded by other wolves. Then one of the wolves in the lead ran off. Eric blended in with the lodgepole pines, oaks, and shadows so the women wouldn't see him unless the wolf forced him to go to the rocky bank.

Which he did.

When Eric drew near enough, he saw five women in goddess-like semi-sheer dresses. He knew he had to be dreaming. Their silky pastel creations—in blues and pinks and mint green—fluttered about the women in the summer breeze. They were standing in the water up to their calves. Above them, the creek water was mostly gentle with a few small rapids. Down here, the rapids were much more common and significant, creating warmer pockets of water. The women were laughing and talking. A petite brunette with short, curly hair really caught his eye. She was wearing a robin's-egg-blue dress, the water sensuously plastering the bottom half of the gown to her calves and thighs.

Another woman with her back to him had long, brown hair and a mint-green dress. She moved deeper into the water, which effectively blocked his view of the woman in the blue dress.

The area was great for fishing, and he was mesmerized by the woman in blue, thinking what a delicious catch *she'd* make.

"You know, Pepper," a blonde said to the woman in the blue dress, her voice darkening, "he wants you for his mate."

Eric straightened a bit. No one used the term "mate" except *lupus garous*. He couldn't smell the women's scents from where he was, nor could they smell his. He would have to cross the creek upwind of them to learn if they were really wolves. But he suspected the woman he was carrying must be a member of the same wolf pack as these women. Why else would the wolf lead him in this direction?

The male wolf suddenly detoured, and Eric was taken away from the creek and back into the woods on a path that led straight to a small cabin. A few more people were there, warily watching him. So the pack was camping here, not just visiting for a few hours. As many of them as there were—he'd seen about fifteen—they must have rented a couple of cabins.

To reach these more isolated cabins, the pack would have had to hike in on foot. No parking was allowed next to the cabins, so no vehicles were in the area. That was another reason why he would have preferred to take her to his vehicle so he could drive her to see Dr. Weber in Silver Town.

The door opened for him, and a man stepped aside so Eric could carry the wolf inside. The wolf in charge ran into a room, then came out wearing a pair of jeans. "I'll take it from here," he said. "Just lay her down on the sofa."

"Is your pack from around here? Our town is only two hours south," Eric reminded the man, hoping he would listen to reason. If the pack didn't have its own doctor, Dr. Weber would welcome the chance to take care of the injured wolf.

"We'll take it from here," a woman added, and Eric swung around to see the brunette with the short, curly hair from the creek—Pepper, the other woman had called her. The other women were with her and some of the male wolves were at her side, as if guarding her. "Thank you for bringing Susan here."

She was even more enchanting up close, and his image of her as a goddess remained the same. He wanted to make an impression on the beautiful she-wolf standing before him, who was obviously in charge and not the least bit hesitant. She was an alpha, and he was in love. It was the first time since he'd lost his mate that he'd felt any interest in another she-wolf.

Eric bowed his head a little to her. "I'm Eric Silver, a park ranger, and I'm with the Silver Town pack. I was telling this gentleman we have a wolf doctor in town if you don't have one of your own who can see to her."

"We're fine, thank you. We'll take care of her."

Did that mean they had someone in the pack with some medical training, maybe a nurse or an emergency med tech? Most packs did, but not many that he knew had actual physicians.

Eric turned and said to the injured wolf, "Take care, young lady. I hope you heal up soon." Then he took one last, long look at the she-wolf in charge and inclined his head again before taking his leave.

The whole way back to his truck, he couldn't stop thinking about Pepper. Was she running the pack? Or was she just a sub-leader when the pack leader wasn't around? Either might be the case, since she had made the decisions once she arrived, rather than the male who had led Eric there. She didn't seem interested in mating the other male, who was clearly interested in her. Which would be good if Eric met up with her again.

Then his law enforcement training kicked in. What if the woman didn't want him to take care of her pack member because they were involved in the illegal activities in the park? Perhaps she didn't want anything to do with anyone in law enforcement, particularly when that someone was also a wolf and could smell things that humans couldn't.

Hell, he hated when his law enforcement training took control. He really wanted to listen to his wolfish side on this one. Damn it.

When he reached his truck, he tossed his medical pack inside, stripped off his clothes, and looked at the bloody bandage on his waist for a second before yanking it off. Stinging and a roaring ache accompanied every movement, but he bit back the pain. Then he locked up his truck and shifted.

If the wolves had been foraging for new places to take cannabis plants, he wouldn't smell anything in the camp. But he hadn't smelled all the wolves who were there either. He couldn't clear them for certain by checking out the campsite, but if the campsite was clean, the possibility of another pack's involvement in the illegal operations would seem more viable.

He raced back along the path, and when he finally reached the area near the cabin, he slipped around to where he could see it from a distance. They were packing up. *Good.* The campsite would be cleared out, so he could sniff around to his heart's content.

He remained silent. No one would be able to smell his scent unless they ventured in his direction. He watched the pack members as they all hoisted packs and began to move the injured lady. Their movements were quiet but complementary, as if they'd been together as a pack forever.

A few of them were taking off down a trail leading away from him when Eric saw a flash of gray and beige fur in the woods off to his right. Before he could react, the large, male gray wolf lunged from the trees and attacked him. Why would they need to post a guard?

"Ohmigod," one of the women said as the attacking wolf growled and snarled.

Adrenaline pouring through his veins, Eric shot around to defend himself against the male wolf's vicious attack.

Eric didn't know if the pack continued to move away or if they were monitoring the situation, but he couldn't understand why the male wolf would attack him. Unless they were doing something illegal. Or maybe this wolf didn't know Eric was the same man who had carried the injured wolf to the cabin. Unless he'd seen him before as a wolf or could smell he was the same man who had helped the pack, he could be anyone. Even a wild wolf.

The hostile wolf was aggressive, alpha, not like any of the beta wolves Eric had met in the pack. Eric snarled and bit at him, telling him to back off. Since Eric hadn't met this wolf, he wondered where the wolf had been all this time. If he was the pack leader, he should have been helping the injured wolf long before this.

Eric intended to take off, his stance firm as he eyed the snarling wolf, who now stood still, half listening to the people clearing out of the cabin, half concentrating on Eric. But Eric didn't dare turn his back on the wolf just yet.

He didn't take a step forward to dominate the space, instead waiting for the wolf to give up and take off with his pack mates. When the wolf didn't, which was real alpha posturing, Eric had a choice: run off and leave the wolf's territory, or wait until the pack was far enough away that the wolf felt the need to keep up with them to protect them. Without proof the wolf was involved in anything illegal, Eric didn't want to take him down. Protecting his pack would be a natural instinct for the wolf, one Eric could understand.

The wolf took a few steps back and turned as if to go, making Eric assume that the wolf wanted to rejoin his pack. Eric turned slightly to race off toward his truck, with every intention of returning when all the wolves were gone so he could conduct his investigation. But then the wolf swung around and lunged at him, biting Eric in the shoulder.

Hell and damnation!

Sharp pain racked his shoulder, and he could swear it raced straight down to set the nerves on fire in the wound to his flank. Eric pivoted and clashed with the wolf. Snarling and growling, he matched the alpha's anger, the pain of his wounds fading as their teeth clashed.

Eric didn't want to kill the wolf and upset the pack when he was damned interested in the she-wolf named Pepper. Even so, he wanted to prove he wasn't about to be bullied by another wolf. *Any* wolf. He'd had his fair share of wolf fights over the years, and he never backed down from a fight another wolf started.

Rather than tearing into the wolf and killing him for the unprovoked attack, Eric ran off, his tail straight out behind, not tucked between his legs. It was a wolf way of saying he wasn't afraid in the least, but he wasn't going to fight.

The wolf doggedly tracked him, despite Eric's lead of several hundred feet, until Eric heard another wolf growling and snarling at his attacker. Eric figured the other wolf was warning the alpha that the wolf he was chasing had just helped them out, and he didn't want him fighting Eric. Or maybe they were afraid Eric would get suspicious of their activities because one of them had attacked him.

Then the woods grew quiet. Eric assumed the guard wolf and the other wolf had caught up to their people.

His shoulder and flank still burning where the wolves had bitten him, Eric finally stopped and listened to the breeze rustling the tree limbs and the crickets chirping. He heard an owl hooting in a tree several hundred feet away.

Despite how much he hurt, the woman in the blue gown—Pepper—fascinated him. He was dying to know more about the mystery wolf pack and this woman who had pinned him with a look that said she was in charge and he'd better mind. She could challenge him any day. He couldn't help but love it. Then he wondered if the wolf who had attacked him was the one who wanted to mate her.

Ah, hell, that would be his luck. He wasn't into stealing another wolf's potential mate—at least not normally.

Still, he was dying to check out the wolf smells at the campsite. But he had to take care of his injuries first.

When he reached his truck, he shifted, got his clothes out, and quickly threw on his briefs, jeans, socks, and boots.

Tomorrow early, he'd go back to the campsite.

Then he pulled out his medical pack, reapplied a bandage to his waist, and did the best he could to bandage the shoulder wound. He pulled on his shirt just to keep blood off his seat, climbed into the truck, and drove to Silver Town to see Dr. Weber.

Eric would never have thought he'd be the one injured when he only meant to help a wolf in need. Now *he* would have to see Dr. Weber about his *own* injury instead. He was about to call CJ with an update when the truck's digital screen lit up with an incoming call. It was his brother Sarandon, and Eric knew he'd have to tell him what had happened, even though he'd rather not mention the second wolf fight to anyone. His own pack would be furious that he was attacked while helping another wolf pack.

Chapter 2

PEPPER GRAYLING COULDN'T BELIEVE IT WHEN SHE HEARD two wolves fighting in the woods. She'd caught a glimpse of both male wolves, the snarling, big tan and gray that bit at Waldron Mason, and Waldron himself, a beige wolf with a white front and a smattering of gray hairs. The mystery wolf had snapped at Waldron before he raced off. The way he didn't tuck tail meant he wasn't cowed by the aggressor. And that had intrigued her.

She was furious that Waldron was pulling her away from her own pack to deal with him when she wanted to ensure Susan was properly cared for. As quickly as she was able, she stripped off her clothes, shifted, and ran like the devil to chase Waldron down. Whoever the other wolf had been, he had posed no threat to them. When she ran after the two wolves, she smelled their scents. The mystery wolf was indeed Eric Silver. No way would she want Waldron to hurt Eric after he'd helped Susan!

She was so angry, she could have killed Waldron for his unwarranted actions.

When she spied Waldron still chasing after Eric, she tore into him, growling and snapping to let him know just how angry he'd made her. He whipped around as if to attack, then recognized her and realized that by attacking, he'd lose any chance of courting and mating her—not that he had any—so he backed off. From his narrow-eyed, harsh gaze, she could tell he was irritated to the max with her. If he could have, he would have continued to hunt the other wolf down and finished him off. She worried about Eric—she smelled his blood on Waldron. How badly had Waldron hurt him?

But she knew Eric had been injured even before this because she'd smelled both an antiseptic and blood on him when she first met him.

She listened but didn't hear any sign of Eric. Growling at Waldron again, she turned and ran off. She continued to pay attention to the sounds around her, making sure he wasn't following her back to their campsite. She didn't want to have to say a word to him about any of this when she reached camp. All she wanted to do was see that her cousin Susan was taken care of.

When she didn't hear Waldron following her, she wondered if he had gone back after Eric.

As for Eric, she already had trouble with one alpha male wanting to court her. She sure didn't need a second one bugging her, if Eric had any such notion. Still, she felt bad that Waldron had attacked him, and she really hoped he wasn't hurt too seriously.

Later that night, after a doctor had x-rayed Susan's leg and found a hairline fracture, Susan and Pepper settled on the couches at Pepper's home in the woods for a late-night glass of wine and chips. Susan had her wrapped leg propped up on Pepper's coffee table to help reduce the swelling.

"You should have played in the creek with us instead running off and starting a rock slide," Pepper said, unable to let go of her annoyance with Waldron. "It would have been safer that way." Had Waldron been watching the women playing in the creek before he attacked Eric? Most likely. She was certain Waldron wouldn't have been spying on the rest of the pack.

She still couldn't believe that Eric Silver had stood up to her about taking Susan to see his own pack's doctor. The challenge in his expression had said he didn't agree with her and that he wanted to do things his way. She didn't know anything about Eric's pack, and she had no intention of relying on a doctor she didn't know. She and her pack might not have a wolf doctor, but they trusted the human ones they saw. Not that their doctors knew anything about the *lupus garous*.

She still could envision Eric finally bowing his head in concession, giving in to her ruling.

"Yeah, but then the most handsome of wolves wouldn't have carried me back to the cabin," Susan replied. "I couldn't believe it when Richard told Eric he couldn't take me to see their doctor. Their pack actually has a doctor! Now how cool is that?"

"Cool." Pepper thought it was great, but she didn't want to get involved with another pack. She was surprised another one lived only four hours south of where she and her people lived. Still, since each pack tended to run in its own territory, Pepper could see how they wouldn't have encountered each other before.

Susan snorted. "You wouldn't know a hot wolf if he knocked you down and licked you all over." She smiled. "Now that gives me some interesting ideas. Let's see." She lifted her phone off the table.

Pepper wondered what she was up to.

"He said his name was Eric Silver, and he's a park

ranger." Susan pulled up an Internet browser. "Yep, here he is. Giving a lecture to a group of senior citizens. With his dark hair and eyes, his height, and that gorgeous smile, he looks like every woman's fantasy." She sighed dreamily. "And," she said in a pointed way, "he's all smiles with the gray-haired women and men, so he wasn't putting on a show just for you."

"He *wasn't* putting on a show for me. He wanted me to do what he said. If he'd wanted to put a show on for me, he wouldn't have suggested taking you to Silver Town."

"He's clearly an alpha wolf, not a beta. And he's a park ranger, so he knows something about taking care of people in the park who are injured." Then Susan frowned. "Ohmigod, you don't think he's the wolf Waldron attacked, do you?"

"Yeah, he was. Though I'm surprised Eric returned to our campsite as a wolf."

"See? He's interested in you. Or, well, maybe he ditched his clothes somewhere nearby and was watching us as a wolf. *Although*"—Susan elongated the word, putting her phone over her heart and looking up at the ceiling—"in *my* fantasy of him, he would be thinking only of me and not of you."

Pepper laughed.

"Did you bite Waldron?" Susan asked. "Richard said you took off after him, and you smelled of blood when you returned. Not your blood. I was in the car by then and missed out on all the action."

"Waldron was chasing him, though I didn't see any sign of Eric. Waldron had bitten him, and I had to do something to get Waldron's attention. He was definitely in hunting mode and determined to catch hold of his prey."

"And kill him?" Susan sounded horrified.

"If he could have gotten hold of him, I'd say that was a good bet." That brought back memories of the alpha who had killed her mate—though her mate had been a beta—and Pepper shuddered.

Susan closed her gaping mouth. Then she set her empty glass on the table. "So, where did you bite Waldron?"

"His tail, the first part of him I reached. I didn't bite too hard, but I still drew some blood."

"Was he pissed off at you?"

"We had a wolf-to-wolf confrontation. Yeah, he was pissed, but I wasn't backing down either, and if he wants me to look at his courting favorably, he has to mind me."

"Oh, wow, I bet that nearly killed him." Susan shook her head, taking another chip from the bowl and biting into it.

"Yeah, he didn't like it. If we'd been mated wolves, I'm certain he would have growled and snapped at me to back off."

"You're not going to, are you? Consider courting him?"

"No way. Look how aggressive he was toward another male wolf who hadn't provoked him in any way. We aren't even courting."

"Agreed. But now, Eric? He's my kind of guy."

Pepper waved a potato chip at her. "You should have given him your number."

"I would have, but I was a wolf. I wish he'd given me his business card."

"He might have. But you were a wolf."

"I should have shifted and given him a big smile and a big thank-you for his help."

Pepper laughed. "You're way too shy to have done that."

"Yeah. I keep telling myself I need to overcome that. I couldn't believe Waldron was watching our pack tonight. Well, and that he tore into the other wolf. He's becoming a real stalker."

Pepper refilled their wineglasses. "He thinks he's protecting his 'property.' But I won't be his mate no matter what."

"Richard said Eric growled and snapped back at Waldron. I've never seen anyone stand up to him. *Besides you.* I wish I'd been there." Susan sighed.

"Eric is a real alpha wolf. I was surprised he didn't stay and fight Waldron to the end." But Pepper was glad for it. She wouldn't have wanted to see Eric hurt further since he'd already been wounded. Even now, she wondered if he was okay.

She didn't want to call and check on him though. She let out her breath on a frustrated sigh.

She hadn't expected to have any trouble on their camping trip into the national forest. She was a forester and used to working with groups on forest management. Many of her pack members worked in some forestry job or another, with Susan supervising their own forest nursery and Christmas tree farm. Some of the pack members worked there or on other tree farms, and some worked on other forestry projects, such as tree removal. But they hadn't had a chance to visit this forest together as a pack in five years or so. It had been a vacation, and before Susan injured herself, they'd been having a blast.

Pepper had a lovely log home for pack meetings, with 250 acres of woods and a covered stone patio for outdoor gatherings. Most of her pack members had log homes of their own situated all over the territory to give them privacy, but close enough together that they could gather as a pack whenever they needed to.

"What if Eric could chase away Waldron permanently?" Susan asked.

"Then what? What if he expected something in return for his help? Our pack? Our land?"

"You? If I were the pack leader, I'd seriously consider it."

"Yeah, well, I'm not interested. We'll continue to deal with Waldron like we have since he moved into the area with his pack two weeks ago."

"I don't think Waldron will get the message without someone taking him to task physically. As alpha as you are, you couldn't beat him as a wolf. Not one-on-one. Not like you took that other wolf down." Susan moved her leg off the table and winced. "I'm going to call it a night. When do you see the Boy Scout troop tomorrow to talk about being a forester?"

"First thing in the morning, and another after that. And I have two sessions after lunch, so I'll be hanging around the area. I'll have someone stop in to feed you while I'm gone." Because Susan was using crutches, she was staying with Pepper for a couple of days. Longer, if she needed to.

"Thanks for putting me up for a couple of nights."

"No problem, Susan. You know I always enjoy your company. If you think of it tomorrow, you could give Eric Silver a call and tell him that you're all right. I'm certain he'd like to know that. While you're at it, you can thank him for the rescue and, if it comes up in the conversation, ask him if he's okay."

Susan smiled broadly at her. "You *are* interested

in him! But I doubt he'd want you to know if he was injured. Macho wolf syndrome, you know."

"Possibly. Unless he wanted to get our sympathy. The doctor said it should take about four weeks for your leg to mend, which means half or less time for us. Just don't put any stress on the leg for now. You don't want to increase the fracture."

"No, that's for sure. It already hurts enough. I hope Pauline can run things until I return to work."

"Pauline will be fine, but I'll run over there to check things out. You don't have to worry about anything. Just rest." Then Pepper raised her brows. "You didn't do this on purpose to get some time off, did you? You know I'd spell you for a while if you needed vacation days."

Susan laughed and hobbled off to bed, saying good night.

Pepper retired to her bedroom, hoping she could figure out how to keep Waldron away from her pack and her lands without having to take more drastic measures. He'd been scent-marking all over her territory and so had some of the males of his pack. She'd taken him to task for it, but what else could she do? They outnumbered her more than two to one, from what he'd said. And she couldn't complain to human law enforcement about Waldron and his men peeing all over her property. She still wouldn't give in to him no matter what. But his actions could be a real problem for the wolf pack if they ignored them.

She tucked herself into bed, thinking about Waldron attacking Eric and drawing blood. She should have told Susan to call her when she learned how Eric was, *if* he was willing to tell her the truth.

—◦◦◦—

His injuries throbbing, Eric answered Sarandon's call while he got on the road to return to Silver Town. "Hey, what's up?" Like Eric, his brother loved the outdoors. He was a guide for anyone who needed one—photographers, nature lovers, hikers, and rock climbers. He loved doing it all.

"Just a heads-up. I might be a little late to the forestry careers talk tomorrow," Sarandon said. "I've got a Lepidopterist Society meeting first thing in the morning so the members can count butterflies and identify different varieties. If we have a big showing, we'll be there a while. So I might have to talk after you do."

"I'll let the Scout leaders know," Eric replied. "I have something to do after I speak, so if I'm not there, just give your lecture and I'll meet you after lunch at the next Boy Scout campground. They'll love hearing what you do."

"I thought you said you had the whole day scheduled to talk to troops."

"I do. We have two other Scout troops to meet in the afternoon, but when everyone's busy with lunch, I have other business to take care of."

"I thought we could get lunch together. We don't often see each other during the duty day."

Eric suspected his brother sensed something was up. He couldn't get anything past Sarandon. His younger brothers, sometimes yes, but not Sarandon. Even though the quadruplet brothers were born only minutes apart, he and Sarandon were the closest to each other, just like Brett and CJ were close.

"Okay, so what are you going to do that's so important?" Sarandon asked.

"Nothing. Just checking out an area on the nearby creek." He wanted to learn more about the pack that had rented the cabin, like where the wolves lived. Which meant checking their reservations. Since he worked for the park, that would be easy to do. He needed to know if they were involved in the illegal cultivation of cannabis.

"For…what?"

Eric couldn't lie to his brother. After the way their father had lied to Eric and his brothers, Eric wouldn't do that to them. But he wasn't about to tell Sarandon he'd seen a fantasy in the forest that he wanted to know more about, and that he wanted to prove to himself in the worst way that Pepper was innocent of any wrongdoing. Pepper was the only name he had to go by. And she was just as hot and spicy as her name. "Just checking it out."

"Okay, well, let me know if you discover anything interesting."

"Will do."

"I bet," Sarandon said, sounding skeptical.

Eric knew he had to get his injuries looked at, and better that Sarandon hear about the fight from him rather than through pack gossip. "A couple of wolves bit me."

"Is it bad? It has to be, or you wouldn't have told me. Do you need me to come get you?"

Sarandon knew not to make a big deal of it.

"Not a problem. And I wouldn't have mentioned it if I hadn't wanted Doc to look at it."

"Hell. It is bad or you wouldn't be seeing Doc."

"Just to be on the safe side."

"How bad—"

"Minor." Though both wounds were still bleeding and hurting like crazy.

"This has to do with the drug wolves."

"One of them, yeah. CJ and the rest of the sheriff's department are checking into it."

"One? What about the other?"

"He was a…guard wolf for another pack, just visiting the park."

"You're going after him tomorrow then?"

"No." Not *that* wolf. The she-wolf.

"Then—"

"I think he was protecting his pack. Anyway, I was just curious where his pack is from." Eric pulled onto the main road going to Silver Town.

"Related to the drug business?"

"I don't believe so." He sure as hell hoped not.

"Any woman you're interested in seeing more of in particular?" Sarandon asked, his tone bordering on amused, but he was also curious. "You wouldn't be interested if there wasn't more to it than that."

"As if it's any of your business, but yeah. There were some women in the pack."

"Hell, Eric." Now Sarandon sounded surprised. Which, given Eric's lack of interest in women for the past two years, was understandable.

"They might be mated." Eric knew Sarandon would assume he was interested in one of the women. He didn't want to tell his brother that her pack, or some of her pack, could be involved in illegally raising cannabis. Not without proof.

Then again, Pepper had been the leader of the group

at the creek, not necessarily a pack leader. The other women had fluttered around her like she was a goddess, everyone attentive to her, and when she entered the cabin, she'd definitely been the one in charge.

"Do you want me to go with you when you check the area out?" Sarandon sounded worried.

"No."

"The wolf who attacked you could be her mate."

"She didn't have one. Apparently some wolf has been wanting to court her though."

"Do you have a name for her?"

"Pepper is all I got."

"All right. Let me know what Doc says about your injuries."

"Sarandon…"

"All right, all right. See you tomorrow if we can get together. Otherwise, I'll talk to you later."

"Sounds good." They ended the call. Despite the fact that Eric's shoulder hurt like crazy, he was trying to see the point of view of the wolf who had bitten him, but he was having a difficult time with it. He called Doc, hating to make this a late-night call, but Dr. Weber always took calls anytime of the day or night. Not that he would be happy about it. Doc wasn't a late-night person.

Still, Eric was damn glad they had a wolf doctor in their pack. Reporting that a wolf had bitten him to a human doctor would be bad news all the way around for wolves, his kind and otherwise. And lying and blaming a dog could cause problems too. Of course, Eric could have called their pack vet, because he didn't mind taking care of anyone any time, but Eric really didn't want to see the vet.

"Hate to be calling you like this," Eric began.

"Another snakebite?" Dr. Weber asked, sounding grouchy.

Eric was still irritated with himself for not spotting a coiled-up rattler only a week ago while he had been out searching for a missing hiker. He'd been wearing heavy-duty, snake-proof boots, but the rattler had struck out at him from a stack of rocks and dug his fangs into Eric's thigh.

"A couple of wolf bites this time. I probably shouldn't even be bothering you with them."

"Wolf bites? While you were in the national park? A regular wolf? Couldn't have been one of our pack. If you're calling me at this hour, it needs to be seen. How long before you get here?"

"Half hour. Yes, I was at the park. No, it wasn't one of our people, and before you ask, it was a *lupus garou*."

"I'll be ready."

"You don't need to tell Darien." Eric knew he would anyway.

"When a wolf bites one of our people, Darien needs to know about it. I take it you didn't provoke the wolf."

"One of them is involved in the drug business. The other bite happened in a different location, and the wolf was just being protective of his pack." Eric didn't want Darien sending out a hunting party to take down the "dangerous" wolf.

"All right. I'll let Darien know."

Fifteen minutes into the drive, Eric got a call. *Darien.* Eric let out his breath and explained about the woman's injury and the subsequent events.

"It's a national park, not a place a *lupus garou* pack

can claim for its own," Darien said angrily after Eric had finished. "And you didn't act aggressively to the wolf or threaten his pack in any way."

"I know, but it's okay."

"I know you, Eric. It's not okay. You're going to try to locate the pack."

"Yes, as a human and in my capacity as park ranger, I am checking on the status of the woman's injury. I won't be running as a wolf. They have to respect the uniform."

Darien didn't say anything. Eric knew Darien didn't want him going alone, not after what had already happened between him and the wolf. Eric *was* concerned about the woman's injury, but he was also bothered by the notion that some wolf was hassling Pepper. Not that she'd appreciate Eric stepping in and chasing off the other wolf if she thought she could handle it herself, but if it worked out well for her, he was certainly willing to help her out.

"I haven't had a chance to check in with CJ. What happened when he and the others investigated the trouble I had up on the cliffs?" Eric asked, not assuming Darien would have gone himself, as busy as he was with pack matters.

"No bodies. No marijuana plants. But all the wolf prints and trace evidence of blood, including your own, were there. The wolf pack had to be close by to clean it up as fast as they did and move out. Eric, you're not to investigate these people on your own any further. You're not immortal."

"I had to take a chance. This is the first time any of us have actually encountered the wolves responsible." Not that it did a whole lot of good, since the wolves were now dead. What if Eric learned Pepper and her pack were involved up to their wolf ears in this shady business?

"Take Sarandon with you," Darien said, breaking into Eric's thoughts. "You said you both were giving talks to Boy Scout troops in the area. Take him with you when you investigate this visiting wolf pack."

Darien was giving a pack-leader order, and Eric didn't like it.

"Eric? I know you're perfectly capable of handling this on your own, but for my peace of mind, will you take him along?"

Eric was surprised that Darien had changed his tune. Normally he wouldn't alter a command making it a request instead—except with his pack-leader mate, Lelandi. No way did he order her around.

"They packed up and left already."

"Okay, but I still want you to take Sarandon."

"Yeah, all right." What else could Eric do? He had gone against Darien's rule on occasion, but not when it might involve another wolf pack and get his own into trouble.

"Let me know what you learn."

"Will do." Eric hadn't wanted the whole pack in on this. Sarandon would keep Eric's injury a secret from their younger brothers, Brett and CJ. But Eric was afraid news would somehow get out that he'd been bitten by a wolf from a neighboring pack and now was trying to track down the pack.

Others in the Silver pack would want to help him. Including his brothers. He really didn't want anyone's help in this. The more who got involved, the more the she-wolf would feel he was being too pushy. He'd been accused of it—well, of being too bossy—when he wanted to help the three new she-wolves in the pack to renovate the Silver Town Hotel. He wasn't one to stand by and not offer advice when he came up with brilliant ideas of his own.

Eric was also worried that if the wolves *were* involved in the drug business, they might get spooked and run off to another park that he didn't have jurisdiction over.

When he arrived at the clinic, Doc Weber let him in, glanced at the blood soaking his shirt, and shook his head.

"Did you call Darien about this?" Doc asked as Eric stripped off his shirt in the exam room. He then removed the bandages Eric had applied.

"I did."

"So how did it happen?"

Eric had to explain all over again.

Doc stopped stitching him up for a moment to consider him, his white brows deeply furrowed. "I'll have to give Darien a medical report."

"Over a couple of lousy stitches?" Eric snorted, wishing he could have pretended nothing was wrong, but because of the location of the second bite, he couldn't have stitched the wound closed himself. Plus antibiotics could help keep the bite from becoming infected. Suturing it would help it heal faster than if he'd just let his enhanced wolf-healing abilities take care of it.

"Twelve on one shoulder, ten on the other. And they're fine stitches, if I do say so myself. I could tell you to take it easy for a couple of days, no running as a wolf, and by the end of the week you should be mostly healed. But I know you won't listen to me."

Eric grabbed his shirt but didn't put it on. With the suturing and the new bandages, he wouldn't bleed on the driver's seat, and he didn't want to wear the bloody shirt.

"Take it easy, and if you need anything for pain…"

"Nothing. Thanks." Eric left the clinic, and when he arrived home, he called Sarandon one last time for the night. He really didn't want to take his brother with him tomorrow, but pack leader orders had to be obeyed. He'd begun washing the blood out of his shirt when Sarandon answered.

"Hey, what did Doc say? You must have already seen him by now."

"Couple of stitches. Why don't you come with me to try to locate the pack tomorrow? I want to check on the woman and see how she's faring."

Sarandon was so quiet, Eric thought he'd lost the connection. "Okay?"

"I know you didn't threaten the women or this wolf, or you would have taken a chunk out of him. You didn't, did you?"

"No. I just left the area."

"If he's a *lupus garou*, he shouldn't have reacted so aggressively unless he was provoked."

"I *didn't* provoke him."

"I know. I'm just saying, it seems odd. He seems to have more at stake here."

"Alpha male pack leader, I suspect. Anyway, no big deal."

"And the woman you're interested in?"

"Yes, she's alpha. At least around the women she was with at the creek, and then later when she met up with me at the cabin."

"You were alone together?"

"No. Give me a break."

"Then the guy was most likely her mate."

"One of the women said a guy wanted to court her but she wasn't interested."

"How many are following *that* wolf then?"

"The one who attacked me was probably with her pack. She might be a sub-leader or just another alpha in the pack. He might be the pack leader or a sub-leader or just another alpha in their pack. We have several alphas in ours. She might have several in hers. And if he's not with her pack, he could be a lone wolf."

"All right. I'm just saying don't get your hopes up. Wait, you've been trying to catch up with the wolves growing pot in the remoter areas of the park. Don't tell me you think this pack has anything to do with it."

"Do you want to come with me or not?" Eric couldn't help being annoyed. He wasn't declaring his interest in courting the she-wolf. Yeah, he found her attractive, and just the fact she was an alpha intrigued him. But she hadn't trusted him enough to let him take her pack member to Dr. Weber. Then again, maybe that was his problem. The need to prove he was trustworthy and not in the least bit bossy. As to the other matter, he wasn't going to say they might be the wolves who planted the weed if they could be innocent.

"Did Doc say you should rest up a bit?" Sarandon asked, abruptly changing the subject as if he knew Eric was about to leave him out of this.

"Yeah, he did. But you know him. He always thinks anyone who has been injured should be in bed for days afterward."

"Of course he does, because he doesn't want to have

to redo his work if the wolf doesn't listen to him and pulls out the stitches. And, hell yeah, I want to go with you. Did you want to ask CJ to come with us? As a deputy sheriff, he would lend a little extra weight."

"No. I don't want to escalate this into something more than a case of reaching out to show friendship."

"All right. I'll make sure the group I'm working with gets an early start counting butterflies so I can make it in time to give my lecture, and then we can see to this other matter at lunchtime."

Chapter 3

ERIC SETTLED INTO BED, BUT HE COULDN'T QUIT THINKING about the she-wolf in charge, the injured woman, and the wolf who had bitten him. He couldn't understand why the pack had been so wary of him.

With the bite wounds still throbbing, he kept replaying the attack scenarios in his mind. If he hadn't moved as quickly as he had, the guard wolf could have crushed his shoulder. And Eric believed he would have done so without hesitation.

He hoped he hadn't scared the pack off so they wouldn't feel safe to return to the park. In the worst way, he wanted to rectify the situation with the pack and let the wolf who had bitten him know there were no hard feelings. He understood the wolf felt compelled to protect the pack, hoping beyond hope they were law-abiding wolves.

He closed his eyes and envisioned the five ladies splashing in the creek, unaware of his presence. Then he imagined seeing the enticing she-wolf's face up close, her eyes narrowed just a hint, her voice pack-leader firm, telling him she and her pack didn't need his help.

He groaned and rolled over on his back. He'd never get to sleep at this rate.

The night faded into nothingness, his mind clearing of everything, and then it came to life again.

*He saw the she-wolf goddess with the short, dark curls
as four women encircled her. This time when he met
her, he'd tell her who he was but also learn who she
was, reassuring her he was one of the good guys. And
she would trust him to do what was right—which was
seek the best help for the injured she-wolf.*

*As soon as he walked into the water, the women
turned to gaze at him, but he only had eyes for the goddess in the middle. Her handmaidens stepped aside,
leaving a clear path for him that led straight to her.*

*He moved toward her then, and she took hold of his
hand and pulled him close. Her hands slid up his chest
and settled on his shoulders. She lifted her luscious
lips, offering them to him as a way of thanking him for
helping the woman in her pack. He pressed his mouth
against her and was enjoying the warm, silky sensation,
the heat between them, when a gray wolf came out of the
woods, raced into the water, and attacked him.*

*As a human, Eric wasn't equally matched. The wolf
shoved him onto the rocky beach, and the women rushed
off as if Eric were the real threat.*

*Before he could defend himself against the wolf, it bit
into his shoulder and Eric cried out in pain.*

Then a ringing noise in the distance stirred him from his
dream. As hot as he was, Eric felt like he'd had the fur-
nace on high although the house was normally cooler this
time of morning. He heard the ringing again and realized it was the doorbell. The front door opened, and Eric
roused enough to glance at the clock. Half past eight?

"Hey, Eric, it's just me," Sarandon called. "I wanted
to drop by and see how you're doing."

Eric groaned. He didn't need anyone checking up on him. Especially when he felt this bad. He'd rather suffer without alarming anyone because he knew he'd soon feel as good as new again.

"Eric?"

Ah, hell. Eric felt like he'd tied one on when normally he was out of bed in a flash, getting a million things done before he headed out to the park. He was usually up around five. Six at the latest. But he was burning up and felt like he needed to sleep for another eight hours straight. Now he wished he'd bitten the wolf back, just on principle.

"Yeah, be there in a sec. I'm just getting up. Had a rough night of it." Between the soreness from the bites and trying to meet the goddess of his dreams, he didn't believe he'd gotten more than a couple of hours of sleep.

Sarandon called out from the kitchen, "I brought us some breakfast."

Eric smiled a little. Sarandon's idea of breakfast was coffee and doughnuts.

"Did you get me a couple of blueberry muffins?"

"Yep. Are you okay to go in today? Doc said to take it easy for a couple of days, and he said you had nearly two *dozen* stitches. Since when does a couple even come close to a couple dozen?"

Eric put on his uniform—green shorts and beige shirt—then joined Sarandon in the kitchen.

"How come Doc told you my confidential medical information?"

As if anything was ever really confidential among the wolves. They had to look out for one another, so Doc would ensure family and the pack leaders knew of any injury. Eric wasn't upset about it. He just liked to give Sarandon a hard time because his brother was giving him one right back.

Sarandon shook his head as he poured himself a cup of coffee. "We all know you, and we know you won't take care of yourself."

"Doc always exaggerates our conditions. He's like a mother hen. You know that."

Sarandon was frowning at him. "Your face is flushed. You're running a fever." He searched through the drawers.

"What are you looking for?" Eric grabbed a cup of coffee and his muffins, and took a seat at the kitchen table.

"The thermometer."

"I'm fine. The antibiotics and our wolf healing should knock it out."

Sarandon found the thermometer and held it up. "Here it is." Then he handed it to Eric, folded his arms, and waited for his brother to check his temperature.

"Now *you're* being a mother hen," Eric said, annoyed.

"After your little lie about the stitches, I don't trust you. Just take your temperature."

Eric grunted at his brother, then stuck the digital thermometer in his mouth. But only because he was curious as to how high his temperature was, not because Sarandon wanted to know.

When it beeped, he took the thermometer out, but before he could read it, Sarandon snatched it away. "One hundred and three. You need to stay home for the day."

"The thing is broken. And I'm not staying home for the day. If I feel worse as the day goes on, I'll come home early. But I'm not disappointing the Scouts if I can help it."

"They'll suffer through it. The real reason you're going is that you're not giving up on looking for those women. Or one in particular."

"I'm not going in search of them. They packed up and left. I was just going to find out if their park cabin reservations showed where they were from. If they've moved into the area recently, they're going to have to learn to get along with me—if they want to use the park for camping. I won't take any crap from that alpha male again. I was only trying to help out when he attacked me."

Eric also wanted to smell around the campsite to see if the alpha male was part of the pack. The wolf hadn't been around when the female told Eric she didn't need his help. And if she was having trouble with an alpha male who wanted to court her and—ah hell. Maybe the wolf wasn't the leader or part of her pack and had fought Eric to claim Pepper for his own. If so, Eric wasn't having it.

Especially not if she didn't want anything to do with the male wolf. He smiled a little.

"So they were camping in the area?"

"Yeah, at Cabin 5. I'll check with the lodge about their reservations. I want to see how the injured woman is faring too. You know I'm supposed to file a report."

"Yeah, if they weren't wolves. I can just see you filling out *that* report. You're not really going to try to confront the alpha male without backup, are you?"

"If he's part of the pack, and only if he was protecting them because I was in wolf form. He wasn't there earlier to learn the whole truth, so I'll let him know there are no hard feelings."

"But you're thinking there's some other scenario going on here."

"Maybe." That would certainly explain the unprovoked attack and then another wolf attacking that wolf. Which made him wonder which wolf had told the other to back off. Eric told Sarandon about that too.

His brother shook his head. "Somehow I knew there was more to the story than the wolf just being part of the pack." He took a bite of his cream-filled doughnut. "What if the wolf that bit you is just as willing to attack you again? If he was with her pack, she could probably tell him to cease and desist. But if he's not?" Sarandon shrugged. "Just don't forget about the trouble he could be."

"The way my shoulder hurts, no, I'm not forgetting about the wolf anytime soon." He couldn't remember when he'd felt this bad.

"If he's not part of her pack, maybe he's involved in growing marijuana in the park. But you would have recognized his scent then."

"You're right, and I didn't recognize any of the wolves' scents who had been around the plants."

"At least that you smelled."

"Right."

"Are you sure you don't want to bring CJ along as a deputy sheriff? If the wolf tries to pull anything else with you, CJ can arrest him. Or if we locate one of the wolves involved in this other business. Thankfully, our jail is equipped for our kind."

"Not this time. I doubt the wolf will be anywhere near the woods. He'll have to work somewhere, and he's probably at the day job now." Eric finished his coffee and second muffin. "Are you ready to go?"

"Are you sure you're going to be all right?"

"Yeah. I'll see you after your butterfly meeting."

"Call me if you feel worse and need me to help out."

"I'll be fine. And *quit* sounding like Doc."

Sarandon snorted. "Yeah, well, someone needs to watch out for you since you won't."

Sarandon left, and as soon as Eric finished other business, he headed to the first Boy Scout camp. He wished he'd gotten up earlier. Now he'd have to wait until his lunch break to check out the campsite.

When he arrived at the parking area for the Scout campground, he called the lodge reservation desk and asked about the person or persons who had reserved Cabin 5.

"Oh, Pepper Grayling? She reserved three cabins, all of which are capable of accommodating six people. There were fourteen adults and five children. They said fitting in the extra child wouldn't be a problem. Anyway, they were scheduled for three days but cleared out a day early. Said it was a family emergency. Why do you need her phone number and home address?"

"One of the women hurt herself in a small rock slide. After I carried her to Cabin 5, they wanted to get her to the hospital, and I had another call to take care of." No way could Eric mention he'd been bitten by a wolf. "When I returned, they were all gone. I thought some of them would have remained in the area."

"That's not like you, Ranger Eric," Lois said. She was a nice older woman, and he wished he could tell her the truth. "So did you want to file an incident report?"

"No. It wasn't serious enough."

Silence.

"I just want to check on the woman who was injured as a follow-up. She might have just had a pulled muscle, but I want to learn what happened."

"Of course." Lois's tone indicated she believed he was more than interested in the woman who had been injured. Lois was always trying to get him to take her granddaughter out. She was of college age, and the picture Lois had showed him seemed to indicate she was a vivacious, fun-loving blonde—but she wasn't a wolf. "Okay, have pen and paper? Here's the information."

"Thanks."

"You owe me."

He hoped she didn't mean by having a date with her granddaughter. He wondered if her granddaughter even knew her grandmother was soliciting dates for her.

Lois gave him a post office box number for Pepper.

He groaned. It gave him a town, but it didn't tell him where she really lived. "Talk to you later."

Eric hiked from the parking lot to the first Boy Scout troop camp. A woman with her back to him was talking to the Scoutmaster and looked suspiciously like the goddess he'd met last night. It couldn't be, yet the appearance of her hair—short and curly, dark chocolate-brown with sun-streaked caramel highlights—and her long, shapely legs and slim figure dressed in green shorts, boots, and a tan shirt made him think of her. She worked for the park in some capacity?

He was sure it was her. If so, she probably had nothing to do with the weed in the park. Though he reminded himself that working there would be a pretty good cover.

The gray-haired Scoutmaster turned to see Eric, smiled, and waved him over. "Pepper Grayling, this is Eric Silver, if the two of you haven't met."

Pepper turned, her pink lips parted in surprise, and Eric was captivated by her wide brown eyes. Not believing his good fortune, he stalked forward, offering his hand before realizing how much that would hurt, and winced with the pain in his shoulder and side.

"We've met," she said, sounding surprised to see him there.

"Yes, on park ranger business," he said, trying to put their meeting in perspective. He wanted her to know he wasn't hotly pursuing her. Maybe a little bit, but not like his life depended on it. Unless that worked for her. He was thinking it sure would work for him.

She lifted her head slightly and took a deep breath of the air, smelling his scent and maybe the blood on the new bandages. Wolves could smell other things too—like the interest he had in her, and sickness—and she probably sensed his pain. It really was remarkable how much a wolf could catalog by scent, taste, and visual cues.

She immediately took his hand, shook it with a firm grip, and then quickly released it, as if she wanted to show him she was not afraid of him but did not want to cause him more pain. Then she turned her attention to the Scoutmaster as he introduced her to the troop of twelve eleven-year-olds ready for her talk. She moved in front of the group seated cross-legged before her and began talking about what she did as a forester.

A forester. So she worked for the county.

Eric stood by, arms folded across his chest, totally lost in her words, her mannerisms, her voice. He couldn't help himself. He found her wholly appealing on several different levels, and despite how poorly he felt, just seeing her gave him a boost of energy.

"I earned a bachelor's degree in forest ecosystem management and conservation," Pepper said to the Scouts. "After that, I worked on a forest inventory project and timber cruising, which means I examined a stand of timber to determine its potential value. What I do now is make presentations, like to all of you. One of the things I do is show people how to identify trees." She paused and motioned to them. "Come with me."

She led them to a pine tree and explained how to tell it was a red pine. Then she pointed off in the distance and said, "That slender tree—the quaking aspen—provides one of the most beautiful fall colors, turning gold in the autumn. It also protects other tree seedlings—such as spruce, fir, and pine trees—from the hot, dry sun so they have a chance to grow up big and tall."

"She's good," the Scoutmaster said to Eric. "We've had her come out and speak to us for about five years now. Every time she comes, she lectures about something different and the kids love her."

Five years? If only Eric had known she'd been coming here all that time. He had either been working at another national forest or had stayed in his pack's own wolf territory. Besides, he could have run for years in the park's million acres and not come across her. This was Eric's first year to do this with Scouts, and he hoped the kids would enjoy his lecture just as much. He did work with the kids in their pack on the kinds of things she was discussing with the Scouts. Everyone who had some field of expertise in the Silver pack shared their knowledge with the homeschooled kids.

But more importantly, he hoped Ms. Grayling lived in the general vicinity and wasn't actively courting a wolf or doing anything illegal. He hadn't felt this kind of initial attraction to another she-wolf in years. Despite her telling him she hadn't needed his help, he'd felt a connection right away. Maybe because he'd challenged her authority, which had seemed to intrigue her a bit.

He followed her, listening to her talk in case she had some good ideas he could use in teaching the kids in his pack. Since they were wolves, they also taught how to smell for certain signs of decay or injury to trees, and how to identify the smell of different trees and of birds and other animals.

Pepper brought the boys up close to a tree and showed where a woodpecker had been pecking for insects. She pulled out her iPad and showed them pictures of the kinds of woodpeckers that could have pecked away at the tree. Then she pointed out some of the insects crawling about the tree bark and the difference between healthy and diseased trees.

"See the fungus on this tree? Sometimes you'll see these fanlike fungi growing on dying or dead trees. The pine beetle borers have really destroyed a lot of pine trees in Colorado, and they multiply so quickly, we have to catch them right away or we lose the tree. So the park service now uses insecticides to protect the pine trees. The beetles are attracted to the sap. If a pine tree has been damaged because of lightning, humans, drought, disease, or other insect damage, even a woodpecker pecking on it, this increases its chance of being attacked by pine beetles.

"We want the trees to remain healthy, so we remove the diseased ones from the forest." Then she began showing them pictures of evergreen tree varieties at a Christmas tree farm and asked which kind of tree they'd like best if they got to cut one down for Christmas. Or even better, have a living tree they could plant outside after Christmas.

Eric was impressed with all she was qualified to talk about, and he did get a couple of ideas to add to his home-school lectures, but she had him beat on the show-and-tell aspects of her talk.

"We also manage the deer to ensure the forest survives. The deer population had destroyed the forest. Here's a video of how a few wolves were introduced into the area and how they helped the forest to grow back. The wolves only killed off a few deer to sustain their pack, but the deer quit eating the trees in the areas where the wolves were and the trees began to grow. Lots of wildlife lives in the forest, so the wolves made a really big impact on the return of wildlife to the area."

Now the kids were really in awe. Eric was too while he watched over their shoulders as the wolves chased after the deer and the trees had a chance to renew. Other animals began to return to the forest, and the trees helped to stabilize the riverbanks and changed the course of the rivers, making them deeper and healthier too. Which allowed for the increase of bird and other wildlife populations such as the beavers to return.

"We have programs for kids to study shrubs and trees, to learn more about how important our natural resources are to us." She pulled a tiny pine tree out of the side pocket of her backpack. The roots were wrapped in wet newspaper and sitting in a plastic bag. She unwrapped the roots and showed the boys what they looked like. "One tiny sapling," she said, rewrapping the roots in the damp newspaper and motioning to the forest surrounding them, "is just the beginning of the growth of an entire forest. How many of you have been to the amusement park Wally Land?"

Several of the kids raised their hands.

"Well, big companies and small ones and individuals like yourselves can help to reforest acreage that has been burned off during a major fire. Over seven hundred acres in a Colorado national forest are being replanted with the help of Wally and others. Trees produce oxygen, the air that we breathe, so it's important to have our national forests to help take the carbon dioxide out of the air."

Which had Eric's thoughts winging back to the weed growing in the park.

He smelled his brother's scent and looked around to see him watching the show. Sarandon raised his brows a little and smiled at him. Eric wondered what *he'd* brought for show-and-tell. But his brother probably realized that if Eric was listening in on the she-wolf's talk with such interest, he was intrigued by more than Pepper's lecture.

The Scoutmaster thanked Pepper for her talk, and Eric was afraid she'd leave before he could speak with her privately about last night. He was going to suggest Sarandon go first, but the Scoutmaster introduced Eric next.

Eric thought the kids would be interested in some of his adventures, so they were what he'd planned to discuss. No show-and-tell.

"As a national park ranger, I give lectures like Ms.

Grayling does as a forester. A number of accidents occur every summer in the park, so part of my job is search and rescue, fire safety, first aid, and the like. Last year the rangers had 190 search-and-rescue operations. Search and rescue are really two separate missions. In the one, the visitor is missing and it can be really difficult to locate the individual. Lots and lots of acreage. Lots of trees. Cold nights. High-altitude sickness for those not used to the area. Just lots of dangers for someone who gets lost and doesn't have the survival skills needed to last out in the wilderness for any length of time.

"Often someone who is lost will think they can find their way out or reach a location that will help others find them. We might have some idea of where they were initially, but if they continue to move, our search area grows wider and wider with each passing hour and the person is more difficult to locate."

"Hug a tree," one of the boys said. "We learned about a nine-year-old boy who died in the mountains and so some of the searchers started a Hug-a-Tree and Survive program."

"Right. If you're lost, hug a tree. That way you know you're not alone. Talk to the tree."

Some of the kids laughed.

"Seriously. If you're all by yourself and feeling scared, talk to a tree. Let him know how you're feeling. Give him a hug. It can make a world of difference. By staying put, you won't fall and injure yourself. Or stay with a vehicle if it breaks down somewhere. The vehicle can protect you from the cold winds, for one thing. We had a case where the woman and kids stayed with the car during a snowstorm. Their vehicle had gotten stuck in a snowdrift. The woman's husband went looking for help. The husband died because of the freezing weather conditions. His wife and kids were fine, and we found them much more quickly than we found him. So it's really important to stay put.

"We also conduct rescue missions. Often we have highly trained rescue specialists. But sometimes the park ranger is the first one on the scene and must give first aid. We deal with falls, avalanches, rock slides, snow, ice, and vehicle accidents. But we also help animals when we can.

"Last winter, I got a call that a deer was stuck on six-inch-thick lake ice. He kept slipping and falling, and couldn't stand up. For us, walking across ice can be treacherous enough, but to approach a wild animal on ice is downright dangerous. There's also the possibility of the ice breaking through. I watched for a long time before I approached the deer, hoping he'd make it out on his own." Eric also knew the deer would smell Eric's wolf half and was afraid he would frighten it further.

"I donned an ice rescue suit and slowly made my way across the ice. I tried to shoo the deer away, but he just couldn't make it on his own. I finally lassoed his antlers, shuffled back to shore, and then pulled the deer to shore. I tugged off the lasso before he ran off, and then he dis-appeared into the forest."

"Cool," one of the kids said.

Eric could see his deer story was more fascinating than the pine tree sapling, but maybe not as entertaining as the wolves changing the course of the river.

"Then another time, a man from south Texas was snowshoeing in the Rockies alone. You have buddies when you go places, don't you?"

"Yeah, we always have to take a buddy," one boy said. "Even to go to the bathroom."

"Right. It's really safer to go with a buddy. And that's for your protection. So he had no buddy, but he had his cell phone with him. He called, told us his location, and wanted to get directions. We gave them to him, assuming he would manage to get out on his own as confident as he sounded, but a little while later, he called back. He had become so disoriented, he didn't know which way he was going. Worse, he wasn't prepared for the cold at night. And as the temperature dropped, he was afraid he wouldn't make it out at all." Eric paused to ask, "What's your Scout motto?"

"Be prepared," all the boys chimed in.

"Right, so what would you have done if you were him?" Eric asked.

"Taken a buddy."

"Had warm clothes and lots of food." The other kids laughed at that.

"So you had to go and rescue him?" one of the boys asked.

"Yeah. Me and three other rangers. We followed his fresh snowshoe tracks and located him in a heavily forested area near a creek. It took us three hours to hike him out."

"Was he tired?"

"He was. We brought warm clothes and food for him, and just being with people who knew where they were going lifted his spirits."

Because of the severity of summer storms, Eric wanted to talk about lightning and the dangers for the kids hiking in the backcountry during school break. Even as recently as last night, they'd had a huge storm pop up in the area. "You might have been out here during your summer camping when a thunderstorm cropped up. You should always move to a safe place—a building or vehicle—and avoid hilltops, ridges, or flat, open areas. Once, a group of people clustered together beneath a tree to protect themselves from the rain. In a similar case, a group of cattle did the same thing. In both situations, the lightning hit the trees, and the electricity spread through them and across the ground beneath them. All of the people and the cattle were hit by the lightning.

"You want to seek shelter under a thick growth of small trees in a low area, rather than stand beneath a single tall tree. You don't want to hold on to anything metal—like a bicycle, metal fence, or metal canoe. The same with water. You want to get out of water immediately if a lightning storm comes up. If you're in a canoe, take it to shore, and tuck yourself close to a rock overhang or anything that can provide protection."

The kids started asking him a million different questions. Had he rescued a bear cub? Was he ever attacked by a cougar? Who else did he rescue? Did he ever get struck by lightning?

Of course, his first thought was about trying to rescue the wolf last night and then being attacked by a wolf later. But those were the kinds of stories he couldn't tell.

He glanced at Pepper to see her smiling as she stood next to his brother. At first, Eric was so distracted by the boys' questions that he didn't think about what Sarandon could be telling her. Maybe just about himself or the Silver pack. But what if he was telling her about him?

Eric didn't want her to hear about Sarandon's version of him.

Chapter 4

PEPPER HAD TO ADMIT THAT ERIC HAD WOWED THE KIDS. AND her too. She was in charge of protecting the forests. But he protected them, the people visiting them, and the animals that made the forests their home. She admired that about him. And she loved how good he was with the kids—a true storyteller. He didn't act like he wanted to tell his story and go, but instead hung around to answer all their questions. She couldn't help but see him in a new light.

She got the impression he really was interested in her lecture, which won her over a little more. Sarandon was a real outdoorsman like Eric, and the two brothers seemed to be really close. Family meant everything to her and so she liked that about them.

She also appreciated the fact that Eric had known just what to do when he learned Susan had been injured. Pepper always had to make all the decisions for the pack, so it was nice to meet someone else capable of doing so—as far as carrying Susan back to camp. She suspected that with the kind of work Eric did, he was always ready for any contingency.

She was amused that Sarandon was telling her all about Eric, as if he was the best brother anyone could have. She thought he was giving her a sales pitch and realized Eric must have said something about her that made Sarandon go straight to priming the pump. But how did he know Eric had met her? She hadn't given

Eric her name when she'd met him the other night, and Sarandon hadn't been here when the Scoutmaster was making introductions.

"Eric wanted to tell you he hadn't meant to intrude on you and your pack last night," Sarandon said.

"We appreciated his concern."

Sarandon looked surprised to hear it. "Yeah, well, he understands why you'd have a guard wolf protecting your backs and that the wolf was only doing his job. So Eric wanted to let him know there were no hard feelings. Most of all, he wanted to learn how the injured woman was faring."

"Susan is all right. She was going to call him this morning and thank him, but she might have still been sleeping. Thankfully, it was just a hairline fracture. It should heal quickly. As to the guard wolf? We weren't sure that was Eric he attacked—at first. But the wolf doesn't belong to my pack. He's from another one." She wasn't going to say anything more. She had no intention of getting tangled up with a new wolf pack when she was having trouble with another. And she didn't want the two alpha males to duke it out, thinking her pack and lands were the prize.

She studied the two spots of blood on Eric's shirt, indicating he'd been bitten twice, and had smelled fresh blood when he stood closer to her. That bothered her. She could see that Waldron could become a real danger to another male who was the least bit interested in her. But she was certain Eric had been wounded before the confrontation with Waldron. As to this business with Waldron, she couldn't allow him to intimidate other wolves. "Did Waldron hurt him badly?"

"Nah. Eric just had a couple of stitches."

She thought it must have been worse if Eric was still bleeding from the wounds. And he probably wouldn't have gone to see a doctor if he'd only needed a couple of stitches. Worse, his face was flushed and she swore he was running a fever. Yet here he was, giving his lecture to the kids and looking like he really loved his job, despite how under the weather he must be feeling.

"He looks like he's running a fever."

Sarandon didn't deny or confirm her comment.

She glanced at him. The brothers were similar in appearance: both had dark brown hair and eyes, but Eric was taller by at least an inch. Six-one, she guessed. Eric was dressed in a park ranger uniform, shirt and shorts, making him look dashing and official. He had the sexiest legs—well-defined calf muscles that said he was a runner, good-looking knees, and well-developed thighs. His brother was wearing jeans, a brown T-shirt, and hiking boots, looking casual and carefree.

Sarandon was studying Eric, a frown furrowing his brow.

"Shouldn't he be home in bed?" she asked.

Sarandon sighed. "I thought so, but he didn't want to disappoint the boys."

She admired Eric for wanting to speak to the boys when he would have felt better resting up. If the roles were reversed, what would she have done? Probably stayed home. Mostly because she had a pack to run and couldn't afford to be sick long-term.

Eric concluded his talk and introduced his brother before the Scoutmaster could. Then he stalked toward Pepper as if he had a new mission in mind, while Sarandon smiled at him and took his place in front of the boys.

"Sorry if I concerned you and the others last night,"

Eric said. "I only wanted to offer my assistance, as I would with anyone who needed help in the park."

"How bad are your bite wounds?" Pepper asked, ignoring his comment. She wanted to get to the point of the matter. As far as she was concerned, he shouldn't be here. Sleeping and resting would help him heal faster. *Lupus garous* might have faster healing capabilities than humans, but they still could prolong the healing process if they didn't take care of themselves.

"It's no big deal."

Typical macho alpha male. "How many stitches?" She didn't believe he'd had only a couple. She'd been worried last night about her cousin and concerned about another alpha wolf hassling her, and she realized she must have sounded a lot harsher than she had intended. Now that she knew Eric truly was with the park service and one of his jobs as a ranger was to ensure visitors to the park remained safe—so in reality, he belonged there—she wished she had schooled her emotions a little better.

She was still angry that Waldron had attacked him. Even if Eric had been a problem for her, he would have been *her* problem to deal with, not Waldron's. His actions were tantamount to proclaiming she was his. She wouldn't soon forget the anger in Waldron's expression either. He didn't like that she had bitten him, telling him to leave the other wolf alone. To leave her alone. She hadn't liked his response, and she worried it would escalate.

"How many stitches did I get? Now you're sounding like my brother." Eric smiled at her, not answering her question.

She didn't smile back. She wasn't going to let him

make light of it. "You're running a fever, and you have two spots of blood on your uniform."

He glanced down at his uniform. "Ah, hell."

"How many stitches?"

"The guy was just doing his job."

She was impressed that Eric was protecting Waldron's reputation. "You're thinking he's one of my…people?"

"Sure." Eric frowned at her. "Isn't he? Why else would a… Wait, he's a suitor? I thought maybe he was your mate."

She saw the change in expression. She knew that look. He had to have considered that Waldron might have been a suitor, not a pack member. "No."

"An unwelcome suitor?"

She gave Eric her pack leader look that said she didn't want to discuss suitors and to back off.

If Eric had been a beta, he would have done just that: looked a little chagrined and turned to watch his brother talking about identifying butterflies. Sarandon had pulled out pictures that their cousin, a professional photographer, had taken of butterflies and was explaining about the various kinds.

Instead of backing off, Eric smiled at her. Just a little. Like he was glad her potential wolf suitor—who was really just a stalker as far as she was concerned—wasn't the one for her. Like he was hoping he might have a chance with her if she wasn't interested in the other wolf.

"Well, that's good to know," Eric said, ultraserious. "Then if he bites at me the next time, I won't hold back."

She didn't want Eric to get the notion he could court her next. But she hadn't expected him to say what he did. It was understandable, but she hadn't expected that response. She certainly didn't want the wolves fighting over her.

She had been happily running her pack for seven years on her own. Real she-wolves were known to do that. And she'd never met a male wolf she'd been remotely interested in. Harold had been the perfect mate, coleading the pack in perfect harmony with her. Well, if she could call it coleading. He had looked rough and tough as male wolves go, although he had really been just a beta. But he had been perfect as far as being mostly agreeable.

The only thing she had regretted was that their mating had never produced offspring. But two of the women in her pack had twins, and another had one child—all males. She didn't have to have children of her own, because she played with and helped take care of all the kids so much that they were like her own.

On the other hand, she didn't want Eric to believe he had to take that kind of beating from another wolf, just so the other wolf wouldn't hassle her. Even so, she couldn't tell Eric what to do if Waldron was intent on fighting him. "With regard to Waldron, be my guest. Maybe another male wolf could knock some sense into him."

She doubted it. When two males wanted the same thing, one could kill the other. That's the way it was in the wolves' world. Then she looked at Eric and asked, "Where did you get the other wound?" She wasn't sure why she hadn't considered it could be something other than a bite wound. What were the odds that he'd had an earlier wolf fight with some other wolf in the park or elsewhere?

"Nothing important," he said.

She didn't believe him. Maybe he'd injured himself on the job, but she doubted it.

"One time, I had a group ask me to take them on a hike through the mountains in search of Bigfoot," Sarandon said to the boys, drawing her attention away from Eric.

"Did you find him?" one of the boys asked.

"Nah. If he exists, he didn't want to be found." Sarandon started talking about other guided tours he'd taken people on.

"Are you from this area?" Eric asked Pepper. "The Scoutmaster said you'd been presenting programs for five years."

"Nope. Not from this area." Which was true. They weren't originally from this area.

Again, he cast her an elusive smile.

She smiled back this time. Their conversation reminded her of a cat-and-mouse game between wolves. He wanted to know where she and her pack were located without asking overtly. As a wolf, he'd easily picked up on her reluctance to get to know him better—the scent she was giving off, her arms folded defensively, her focus on Sarandon and the boys. Though when she did turn her attention to Eric, her eye contact was direct—total alpha posturing. She suspected he had already checked her cabin reservations, since he could as a member of the staff. He could even use Susan's injury as the excuse to get in touch with her. Pepper was glad she'd only used their P.O. box.

"First time to actually camp in the park?" he asked.

"We've been here before. But it's been maybe five years since the last time."

"To…the campsite or the park?"

She chuckled. "The campsite. We've been to the park, but not all together as a pack."

"Lots of times?"

"Yes." Which meant she lived nearby, and he would deduce that. Which made her wonder why she hadn't run into him before. "Have you come here a lot?"

"No. I've only worked here since Thanksgiving. Before that, I worked jobs in Silver Town—with the ski resort and elsewhere. We have our own lands to run on and I've visited most of the national parks at some time or another, but I wouldn't have come anywhere near campsites when I was running as a wolf. Now I'm regretting that I hadn't been up here more. I must have gotten extra lucky last night."

"Right. And you have the wound to prove it." She couldn't help but be annoyed with Waldron all over again. Where had he been when Susan needed help? He'd only been around to annoy Pepper and injure another wolf who had helped her out.

Eric shrugged it off. "No big deal. I wouldn't have bothered seeing Doc, but I felt it wouldn't hurt to get some antibiotics."

"I can't believe you have a doctor in your pack." That was the only thing she really wished. That they had a wolf doctor who could take care of injuries or sickness and delivering babies, instead of going to a human doctor for their care.

"Doc Weber takes any wolf patients. Humans too, but he transfers them out as soon as he can. We run Silver Town. As a pack."

She closed her gaping mouth. She knew of Silver

Town, but she really couldn't believe they ran the whole town. She'd never had any reason to visit. Then she wondered about Eric's name. Maybe he was the pack leader and didn't need to be a leader of anyone else's pack. Wouldn't that be a joke on her when she'd been worried about his intentions?

"Silver? Any relation to the town's name and founding fathers?"

"Yeah, my cousin Darien and his mate, Lelandi, are the pack leaders. He has two brothers and I have three. Our family started the town in the old days. It was first a silver mining town. Since then, we've done tours of the mountain in the mining cars, and we started a ski resort. We don't have a lot of accommodations for out-of-town skiers. Mainly we to try to keep the non-wolf ski population from visiting since we're rather remote from other Colorado cities."

"Yeah, I know. That's probably why I've never been there. It's not on any of the main highways. I never even considered that it would be wolf-run. Or that any pack would run a town."

"It's perfect for raising kids. If you and your pack ever need a home, I'm certain Darien and Lelandi would welcome you to the town."

"No, thanks. We're fine."

"I thought the male who attacked me ran the pack you were with."

"He'd like to, I'm sure, but no."

"Then you run it?"

"Yes."

"Alone?" Eric had such a speculative gleam in his dark-brown eyes, his lips curving imperceptibly, that she figured he was putting all the puzzle pieces together.

"Yes. And I'm not looking for a mate. Do you have your own police force?" If they did, Eric could easily have her license plate checked out, even get her address that way, if she was parked in the same area that he was. Since he was a law-enforcement park ranger, he might be able to run the tags himself.

"We sure do. Two deputies, one being my youngest brother, and a sheriff."

"That's nice. Well, I've got to run along. I suppose you're meeting up with another Boy Scout troop after this one, and two more this afternoon?"

"Sure am. What about you?"

"Same."

"Great. Sarandon and I will see you then. I'll walk you to where you're parked."

She had parked in the farthest lot out, figuring she could use the exercise after she and Susan ended up having too many chips and too much wine last night. "Not necessary. See you at the next campsite." She stalked off, feeling the wolf's eyes on her back.

As soon as she turned left into the woods, she glanced back in Eric's direction. Yep, he was watching her. He shoved his hands in his pockets and smiled.

She shouldn't have glanced in his direction, telling him she was interested in what he was doing. Every action a wolf took would be recorded by others and analyzed. She didn't want him drawing the wrong conclusions.

Pepper made her way to her vehicle, glad Eric had abided by her wishes and hadn't followed her. She'd give him high marks for that. Not that it would change her mind about him or any other male wolf who thought he might take her mate's place.

She got into her mini-SUV and drove to the next campsite, realizing he could still find her vehicle if he really wanted to by smelling her scent on it. She sighed. What difference would it make anyway? She wasn't going to have anything to do with him beyond talking to him a little at the campsites in between lecturing.

When she arrived at the next troop encampment, she was shocked to see Eric already there and lecturing. He must have known a shortcut, maybe a road only park officials could use. He didn't even glance her way, though she was sure he knew she was coming up the trail to the campsite because the breeze was blowing her scent in his direction. For an annoying fraction of a second, she realized how much she wished he had glanced her way, smiled a little, and continued on with his talk.

She was used to being acknowledged when her pack members were around. When Waldron was around, he paid constant attention to her, as if she was the only person in the world. But that annoyed her. She was puzzled by Eric's behavior. He appeared to be giving up on her way too easily—for an alpha. Unless he had just been trying to be friendly and didn't have any deeper goals in mind.

Nah. He was totally intrigued by her. She'd smelled his interest. But he was different, not pushy like the others she had known.

The Scoutmaster spoke to her, but she barely heard a word he said, instead listening to Eric pull the boys into new tales, all different from the others she had heard.

Right now, he was talking about the time he was chased by a bear when he was a kid and climbed a tree, but the bear did too.

The boys were sitting cross-legged in front of him, and he sat the same way to give his lecture, as if he were just one of the boys. The boys looked enraptured, their mouths gaping, their eyes wide. She was just as caught up in the tale, wondering how he got out of the predicament he'd found himself in. She wondered if he was giving a new lecture so she wouldn't have to hear the same old stories again. She had to admit she was fascinated with his adventure stories.

"Mr. Silver is new to us," the Scoutmaster said to her. He chuckled. "He sure has some tales to tell."

Considering how long *lupus garous* lived, at least until lately, she knew why Eric had so many tales to tell. She let out her breath on a long sigh. No way would her wolf video or little pine tree sapling garner the attention Eric did.

She wished she'd gone first like before. Unlike him, she didn't have another lecture prepared, and she wasn't good at impromptu speeches.

She sighed again and saw Sarandon coming down the same trail she had. He was all smiles—directed totally at her. Maybe *he* was the one she should watch out for.

Chapter 5

AFTER THE LECTURE, ERIC GAVE PEPPER A BRIEF SMILE IN greeting, then joined Sarandon as he waited to talk to the troop. Pepper was speaking to the boys now, and Eric asked his brother, "Did you want to meet me for lunch after this?"

"Certainly. Guess you don't need to do what you were going to do now." Sarandon was careful not to be specific in case Pepper could catch any part of their conversation. "Did you want to wait for me?"

Eric thought about it. He really had wanted to track down where her pack was from. But he was feeling so wiped out, he figured he needed to eat. Then after the last lecture, he'd swing by the cabins Pepper had rented and check them out.

"Yeah, sure."

Like Eric, Sarandon would be telling all new tales so Eric didn't mind hearing them, especially since some would be new to him too.

"Do you want to ask Pepper if she'd like to go with us? We'll all be at the next troop campout after that."

Pepper glanced their way, probably having heard her name mentioned.

"I'm getting strong vibes that she's not interested in seeing anyone," Eric said, lowering his voice so only his brother could hear.

"And that's stopping you, why?"

Eric frowned at him. "She already has trouble with another male wolf. I don't intend to add to her problems."

"So take care of the other male wolf."

Eric snorted. "I would in a heartbeat if I thought she wanted or needed my help. But I don't believe she does." If he learned Waldron was the one illegally growing crops in the park, that would be the perfect scenario. Eric could take him down for a criminal venture and get him off Pepper's back. At the same time, he'd be doing it in the course of his job and for the safety of all *lupus garous*.

"Ah, so she would think you'd force the other wolf to leave, but then take his place. Gotcha."

"Right."

"Well, I got to tell you, Brother, you have more fortitude than I have."

Eric wasn't about to let his brother know how much it was killing him to back off. He swore Pepper was surprised he had given her the space she seemed to need when she first arrived. She was probably used to the other male wolf not backing off. Which was why Eric was working so hard at this. And that was a new way of handling a situation like this for him. Of course, she might not care for him, in which case, he *really* wasn't pushing it.

"So are you hanging around to have lunch with me, or do you want to just meet me somewhere?" Sarandon asked.

"I'll hang around. We can leave your vehicle here and take the shortcut out of the park so we can have plenty of time to visit and still be back in time for the next talk."

"Are you sure you don't want to ask Pepper? What if she *doesn't* say no?"

Eric really didn't want to press things with her, but

Sarandon was right. What if she did want to have lunch with them and she felt left out because they hadn't asked if she'd join them? Because of his park ranger position, he could get them out of here faster than if she used the visitor roads.

What the hell. If she rejected the idea, he would remind himself it was just a polite offer, nothing more, like if he'd asked any another wolf to join them, just in friendship and camaraderie.

Who was he trying to kid? All he had to do to know how he felt was envision her playing in the creek last night with the other women and then kissing him back as he kissed her—like in his dream.

When she joined him to thank the Scoutmaster, Sarandon gave Eric a look that said he ought to ask, just to be courteous. Then Sarandon began his talk with the boys.

Eric said to Pepper, "Sarandon wondered if you'd like to join us for some lunch." He thought saying his brother wanted him to ask would make it less of an issue for her. "I can drive us on the official-use-only roads and get us to town quicker, if you'd like. Then we'll be back in time for the next Scout troop, if you're doing the same ones we are this afternoon."

"Is it legal for a nonofficial person to ride in an official truck?" she asked.

He smiled.

She smiled back.

"Sure, if it means getting a Reuben sandwich at that deli on the corner of Fifth and Parker and having a little more time to chill out between lectures," he said.

"You got it." And for a second, Eric thought he had

made a slight inroad with Pepper. "But only if Sarandon likes the place too," she added.

"He does. We both do," he assured her quickly. But he suspected that even if Sarandon hadn't liked the place, he would have gone along so Eric could visit further with Pepper. Even so, Eric was glad both he and his brother ate there whenever they had a chance because the food was so good.

She raised a brow as if she didn't believe him.

"He loves the tuna melt. I love the chili on cold days, the Reuben on hot days."

She frowned at him. He thought she still questioned his veracity but she said, "Are you sure you're all right?"

She was still concerned about him. That was a good sign. "Yeah, sure." His injuries were aching and he was burning up, but no way was he going to tell Pepper that. As soon as he finished speaking to the next two troops this afternoon, he'd go home to bed. Well, after he checked out the cabins.

"You look flushed."

He shrugged. "No big deal."

"The Scouts will understand if you can't talk to them this afternoon."

Now that he had a chance to be around Pepper for longer? No way was he going home this early. "If it was a life-or-death matter, I'd bow out. It isn't. Really." Eric appreciated her concern, but he wasn't about to leave now. Maybe she wouldn't be interested in him. And maybe he wouldn't be interested in her—if they got to know each other better. But he couldn't pass up this opportunity to have lunch with her, and having his brother along would help make her feel easier about it.

"All right."

Before long, Sarandon had finished his talk and Eric drove them to the old-time deli, which featured Chevy convertible toy cars and pictures, checkered tablecloths, a chrome bar, and red vinyl seats. They went to the serving line and considered the menu. Pepper frowned. "Do you have sandwiches in half orders?"

"No, ma'am. Only whole sandwiches," the server said.

Eric quickly said, "We can split one."

Immediately, she began to object. "But—"

"No buts. With this fever, I'm not as hungry as I usually am. I couldn't manage more than half a sandwich."

She looked skeptically at him. Sarandon was smiling like he didn't believe Eric one bit.

They ordered and sat down at one of the tables. Sarandon began talking about their pack as if Pepper might be interested in joining them. But he didn't tell her about their father's misdeeds or anything that could cast a bad light on him or his brothers.

After listening to Sarandon talk almost nonstop for twenty minutes, Pepper turned to Eric and asked, "Were you really chased by a bear when you were human? Or were you a wolf at the time?"

"Both. The time I told the Scouts about, we were human. As wolves, when we were about fifteen, Sarandon and I were hiking up in the mountains and it started storming. Remember my talk on lightning storms? We were up on a peak when a thunderstorm rolled in. We sought lower ground and found a cave, thinking only about protecting ourselves from the lightning. But then we discovered the cave had a resident. A sleeping black bear. We hurried out of there and scrambled down the mountain, figuring we'd take our chances with the storm."

"Wow, I would have been so freaked out."

"We definitely were. What about you? You must have had some harrowing experiences over the years," Eric said.

A server brought their lunches to the table and left.

Pepper said, "Yeah, it's hard not to, given our life spans and as much time as I've spent in the forests. One time I'd taken a couple of wolf pups with me on a hike. The mom needed a break and she turned into her wolf so the twin boys would take wolf form and I could take them for an outing. I was trying to make them mind, but also to get them used to exploring nature and the world around them. So I was observing them like any wolf 'nanny' would, while also watching the area surrounding us.

"Then I saw a cougar. She had two yearling cubs with her, and she was teaching them how to hunt for food. Before she could see us, I moved the pups away from the area quickly. That was the scariest thing that ever happened to me. If I'd had my pack with me, no problem. A wolf pack would have scared them off. But one wolf and two pups? They were only four months old in wolf form, four in human years. I couldn't have fought off the cougar and her cubs. After that, I made it a rule that if any of us took pups out into the woods, we went as a pack."

Eric blew out his breath. "Now that would be a tale to tell the Scouts, if you could tell it."

"I wish I could. Between your and Sarandon's tales, the boys were absolutely awestruck. I think that's the quietest I've ever seen a group of Boy Scouts. I don't remember seeing you giving the lectures before though."

"It's a new job for both of us since Thanksgiving of last year," Eric said. "So we missed the summer when the Boy Scouts are camping. The park service normally hires temps in the summers, but I'd been working up north in the same capacity for a few years, so I managed to get a permanent position down here closer to home." He drank some of his water. "So how long have you been at the job?"

"Nine years. I started giving lectures to troops five years ago. I hadn't expected a park ranger or a nature guide to show up today. That must have been your doing," she said to Eric.

"Well, actually, we both had the idea at the same time." Eric lifted a pickle off the plate. "I was telling Sarandon about what I needed to do, and we both had the idea that he could add something to the talk. Then we'd have lunch after that."

"That was a good idea. I was curious though. Do you often prowl the park at night as a wolf?"

"Yes. I love the woods. It gives me a chance to run in my wilder form." Eric then noticed two male teens looking at them curiously from across the room. Even though they were talking softly—their wolf hearing ensured they could hear each other—the teens seemed to have caught some of their conversation.

Pepper glanced in the teens' direction, then said, "I think they overheard us."

"Only if they're wolves." Eric finished off his sandwich.

"Not any of yours, I take it."

"Nope. And not any of yours?"

"No."

Eric eyed them for a moment, wondering where they were from. He frowned. "What about Waldron's pack? Would some of his wolves be here?"

"In the summer? Teens out hiking in the park, then coming in to have lunch? Could be."

Eric thought it was too much of a coincidence that Waldron would attack him for showing any interest in Pepper, and now two teens—possibly from Waldron's pack—were having lunch at the same place and same time as them.

"But you don't know them?" Eric asked, wondering just how much interaction she'd had with Waldron and his pack.

She shook her head. "He said his pack is thirty members strong. I don't know where they're living, what they do, and I didn't ask. He didn't share either."

"You never met him before? I mean, you haven't known him long-term then?"

"He just moved into the area, from what I understand."

So she and her pack must live close by. Then again, Waldron and his pack must also.

"I wonder why they would move out of their own area," Sarandon said, as if he thought the pack had caused trouble and moved on.

"Yeah, I was wondering the same thing." Though Eric had no intention of bringing it up, because he and his brothers had moved on when their dad had caused all the trouble for the pack. Now they were back, but Eric still felt unsettled, responsible, and angry with his dad, when *they* hadn't caused any trouble. Still, Eric and his brothers had left the pack even though it wasn't their fault, so the same could be true of Waldron and his people.

"Do you want me to talk to the boys?" Sarandon asked.

"Nah. They're just checking us out like we're checking them out." But Eric wondered if they knew who Pepper was and if they were in Waldron's pack, and he knew word would get back to him that two male wolves had lunch with her—one who had even shared a sandwich with her. Though it was all innocent, another wolf interested in courting her might not think so.

"Are we ready to go back and take on the next round of Scout troops?" Pepper asked, setting her napkin on her plate. "And thanks, Eric, for buying everyone lunch."

Eric thought she was elevating her voice a little, making sure the teens knew why they had lunch together. Was she afraid Waldron would come looking for Eric if he learned he was having lunch out with her? And try to take another bite out of him? Not this time.

Pepper and the Silver brothers cleaned up their table, then dumped their trash as they headed out the door. The teens quickly followed but kept their distance. They eyed the vehicle Eric was driving and took a picture.

"They have to be from Waldron's pack," Pepper said, climbing into Eric's truck. "There would be no other reason for their *obvious* interest in us. Like a warning that what we did would be reported back to him."

She'd halfway expected Waldron to saunter in like he owned the deli and tell Eric she was off-limits. She could see that Eric was all alpha, and he was ready for some payback. Waldron wouldn't get off so easily next time—if there was a next time.

Eric snorted. "All the better reason to clear the air, *and* the sooner the better."

Sarandon cast Eric a warning look. "Not in your condition, it isn't. And you know if he injured you again before you were healed, Darien and all the rest of us would tear into him. No letting the two of you deal with this on your own."

"Well, I hope no one does anything on my account," Pepper reminded the brothers. Just because she ate lunch with them didn't mean she wanted anything further to do with them. Yes, they were nice, but she doubted just being friends was Eric's goal.

"This would be strictly on my account. Believe me, no wolf is going to get away with fighting me twice without some payback."

On the other hand, maybe since the teens now knew Eric was on duty—he was wearing a park ranger uniform and driving one of the ranger vehicles—they would relay the information. And Waldron would realize Eric was just taking a break for lunch. Having his brother with them helped somewhat too. Of course, Pepper had no intention of telling Waldron what she was doing that day or any other, but he could guess that if she was with the ranger and another man, she was doing some kind of forestry lecture or project.

Still, she was concerned things would escalate between her and Waldron. Just the fact he was anywhere near her campsite last night proved troublesome. Had he been there for the two days they'd been staying there?

And now this. What were the chances that the kids just happened upon them at the deli?

"I hope you're going to make your brother go home after this," she said to Sarandon.

"Like I could make him do anything he didn't want to do."

They arrived back at the campground, then hiked in to the next troop encampment. "A good night's rest, and I'll be good as new," Eric said as if he didn't want them to get the last word on the subject.

"He won't let me see his bite wounds," Sarandon said. "But after a couple of dozen stitches, and the fact they are bleeding again…"

Eric glowered at him.

"I thought you said there were only a couple of stitches," Pepper said, glancing at the spots of blood on Eric's uniform.

"That's what he told me. He could have a compound fracture and downplay it. He doesn't like being pampered." Sarandon hurried to catch up to his brother.

Pepper rushed to keep pace with the two long-legged brothers.

"I can still hear you, you know," Eric said to his brother.

"I meant for you to." Sarandon waited for Pepper, but his gaze suddenly shot past her down the trail.

She turned to see what he saw. The two dark-haired teens from the deli. She didn't believe it was a coincidence that they had come here to hike and just happened to be using the same trail to go to a campsite. Not when they'd taken pictures of her and the Silver brothers at the deli.

"I'll catch up to you in a moment." Sarandon

obviously intended to talk to the boys. But suddenly Eric was passing her and Sarandon.

Between the two brothers, she had no doubt who was in charge. Then again, Eric did work here as a law-enforcement park ranger and had the authority to question the teens in a more official capacity than his brother did.

She folded her arms and watched the confrontation, curious as to how it would play out. She wanted to know just as much as they did who the boys were and what they were doing here. But she also wanted to see how Eric handled it.

"Are you with Waldron's pack?" Eric asked.

"What's it to you?" one of the boys spouted off.

"I need to know who to call if you cause any trouble in the park."

That made the boys cast each other a look. She thought they appeared a little worried. One shoved his hands in his pockets, while the other lowered his gaze to the ground. She suspected Waldron wouldn't like to hear the boys had taken it upon themselves to chase after her and the Silver brothers as if they were on a spy mission.

"What is your business in the park?" Eric asked, sounding like a pack leader himself.

"Just hiking around," the other boy said. "Not against the law."

"Names?"

"Jonathan Fairhaven," said the first boy, who was slightly fairer than his companion.

"Leroy Fairhaven."

"Brothers?"

"Yeah," they both said.

"Let me see your IDs."

When they handed over their IDs, Eric said, "Says here you're from Idaho. If you're going to stay in the area, you have to get new driver's licenses."

"We're just…visiting for now."

"Do you have jobs?" Eric asked.

The boys shook their heads.

"What about Waldron?"

"Can't say."

"Do you have his cell number?"

"No," Jonathan said quickly.

Pepper knew it was a lie. She was certain now that the boys were keeping the pack leader informed about what was going on with Pepper and the Silver brothers. Eric recorded the boys' previous address and sent a text to someone. "No more following Ms. Grayling, or I'll have to do something more than lecture you," Eric said.

Both nodded, then headed back the way they had come.

"Do you think they'll listen to what you said?" Sarandon asked Eric. He looked like he thought Eric should have hauled them in on some charges right then and there.

"Yeah. I think they're afraid enough of Waldron that they will. But mainly I think they're afraid he won't like that they got caught on their little secret agent mission. If they'd been sneakier about it, he might have appreciated the news."

"They weren't trying to be stealthy," Pepper said.

"No. They were being cocky teens. What can I say?" Eric said, raising a brow at her.

"Like you were at that age?" Pepper could just imagine.

Eric cast her an elusive smile.

"Only you wouldn't have backed down," Pepper guessed.

"Depends on who I was talking to."

Sarandon snorted. "You wouldn't have backed down. Not even with our father or Darien's father when he was pack leader."

Eric looked like he could have socked Sarandon for saying so.

Pepper was amused by Sarandon speaking up about Eric. It made her wonder: If Eric had been a pack leader in his own right, would his mate have had any say in leading the pack? That made her wonder if he'd ever had a mate.

"What?" Sarandon said. "It's the truth. If you felt something needed to be done or said, you did it. And you owned up to it. You never backed down."

"What about you, Sarandon?" Pepper asked, curious.

"Hell, not me. When Father was in a terror, we let Eric stick up for us. Dad was the sheriff of Silver Town. He was pretty much adrift after we lost our mother. Eric tended to be the bossy one. Keeping us in line when we needed someone to do that. We're all only a few minutes apart, but he always made sure the rest of us got fed.

"Normally, we had more than enough motherly she-wolves in the pack to check up on us, but occasionally something was going on and we'd be forgotten. When we were a little older, Eric learned how to cook and taught us. So we became really self-sufficient when we were fairly young. Eric even made us do laundry. And you know how that was done in the old days. No washing machines and the modern conveniences we have nowadays."

"Yeah, I know the days." She couldn't help but be impressed that Eric had taken charge of his brothers when he was the same age as them.

When they reached the campsite, they spoke in turn to the Boy Scouts. Afterward, they went to the last camp and then they were finished with their lectures for the day.

Eric offered her his card. "If you ever need anything when you visit the park, let me know and I'll see what I can do."

"Thanks." She tucked his card in her shirt pocket, certain she'd never have any need to call him. But what if she did? She would keep it in a drawer of a chest in her living room, like she did with the rest of the business cards people gave her.

Despite the fact that Pepper wasn't interested in having a mate, she'd had fun meeting wolves from another pack. They were different, interesting, and she realized how everything had become kind of the same old thing with her own wolf pack. She thought about how Eric must have felt to lose his mother and then take charge of his brothers, and how that must have affected him. Maybe that's why he was genuinely good with the Boy Scouts. Had he been the same way with his brothers? She imagined he'd had to be strict with his own brothers, or they would have gotten away with stuff like all boys would do. But then she wondered if Eric had gotten away with stuff when he was a kid, or had he been super responsible?

She'd had a close relationship with her mother and father, and when they had died she'd inherited the pack. No one would have considered it any other way. Harold had been a wolf with her pack forever. He had been the closest in age to her, and she had cared for him. He'd been more of a beta. Not alpha pushy like Waldron, who had declared from the first time he met her a few weeks ago that he wanted their packs to join as one.

She knew it had to do with her treed land as much as anything. She had wondered why Waldron's pack had left their territory, but since she hadn't wanted him to believe she was interested in him or his pack, she'd hadn't asked.

No way did she want an alpha male in her life. She'd had too much trouble with several over the years. Including her father before he died. She thought some of it was because she was just as alpha and they'd butted heads all the time. Her mother had been more beta, and Pepper had gotten along great with her.

On the hike to her car, Pepper pulled out Eric's card to really look at it and smiled when she saw the wolf's head. It wasn't just any wolf's picture. It was Eric's handsome wolf portrait.

But even so, she just couldn't imagine dealing with another alpha male like any of the ones she'd met so far without wanting to do him bodily harm.

Chapter 6

ALL THAT WAS ON THE AGENDA WHEN ERIC WENT HOME WAS to wash the bloodstain out his uniform and then go to bed. He'd probably get up later, but he was wiped out from the lingering fever. Tomorrow, he'd investigate the cannabis plants further, but before he left the park today, he was driving over to the campground where Pepper and her people had stayed.

Sarandon walked him to his truck. "I'm dropping by Silva's tearoom and picking up some chicken soup, potato rolls, and a pie for you. I already called in the order, and I'll drop it by your place."

"I thought you said I should sleep."

Sarandon turned to leave. "And eat. You need to eat, then sleep. See you later."

Since when did his younger brother dictate Eric's life? Not that he didn't appreciate what Sarandon was doing for him, but Eric knew Sarandon wasn't going to just drop off the food and leave. His brother wanted to talk more about Pepper and her situation.

Eric didn't tell Sarandon where he was going first either. He wanted to know for himself if Pepper or her people had anything to do with the illegal marijuana plants.

When he arrived at the campground, Eric felt a bit apprehensive. He wanted more than anything to clear Pepper and her people of any wrongdoing. He didn't smell any of the wolves who had been at the growing sites. He suspected if Waldron's or Pepper's packs were involved, they now knew that one of the park rangers was a wolf. They might have begun wearing hunter's scent, but it was too late for that. He already knew the culprits' scents. At least five of them.

He only found the same scents as before when he reached the first of the cabins. No one he'd smelled at the marijuana sites. The second cabin, same thing. But as he reached the third cabin, he saw Pepper hiking up the trail, looking as surprised to see him there as he was to see her. Now how the hell could he get himself out of this one? And what was she doing back here?

"Fancy seeing you here," she immediately said, looking wary. "I thought you were going home to bed because you're sick."

"I am, but I wanted to make sure no one was camping here illegally since you vacated early. Sometimes we have folks who will try to use a cabin if the renters leave earlier than expected."

"Really?"

"Yeah. It hasn't happened here while I've been working, but it did up north at another national park. Besides that, I wanted to learn all your people's scents in case I run into them later. I smelled Waldron around here, checking out the area."

"I noticed."

"Did you leave something behind?"

"A pack member said one of her son's favorite action figures was left at the cabin because we were in such a rush to leave. Since I was already close to here, I told her I'd check. I hope you won't report me for using a lockpick on the cabin where her boys stayed so that I can look for it."

He shook his head. "Unless you want me to use mine so your search will seem more legit."

"I'll take you up on that. I wouldn't want to do anything illegal in front of a law enforcement officer."

He unlocked the door to the cabin, then let her go in first. She headed straight for one of the bedrooms while he smelled around the place, trying to locate any scent of a wolf who had been up at one of the marijuana patches. None smelled familiar, and he felt a hint of relief.

She came out of the bedroom smiling and waving a golden-armored action figure. "Pauline didn't think she'd hear the end of it last night, so she'll be delighted to know it was still here."

Eric was glad Pepper had a legitimate reason to be here. Not that he didn't, but he still felt guilty about checking up on her and her people when he really liked what he'd seen of her.

"Are you returning home now?"

He swore she wanted to tell him she'd call his superiors—his pack leaders—if he didn't go straight home and rest. He smiled. "Yeah, I'm done here." And he was glad he hadn't found anything to tie her pack to the illegal drugs.

"Thanks, Eric." And then to his surprise, she took hold of his arm and kissed him on the cheek very quickly, pulling away before he had a chance to react.

"Hell," he said, smiling down at her, "I'm glad I came back to check the cabins."

She laughed. "Well, it won't happen again. I just… wanted to thank you for everything."

Now he was feeling guilty again. If she only knew

why he really was here. He wished he could just accept the kiss as a sweet gesture and nothing more, but, damn it, he wanted something more to come of it. But what if she was trying to bamboozle him into thinking she was all sweet and not doing anything illegal so he would be too stuck on her to arrest her? His law enforcement training was telling him to be careful before making any mistakes he'd later regret.

His wolfish side said screw that, she was the kind of woman he wanted in his life. And if she was doing anything illegal, well, he wasn't going to worry about that now. He just had to prove who was planting the seeds and harvesting the plants and hope that had nothing to do with her pack.

"Eric? Where did you park your truck? I didn't see it at the site where we parked ours before. Is there another official-use road near here?"

"Yeah. That's where I parked when I carried Susan to the camp."

"Oh, okay. I was going to give you a lift because you look so flushed, but you're probably parked closer than I am."

He was touched by her change of heart and glad he had invited her to share lunch with them. Maybe that had convinced her that he and Sarandon were just offering friendship as wolves in the vicinity.

"Thanks. I would have taken you up on it, but you're right. I enjoyed visiting with you and loved hearing your lecture. I was trying to pick up some tips from you to teach our kids, but maybe instead you could talk to them sometime."

"I'd…like that." She shrugged. "It's part of my job."

She waved the action figure. "Got to get going. Nice seeing you again."

"Likewise." He watched her head out as he locked up the cabin. Despite feeling drained physically, he felt a little lighter-hearted about having seen Pepper again.

But when Eric made a wide loop around the last of the cabins, he smelled the scent of one of the wolves who had been at the first marijuana site he had found. He began to explore the area again, hating that he'd found anything that could incriminate her pack. Maybe the wolf wasn't one of her pack members. Maybe he or she was like Waldron, just snooping around.

But what if the wolf *was* in her pack?

When Eric arrived home, he took a shower, careful not to get his bandages wet. He pulled on a T-shirt and gym shorts, ready to retire to bed when Sarandon arrived.

"How are you feeling?" Sarandon asked, bringing in two sacks of food.

"Like I need to be sleeping." Even though all he wanted to do was investigate this business with the cannabis further and prove Pepper wasn't involved. "Soup smells good." Eric sniffed at the air again and smiled. "Silva made me chocolate mousse pie?" Now that sure brightened his evening.

"Yep, just for you. Sorry the word has spread, but several pack members asked me if you needed to hunt down the wolf who attacked you. Now that we know it wasn't a guard wolf and he's causing trouble for Pepper's pack, we might need some backup to handle it."

"We're *not* getting involved. Not unless she asks. Although I did ask CJ to see if he could run down a wolf pack in Boise, Idaho, to check if that's where Waldron and his pack are from. And if Waldron and his pack members are involved in the production of marijuana, I'll need our deputy sheriffs to help me catch the culprits."

"So you think he might be involved?" Sarandon poured the soup into two bowls, then paused and looked up at Eric. "It's okay if I share this with you, isn't it? She made enough for six."

"Six?" Eric brought out spoons. "Yeah, of course. I wouldn't want it any other way." Not after his brother had gone to the trouble of ordering it and paying for it. Eric normally loved his brother's company, but he knew where the conversation would be headed and planned to change the direction right away. "But, yeah, it's possible. The Fairhaven teens wouldn't say what kind of a job Waldron has. So what if pot is his business here? And he thinks that if he takes over Pepper's lands, he can make a real mint off growing weed."

"As far as Pepper goes, it sounds like the perfect setup to me—for you. She's not mated and has her own pack. You need a mate and would be the perfect coleader. You've always wanted to be one. If Darien hadn't taken over the pack, you would have, and done a damn good job."

Eric wondered if things would have turned out differently if his father had been the pack leader. He thought about telling Sarandon that he had to consider Pepper and her pack as suspects too, but he wanted to know what he was dealing with first and not just make wild assumptions.

"It wouldn't work out. She said she doesn't want anyone in her life." Even though she had kissed him, it was purely a thank-you, and despite wanting to read more into it, he knew better. "I'm sure she's used to running her own pack. She doesn't need a male sharing the responsibilities. She may believe I'd be a threat to her position."

"What about to have children? From the sounds of it, she has none of her own."

"Maybe she doesn't want any."

"Maybe." Sarandon sighed. "But you'd be happy either way, wouldn't you? So what are you going to do about this Waldron? Surely you're not going to let him get away with stalking her."

"Sarandon, she doesn't want my help. I'm sure she thinks all I'll do is replace Waldron in his quest to court her and take over her pack."

"You're probably right. Though I can't imagine you giving up on her so easily." Sarandon served a couple of beers. "You know they say beer and baked potatoes—well, or chicken soup—make you feel better when you have the flu. If you had the flu. With the fever. You know what I mean." Then he took his seat across from Eric. "Despite what you think, I could tell she liked the way you were with her: not pushing her to go to lunch with us, just offering her your card in case she, or anyone in her pack, had trouble in the park. That showed real restraint on your part. I didn't know you had it in you." Then Sarandon frowned at Eric. "It's not because you're feeling so poorly, is it? Hell, that's probably it. The fever, the pain from the bite."

"It's not the fever. I want to give her space. Besides, I'm really not in the running for a mate right now." Not that Eric wouldn't be damned interested if Pepper was, but the rest of his pack didn't need to know that. He took another spoonful of the tasty chicken soup. "Silva sure makes the best soups."

"And pie. When I called, she didn't have any left. So she baked you a fresh one and wished you all the best. I have to warn you, CJ and Brett are dropping by in a few minutes."

"Ah, hell, Sarandon. I'm supposed to be resting."

"Yeah, but they're our brothers and they want to see for themselves you're all right."

"I'm all right." Eric felt like hell, but by tomorrow morning, he was sure he'd be feeling fine.

The doorbell rang and Sarandon hurried to get the door. "Hey, CJ, Brett."

"How's he doing?" Brett asked, sounding concerned.

"Grouchy. Which means he has to be feeling better."

CJ was carrying a box of chocolates. "From my mate's aunt's chocolate shop. She sent them especially for you," he said as they entered the dining room. "You look like you're on fire."

"Have you eaten?" Eric asked them, suspecting they might not have, since Sarandon had picked up enough food for six people. Eric should have known.

CJ shook his head. "But we don't want to impose."

"There's enough for six." Eric finished his bowl of soup and took another swig of beer.

"So what's the deal with the wolf?" CJ asked, sitting down to eat with the rest of them. He took his job seriously as a deputy sheriff, and if any of the family was injured by an outside wolf, he and the rest of the sheriff's department would take care of the situation in a heartbeat.

Eric explained what had happened and how he didn't want to get involved unless Pepper asked for his help.

"Ah, now I got it." Brett was a reporter for their local newspaper, and he loved people and stories. "You are the reluctant hero."

"How do you figure that?" Eric couldn't help being annoyed. "If she needs me, I'll be there pronto. But I don't want to butt in where I'm not wanted."

Brett and CJ stared at him.

Sarandon saluted him. "Yep, I told you guys Eric had turned over a new leaf."

"I wonder how long that will last," Brett said, chuckling.

"If everyone's done with their soup, I'll serve the pie and then we can let Eric get some rest," Sarandon said.

"I thought the pie was for me," Eric said, not being serious in the least.

"Now that's the Eric we know." CJ eyed Sarandon with the pie cutter, his plate readied for a slice.

At least Eric hadn't *meant* to sound serious. Was he *really* like that?

Despite how rotten he felt, Eric was glad that his brothers had come by. He wasn't sharing his box of chocolates though. When they left, he collapsed in bed, knowing Brett was wrong. To be a reluctant hero, he would have to be apathetic toward Pepper's situation. He was anything but. He totally sympathized with her. And if she needed him, he would indeed be there without hesitation. Guaranteed. Nothing reluctant about it.

─────

When Susan called, Pepper was afraid it was because of trouble with the pack. She wouldn't be home for another hour and a half because she had to do some grocery shopping since Susan was staying with her for a couple of days.

Waldron had called, Susan told her. "Before you get angry with me for taking the call," Susan started, "remember that you wouldn't return his calls, answer them, or listen to his voice messages. Anyway, he said he now knows who the wolf he attacked is. At the time, Waldron thought the guy intended to do you harm."

"Oh, give me a break." The gall of the man! Did he really think she'd believe him? "By the way, I saw Eric today when I was giving my lecture. He and his brother Sarandon were also talking to the Boy Scouts about nature. We had lunch together. All three of us. Waldron had two teen boys from his pack spying on us. So I'm certain he's upset over that."

"Seriously? He's a real case and a half. But, wow, you had lunch with Eric? Be still, my pounding heart. So how was it? What did you talk about? Have you set another date?"

"I'm not *courting* the wolf. And I only went with them because I was hungry and it would have seemed rude of me to decline when Eric had helped you out." Pepper wasn't about to mention running into him at the campsite again. She was still wondering why she had kissed him if she didn't want anything romantic with him. "I thought you were going to call him and thank him, but I got the impression you hadn't."

"I didn't. Sorry. I slept most of the day. My leg has been killing me."

"Oh, I'm sorry, Susan. I should have asked."

"No problem. I know you've had your hands full dealing with Eric." She laughed. "Okay, so Waldron knows Eric is a park ranger, I guess because of his spies. Waldron wanted you to know the ranger was probably just there on a night run, not there because he intended to bother you."

"Yeah, like Waldron is doing. Did you ask why *he* was there last night?"

"No, but he told me anyway. I'm sure he wanted the news passed along to you. Anyway, he said he often runs in the park since he doesn't have his own territory, and it's normally safe. Then he saw this other wolf spying on you like he was ready to pounce."

"Ha! Who's the one doing the spying?"

"I agree. Now this is the real kicker. Waldron said if the other wolf is interested, you'd better let him know you're not, because otherwise he could make it damn hard for the ranger to keep his job."

"You're kidding." Pepper didn't want to believe Waldron would do anything that underhanded. But then again, if he thought he had a chance to get her prime land…

"So now, what about Eric?" Susan asked.

"He was running a fever."

"From Waldron's bite? I will kill the wolf myself."

"Yeah, and Eric didn't want to disappoint the Scouts by not showing up."

"He sure sounds like mate material to me. You know, Pauline won't be upset with you if you decide to find another mate, Pepper."

Pauline was Harold's sister and had five-year-old twins. Pepper did wonder sometimes whether Pauline felt Pepper owed it to her mate's memory to never take another mate. Not that she'd ever found one, but still, Pepper had also pondered if Pauline's presence in her pack had anything to do with Pepper not wanting to change the status quo. She and Pauline didn't get along all that well, but Pauline still needed a pack to help raise her twins.

"Well, what was he like?"

"He's nice. Not pushy like Waldron. And he has a cute brother."

"Oh, you're interested in both of them?"

"No. Neither. They were just nice."

"They're too beta? I worried about that when Eric didn't fight Waldron."

"Eric thought Waldron might be my guard. He didn't want to cause trouble with our pack."

"Wow, he sounds perfect."

"He's not. He's one of those all-alpha wolves. He'd take charge and I'd lose the pack."

"You don't really believe that, do you?"

"Yeah, I do. He wouldn't be able to help himself. Even his brother said Eric stood up to their pack leader, who is a cousin of theirs, and to his dad, the sheriff. So yeah."

"Well, here I'd hoped he would help us out with Waldron. What's that in your pocket?"

Pepper glanced down at Eric's business card, the edge poking out. She pulled it from her pocket and handed it to Susan. "Eric's card. In case we ever have trouble in the park."

"Are you going to tell Eric what Waldron said?"

"I don't want to get him involved…but since this could affect his career, I need to warn him."

"I wholeheartedly agree. On another subject, Pauline wanted me to remind you about the boys' birthday party tomorrow."

Pepper never forgot the boys' birthday parties. She

wondered if Pauline was subtly reminding her that her brother had been Pepper's mate. Pepper realized she was probably making something out of nothing, but the thought of Pauline doing that still bothered her.

"I'll be there."

After dinner, Susan went to bed and Pepper considered Eric's business card, his wolf eyes gazing into hers. She didn't want to wake him if he was sleeping because he needed the rest. On the other hand, she didn't want to delay telling him in case Waldron and his pack planned some shenanigans tomorrow that could endanger Eric's job.

She called him, and when she heard his groggy voice on the other end of the line, she felt bad she had woken him. "Eric? It's me, Pepper. I needed to tell you something important."

Chapter 7

ERIC WAS ALMOST ASLEEP WHEN HE GOT THE CALL FROM Pepper. A million thoughts raced through his mind: she wanted to see him again; she wanted to check how he was feeling; she was having trouble with Waldron. If so, Eric was ready to shift and take the wolf on. What he hadn't expected was *this* kind of call.

"Eric, I hated to wake you but I wanted to warn you about this. My cousin took a message from Waldron concerning you."

"Don't tell me. He's going to show me what else he can do with his bite, if I don't back off from seeing you. I guess the boys at the deli must have told him we had lunch together."

"They did, but it's worse. He's threatening to get you fired."

"Oh, really."

"That's what he said. And I wouldn't put it past him either. I don't believe he's bluffing."

"Probably not."

"Well, what are you going to do about it? I was afraid to tell you in case you'd do something rash."

"I don't understand why he'd tell you this. I would think your reaction would be to dislike him even further."

"I think he's more worried about you than how I'll react to his threats against you."

"All right. I'll talk to Darien about it."

"Will he get the whole pack involved in this? I didn't want to upset your people."

"No. But we'll discuss the best way to handle it." Eric always took the lead in doing things his way when something had to do with him. So this was really a first for him: reaching out to Darien and Lelandi and asking how they'd want to proceed. He wasn't a lone wolf, after all. Ultimately his actions with another pack could have consequences that would affect everyone.

"Let me know what you're going to do, will you?"

Eric smiled a little. "You didn't give me your phone number or any way to contact you."

"Oh, sorry." She gave him her cell number.

Waldron was really going about this the wrong way, Eric thought. His actions had only made Pepper want to protect Eric.

Eric wrote her number down on a pad of paper on his bedside table. Not that this changed a whole lot between them, but he realized she cared enough about him to try to save him from Waldron's underhandedness.

"How are you feeling?"

"I've felt better. I'm sure by tomorrow I'll be as good as new."

She sighed. "Sorry I had to wake you with this news. I'll let you get some rest."

"Pepper?" Eric wanted to make sure she didn't take any guff from Waldron on his account. "If he threatens you any more, give me a call. From the sound of it, he wants to escalate matters. I know there's nothing going on between us, but Waldron might think that if you aren't interested in me, you might meet other bachelor males in my pack. Even my brother Sarandon, because he had lunch with us. Waldron might worry you're going to find a mate elsewhere before he can convince you that you need him instead."

"I'm not interested in finding a mate, for one thing. But beyond that, I'm *really* not interested in him."

"What if he thinks he can chase you out of your territory?"

"That's not going to happen either."

"All right. Just trying to come up with some scenarios so we can be prepared if he tries something underhanded regarding you and your pack. I'll let you know what my pack decides to do about his issue with me."

"Thanks, Eric. I appreciate it. Have a good night's sleep."

"You too." He ended the call feeling he really had made some progress with Pepper.

He'd had an awful time getting to sleep anyway because of his concern about having smelled a wolf who had been at one of the marijuana sites at her campsite. He had to learn the truth for himself before he confronted Pepper with it. Especially since the wolf could have been with Waldron's pack and snooping on Pepper for Waldron. Maybe none of the wolves involved with the marijuana were members of Waldron's or Pepper's packs, but Eric thought the likelihood of another wolf pack roaming the park was close to nil. Wanting to take Waldron to task, Eric called Darien. "Hey, we might have a problem."

Darien put the call on speaker so Lelandi could hear while she was tucked in his arms in bed. He was certain

Eric's call had to do with the wolf who had bitten him near the cabins. Darien had suspected it wouldn't end with that.

When they ended the call with Eric, Lelandi said to Darien, "Oh…my…God, that is the first time Eric has ever consulted us about something that could cause him trouble."

"He knew the pack would go after this Waldron, which would cause them trouble too."

"Yes, but, Mate of Mine, don't you see the significance?"

Darien loved Lelandi, knowing she was using her extensive psychology training to consider Eric's actions. Darien was thinking more about how they were going to safeguard Eric and the pack from this lunatic wolf and his pack. Which proved how important having two points of view was in leading the pack.

"He's behaving like a pack member should." Darien was glad about it.

"Yes, but why?"

"Because of the woman!" Darien really hadn't been thinking along those lines at first.

Lelandi sighed. "Right. Who would have ever thought a woman would make a difference?"

"Yeah, but she's not interested in a mate."

Lelandi stroked Darien's naked chest, and he contemplated tabling the discussion until after he made love to his mate.

"Right. But people can change their minds," she said.

"Yeah, look at how you changed your mind about me."

"Ha. With us, it was the other way around."

"Mutual, really." He let out a breath.

"I can't believe Eric has found a she-wolf he's interested in after all these years," Lelandi said, sounding hopeful.

"He's found a she-wolf who's trouble. At least for him. Well, and the pack, because we're not going to let this alpha male attack Eric, either on the job or off."

"I think you said the same about me—as far as being trouble."

He smiled. "Only the best kind of trouble."

"It's unusual to find a she-wolf who runs a pack on her own. She must be a natural-born leader and have some good sub-leaders to help her out."

"Exactly. And Eric is a born leader, which is why we butt heads so often. I don't want to see Eric get hurt over this. Also, I'm sure something happened a few years ago—before you were part of the pack—that had to do with a woman. He was gone for a while, then came back, stayed in seclusion, and wouldn't speak to his father or any of us, just Sarandon. I suspect he finally told Sarandon what was going on, since he's Eric's closest brother."

"He fell in love and lost the woman?"

"Possibly. He wouldn't discuss it with me. I've asked CJ, but he said he doesn't know what happened and Eric would never tell him. I didn't ask Sarandon because I was sure he knew and surer still that he wouldn't tell me."

"Hmmm."

"No trying to wheedle it out of him. If he wants to talk about it, he will."

Lelandi sighed. "Yes, but it sounds like he really needs to deal with the issue concerning the woman, if that's what has made him reluctant to get involved with another."

"I agree." Darien let out his breath. "If he bosses

Pepper Grayling around like he did the MacTyre sisters when they were renovating the Silver Town Hotel, I can see her being downright annoyed and chasing him off."

"Well, I hope they find some common interests and much more. Besides, I don't think he felt any attraction to the sisters. He was more interested in the prospect of the hotel being renovated to show off its former glory. With Pepper, something more might come of it. Maybe we could help them along."

"No." Darien wasn't in the matchmaking business, and he didn't want Lelandi pushing Eric.

"Well, maybe you don't want to do anything, but…"

Darien smiled and shook his head. "Eric doesn't need our help *or* interference. And he wouldn't appreciate it. Just let him be. If it is meant to be, it will be."

Lelandi sighed. "Sometimes a little planning can make all the difference in the world. What about the wolf who bit Eric?"

"What do you think we should do?"

"Beyond killing Waldron?"

Smiling a little, Darien raised his brows as he considered Lelandi's serious expression. He'd thought she would offer a more analytical approach, based on a psychological analysis of the wolf and his pack dynamics. Although, Darien agreed that some of what she said had merit. Even if Waldron didn't go any further, his threat was forcing them all to watch their backs. Not only did they have to worry about Eric losing his job, but Waldron might decide to have some of the bigger males in his pack help attack Eric while he was out running alone as a wolf at night. If that happened, Darien and his pack would have to take more drastic measures.

As determined as they all were to locate the wolves growing the cannabis, Darien was sure Eric would continue to do his night searches. Darien had hoped Eric would be able to tie Waldron into that operation, but Eric had assured him the wolf he had fought hadn't been at any of the sites they'd located.

"I was thinking you could analyze Waldron's personality profile and we could come up with a really good strategy to take care of him." Darien caressed Lelandi's soft, silky back.

"You mean, beyond killing him?"

Darien chuckled. "Yeah. If he hurts Eric again the way he did this last time, he's a dead wolf, period. But if he doesn't—"

"Oh, all right. Here's what I'm thinking. Why would he leave his old territory?"

"You're brilliant, you know that?"

"Yeah." She smiled up at him, and he began kissing her and rolled her onto her back. "More talk—later."

—∿∿—

"Did you tell Eric what Waldron said?" Susan asked Pepper the next morning before the pack leader headed out to a Christmas tree farm. They had both been asked to inspect the trees and suggest planting tips to improve production. Susan always assisted when Pepper went to places like this. Since Susan was manager of their pack's own tree farm, she always had a handle on specifics. But this time Susan was stuck at home, unable to maneuver around a tree farm very well on crutches.

"I did. He said he'd talk it over with his pack leaders."

"Oh. What *are* they going to do about it?"

"Not sure. Eric said he'd get back to me—" Pepper's phone howled, her favorite ringtone, and she checked to see who was calling. "Speak of the devil."

Susan raised her brow, but Pepper ignored her. Her outlook on pack leadership wasn't changing, no matter what Susan thought. "Hi, Eric? What did they say?"

"Do you want to have lunch with me?"

Pepper was so taken aback, she hesitated to respond.

"I'm home sick. Doc said I can't go anywhere, and I'd like to talk to you about this."

"At your place?" Pepper thought he sounded somewhat frustrated. She'd feel the same way.

Grinning, Susan winked at her.

"Yeah, that's where I am. At home. And Doc gave me strict orders to stay here until I kick this fever or else."

"Is this part of the plan to stop Waldron from hurting your career?"

He laughed. "Well, if I can't go to work, I guess he can't hurt me."

"What time?"

"Any time that works for you. Just call before you get here so I can get out of bed and fix us something."

"Could you handle another Reuben? I'll stop at the deli."

"Hell yeah."

"I'll bring chips, pickles, the works."

"I'm already hungry. See you in a couple of hours."

When Pepper ended the call, Susan said, "Wow."

"It's nothing. He's still sick from the bite Waldron gave him, and their doctor has restricted him to his house. No going to work today."

Susan was still smiling.

"We'll be discussing what his pack is going to do about Waldron."

"At Eric's house."

"He can't leave the house."

"Okay, all right. I hope he feels better soon. Waldron must have really torn into Eric. I'm amazed he didn't retaliate."

Pepper was too. She really admired him for not doing so because he thought the wolf was protecting one of his pack members. Not every alpha wolf would have stood for it.

"He was burning up yesterday. I felt bad for him, but he was really good about it. No acting like he was dying. No looking for sympathy or to be babied." Pepper remembered how Harold had been when he got sick. She'd thought she suddenly had a kid to take care of.

"Just so he could keep on lecturing the kids? Or because he wanted to stay near you?"

"Oh, come on, Susan. He didn't even know I was going to be there, and yet he was still there."

"Oh, all right. But I really think you shouldn't… well, dismiss him." Then Susan's blue eyes widened. "Forget it. Don't pay him no never mind." Then she smiled. "Maybe you'd like me to go and talk to him. He sounds like he could use some tender, loving care, and you don't want to give any indication you're giving him any. And really, it's probably safer for him if you stay away, so you don't antagonize Waldron."

"*You* can't leave home or drive right now. And if you're serious, he does have two unmated brothers." So if she wasn't interested in Eric, why didn't Pepper want Susan to visit him?

"Yeah, but this one sounds so dreamy. Not your type at all."

Pepper laughed. "If I didn't know you better, I'd say you were using reverse psychology on me."

"As stubborn as you are, I wouldn't even try such a thing." Then Susan frowned. "You don't think he's just pretending he's still sick to get on your good side, do you?"

"As alpha as he is? No. He sounded annoyed he's confined to the house for the day."

"And the night."

Pepper gave her a look not to go there.

"What? I only meant that he was running as a wolf at night before, and he can't do that now either."

"Right."

"Hey, I can't help it if you're thinking of other things."

Pepper enjoyed being around her cousin. They were just like sisters. And she loved Susan's fun-loving nature.

"What do you think Pauline thinks about all of this?" Susan asked.

"She's funny that way. She keeps her feelings to herself. As long as I've known her, I don't think I'll ever really know her."

The winding road to Silver Town finally straightened, and before Pepper reached the actual town, she found the country road that led to Eric's house. It was backed up against a mountain and sitting beside a creek with four other homes, half hidden in a parklike setting. The ruggedness of the forested land suited him.

Before she reached his house, she saw a police SUV

flash its lights and pull over a navy-blue pickup that had been following her for miles.

What if one of Waldron's men had followed her here and was keeping an eye on where she was going and who she was seeing? Now that would really fry her biscuits.

She wondered what the man had been pulled over for. If he had been following her, she hoped the officer would at least find a reason to put him in jail for a while.

Just before she drove into Eric's long, secluded driveway, she saw the Fairhaven boys get out of the pickup. She was shocked to see them. But now she knew what their vehicle looked like, in case they pulled this again. She parked at the curb to watch what happened next. To her surprise, the officer called for backup and two more vehicles arrived, as if the boys had committed a federal crime. The officers handcuffed the teens and put them in the back of one of the police vehicles, and then drove off. A tow truck came and towed the pickup away. She wondered if the boys had illegal drugs in the truck.

The excitement over, she pulled into Eric's drive and headed up the long driveway. She'd told him half an hour earlier that she was on her way to give him time to wake up. When he came outside to greet her, he still looked a bit flushed, so she could understand his doctor's concern.

"The Fairhaven boys followed me here," she said, disconcerted. She started to grab bags of food off the passenger's seat, but Eric got them for her.

"Yeah, my brother called me with an update. He's Deputy Sheriff CJ Silver. He said they followed you for a long time. CJ was checking on their truck registration and trying to find something to charge them with."

"Stalking?"

"Speeding on the way into Silver Town."

"I must have been," she admitted with chagrin.

"No one saw you speeding," Eric said, looking so serious, she had to laugh.

"I can see how running your own town can come in handy. So your brother wasn't able to charge them with enough to keep them in jail?"

"CJ and Trevor Osgood, the other deputy sheriff, found a six-pack of empty beer bottles in the teens' truck. They'd both been drinking. Seventeen, underage. Driving under the influence. Yeah, we've got them. Plus the stalking business, once the deputies realized these were the two kids who followed us yesterday."

"Were they really DUI?"

"Yes. We needed to get them off the road and send a message home to Waldron. If the boys do illegal stuff while stalking you, they'll have to pay the price. Not to mention that following you like that is another offense we take seriously around here."

"What if their parents come to pick them up and don't let Waldron know the trouble they were in? I can imagine he'd be angry with them."

Eric set the table and Pepper brought the food over. "Darien will insist that he speak to Waldron about the kids stalking you twice now. He'll do it with a pack leader perspective, from one to another. I assume Darien's position will have more weight than mine."

She didn't know why Eric's comment touched her so, but it did. He didn't seem upset over it, just resigned to the fact that this was his lot in life. Yet she could tell he was a real alpha leader. "Why don't you start your own pack?"

"My brothers followed me once. But this is home for them. Silver Town. Our heritage. This is where we belong."

She didn't think he meant it. Not as far as *he* was concerned. But for his brothers, yes. He'd brought them home, giving up his own dreams. That said something good about his character. "How does Darien want to handle the situation between you and Waldron?"

"We want to learn more about Waldron's background. Where he and his pack were staying before. Was he part of a larger pack, or did he cause trouble with another pack in the area that ran him off? Darien wants to use Waldron's past against him, if we can learn anything."

"What if he has no past to mention?"

"As long as we've lived, everyone has a past of some kind or another."

"Even you?"

Eric fixed glasses of ice water for them. "Even me."

That made her really curious.

"So have you always run the pack on your own?" Eric asked. "Or did you have a mate?"

She hadn't really planned to share that much about herself. The more she shared, the more trouble she could have. On the other hand, Eric had only helped her cousin out and had earned Waldron's wrath because of it. Though it wasn't Pepper's fault, she felt somewhat responsible and hated that Eric and his pack had been dragged into this. "I lost Harold seven years ago. We had been mated for less than two years."

"Was Grayling his name or yours?"

"Mine. The pack was mine. We decided it should stay in my parents' name since they'd started the pack."

Eric nodded. "That's the hardest part for us. Letting go. Losing a mate we vowed to stay with forever."

She didn't think he could really understand how it felt to lose a mate. She would always love Harold. But her real concern was that she didn't want to have to break in another leader. Once she'd known she could manage on her own just fine, she didn't feel the need to add a new mate into the equation. She had to think of not only herself, but her people. What if a new mate was good to her, but not to her pack members? They'd have to either move away or silently suffer, because once she mated again, she would be with that wolf for life.

At least everyone had known Harold, and he'd been beta enough that she was able to mold him into the leader she needed him to be. With Eric or others like him? Waldron, for one? They were alphas to the max, and that made her take a few steps back.

Not all betas would be able to become alpha enough to lead a pack either. Pauline was lots more alpha than Harold had been. Pepper had had to take her sister-in-law to task a few times over the years because of it. Pepper adored Pauline's twin boys though. When Pauline lost her own mate, Pepper thought she might move on, find another mate, and join his pack. Pepper would miss the boys terribly if that happened though.

"Have you ever wondered what you would have done if you hadn't inherited your parents' pack and become the pack leader? Would you have started your own?" Eric asked.

"Starting your own pack can be really tough. You offer for others to join. They may not care for your style of leadership and move on. You have to make sure that you set up in a territory that's not run by another pack. Sometimes you don't know that until it's too late. My great-grandfather died over a confrontation with another pack in a territory," Pepper said.

"None of them knew there were others in the area, so he didn't know they ruled there until they made it abundantly clear. My great-grandmother had to move the pack to the area north of park. Originally our pack was from New Mexico. There were only ten pack members at the time, including my great-grandmother's triplet sons, one being my grandfather, who took over when she died."

"She had run the pack alone until then?"

"Yes." Which was another reason Pepper knew she could do it. "All this time, we never knew you lived south of the park or that Silver Town was wolf-run. I'm sure we might have run across one of your people at some time or another, but it was just a brief encounter, nothing any of us recall."

"So you've mentioned us to your pack?"

"Sure. I wanted to let everyone know that if they need medical aid, you have a wolf doctor in town who can take care of them."

"And a vet."

She smiled.

"Just saying."

"I'll have to mention that too. In any event, they were glad to hear about the doctor."

"I take it you have land that's safe to run on."

"We do. Thanks."

"Well, we do too, and we use the ski resort for wolf

runs at night when the resort is closed. Feel free to join us anytime. Also, Darien and Lelandi would like to meet you. We have ties to a number of packs. Lelandi's brother runs a red wolf pack in Portland, Oregon. Her uncle runs the pack her father used to run. We're friends with another gray pack in a city close to here. My brother's mate has an aunt with the pack, and we have close ties to the woman who mated the pack leader. Her human family still lives here," Eric said.

"Human?"

"Long story. We never planned it that way, but because of it, we have a lot of pack allies while other packs remain isolated and have to fend for themselves, both against other *lupus garou* packs and with humans. We share resources, like our doctor, with other packs close by that might need one."

Pepper felt a bit of panic. She assumed Eric was offering her something they probably didn't offer to everyone—like to Waldron and his pack. And she had to remind herself she should talk to Darien and Lelandi before her people came here to use their doctor, just as a courtesy. But she couldn't help feeling more was going on here than met the eye—like this was a way for Eric to get to know her better. Still, if her people availed themselves of the Silvers' generosity, she'd be helping them out, not showing any interest in Eric.

"That would be nice."

"Splendid. When would be a good time for you to meet Darien and Lelandi?"

"I have nothing scheduled for this afternoon. I might as well do it while I'm already here, if they have the time and can meet with me."

"I'll give them a call and ask."

Eric called while Lelandi was putting the dishes in the dishwasher, so Darien answered the phone.

"Hey, Darien," Eric said. "I know you have babysitting duty while Lelandi has a couple of sessions with patients, but if you have time, could you meet with Pepper Grayling?" He glanced at her and asked Pepper, "Would half an hour from now be okay?" He quickly added, "Do you mind if the kids are about?"

She smiled. "I love kids." And their meeting would seem a lot less pack leader official if Darien was busy with the triplets. "And a half hour works for me." She figured that would give her enough time to drive around town and see the sights.

"Great," Eric said to Darien. "That works for her. I'll give her directions." He paused. "I'll tell her. Thanks. Later." He pocketed his phone. "He's calling CJ to have him give you a deputy sheriff's escort to his place so you don't have any further trouble—at least in our pack territory."

"Waldron is going to be so furious when he learns what happened to the Fairhaven boys."

Eric shook his head. "It's his fault for causing trouble with my pack."

"He won't see it that way."

"That's his problem."

Yeah, but it was now *her* problem too.

Chapter 8

As soon as Darien told Lelandi that Pepper was coming to see him, Lelandi rescheduled her patients' sessions for later in the afternoon. Everyone was excited that another pack might become their ally. And her patients knew that if anyone could put the she-wolf leader at ease, it would be Lelandi.

She surprised Darien when she returned to the house from the office where she conducted her practice.

"I thought you had two more sessions this afternoon." Darien pulled her into a hug as if he'd missed her for the hour she'd been away.

She hugged him back. "My patients are eager for us to have another wolf pack ally. We're good."

"Should we get someone to watch the triplets?"

"Nah. If Pepper knows you're going to be watching them, she'll probably be more at ease and see this as a social call, rather than business."

"You know best about these things."

"Not when it comes to a she-wolf who's been leading a pack on her own. I've never known one before. How long has she run the pack by herself?"

"I'm not sure. We'll have to ask her. I hear her driving up now."

Lelandi headed for the door and walked out to greet Pepper. She was dying to meet the woman who had intrigued Eric so.

Pepper was a pretty brunette who was wearing an aqua blouse and blue jeans. Her dark eyes were smiling, though she seemed a little wary. Which was understandable. She didn't know them, and the Silver Town pack was large enough to cause real trouble for smaller *lupus garou* packs.

"I'm Lelandi Silver," Lelandi said, stretching out her hand. "We're so eager to meet you. I had to see you for myself after you had such a positive effect on Eric."

"How so?" Pepper asked, sounding surprised.

"Well, truth be told, he rarely asks Darien and me to intervene when he's having difficulty. I just had to meet you to learn how you ever accomplished such a feat."

"I'm not looking for a mate," Pepper quickly said.

"Oh, heavens no. Of course not. Which is a good thing. Eric isn't either." At least that's the way he'd always talked. Lelandi suspected it had to do with the way his father had fallen apart after his mother's death. But she sensed there was more to it than that. As soon as Darien told her about Eric leaving the pack before his father had died and coming back devastated, she'd asked Eric's brothers if any of them wanted to talk about it.

CJ and Brett suspected something had happened to deeply upset Eric. He'd been restless, needing something, yet no one knew for certain what. Eric had gone off several times after his brothers were grown. From what she'd learned, she thought he'd been looking to start a pack of his own, although nothing had come of it. But that last time he left before their father had died, something had changed, the brothers said. CJ and Brett didn't know what, and Sarandon wouldn't say.

After talking to Sarandon about what had gone on with Pepper at the Boy Scout camps and then over lunch, Lelandi suspected that Eric was really interested in Pepper but didn't want to push her away like Waldron was doing. Then again, maybe Eric really *wasn't* interested in a mate. He hadn't shown any interest in the MacTyre sisters. Since Eric had wanted to learn where Pepper's pack was living, Lelandi suspected the former. He was trying his darnedest to be circumspect about it, which was a real change for him.

"I wanted to apologize for what happened to Eric," Pepper said, while Lelandi offered tea. "Thanks, I'd like some tea. Unsweetened, if that's all right."

"Yes, I made it before you got here. Neither of us drink sugar in our tea either. As for the situation with Eric, no apology necessary. If you don't mind, we can sit in the den while the kids watch television. If that's too much of a distraction, I can have someone come over and watch them."

"No, that's quite all right."

Lelandi poured glasses of tea for everyone, then carried the pitcher and a glass while Pepper grabbed Darien's and hers. They joined Darien in the den, where he was overseeing the triplets while they watched cartoons, and he seemed to be enjoying them as much as the kids, Pepper thought.

Lelandi made introductions. "These are our three-year-old triplets: our daughter, Lacey; our son, Dashiell, though we call him Dash; and Lucas."

"Adorable," Pepper said. "They sure take after the two of you. I bet you had dark curls just like Dash and Lucas when you were little," she said to Darien.

Lelandi smiled at Darien as she swore he blushed a little.

"And Lacey with her dark-red curls like yours, Lelandi. They're just the cutest."

Acting shy, Dash and Lacey clung to their dad's legs. Lelandi introduced Pepper to them, and then Darien scooped the kids up and set them back on the pillows on the carpeted floor to watch TV while the adults took their seats on the sofas.

Pepper sipped from her glass, then set it down on the coffee table.

"We want you to know we're here for you if you have any needs we can meet. Medical, vet, home repair, we have a list of services," Darien said.

Lelandi added, "We don't want to sound like we're pushing our wolf services, but it's nice to know that you can get discounted work done in case you need any, and if someone has to shift while they're there, no problem."

Pepper smiled. "No newly turned wolves in the pack, so we're good. But I do appreciate the offer. I'll share the list with my pack members if anyone needs work done on their homes or whatever."

Lelandi nodded. "Sounds good. And if you have any services you can provide, the same goes."

Pepper handed over a business card. "If you ever need trees—Christmas or just trees for landscaping—we have a tree nursery and a Christmas tree farm."

"That's great. I'm sure we can use some, as much as we love the forests. And Christmas will be here before we know it. As to the problem with Waldron and his pack," Darien said, "we're going on the offensive now. We would have let sleeping wolves lie, but with Waldron threatening Eric with further mayhem, we can't permit it."

Pepper took a deep breath and exhaled. "What do you propose to do?"

"Learn his weaknesses. And his strengths. Build a case against him to counter any he might try to hit Eric with. Already we know two of his weaknesses," Darien said.

"The Fairhaven teens," Pepper said with conviction.

"Right. We've got them on stalking charges because they've followed you twice now and we have enough eyewitnesses to verify it. The boys will probably say they acted on their own, but since they must have reported back to Waldron about your lunch with Eric and Sarandon, I imagine he told them to keep doing a good job. Maybe Waldron thought they could intimidate the two of you."

"Hardly," Pepper said.

"They don't really know about Eric. He ran off when Waldron bit him. He didn't stick around to fight. He used his uniform to take the boys to task, but Waldron might think that if Eric had to face him in a wolf-to-wolf fight, Eric would run off again, too afraid to fight," Lelandi said.

"That would be the day." Pepper leaned back on her chair, looking like she was glad Eric would stand up to Waldron if there was a next time. That was good, Lelandi thought, because the way things were going, that probably would happen. "You're right. It would be a fatal mistake on Waldron's part," Lelandi agreed. At least she hoped Eric would come out the winner. She hadn't seen Waldron in his wolf form or otherwise.

"We suspect Waldron would come prepared though, just in case he's mistaken about Eric." Darien set his empty glass on the table.

Pepper frowned. "Waldron would have reinforcements, you mean."

"Precisely."

"So what exactly does Waldron want from you?" Lelandi refilled their tea glasses.

"He wants to take over the forested land I own, increase his pack size by joining our two packs, and have me."

The way she listed the items in order of importance was really telling. Lelandi wanted to give Eric and Pepper a chance to see each other without any other wolf or pack intruding. With their pack allying with Pepper's, what better way would there be to get to know each other than to have a big pack gathering? She hadn't mentioned it to Darien, because she had wanted to meet with Pepper first. Now that she had, Lelandi could see the she-wolf wasn't an isolationist wolf—which some of them were, not wanting their packs to have much to do with others.

A get-together would be a great way for Pepper's people to meet other *lupus garous* and maybe even have playdates for wolf cubs or teen get-togethers. It was really important for smaller packs to have that socialization. And who knew? Maybe they had some unmated she-wolves other than Pepper who were interested in meeting some bachelor males.

"How about if your pack and ours get together for a barbecue? We'll have it here on the property, and that will show our solidarity." Lelandi was ready to throw a big party. It was great for everyone to take a moment out of their busy schedules to socialize. But meeting others from another pack? Even better. She knew her people would be excited. She hoped Pepper's would be too.

"How about if we have it on my land," Pepper said. "That will show Waldron I have another sizable pack I'm allied with. And anytime any of your pack members want to run in our woods, I have two hundred and fifty acres of forested land they can enjoy."

"We'll do it. We'll bring the food."

"We could provide the beef, chicken, and hot dogs. You can bring the rest." Pepper was smiling.

For the first time since Lelandi had met her, the she-wolf looked really pleased, which made Lelandi glad she'd come up with the idea. Now Lelandi was excited about how this would all play out.

"A show of solidarity should really help to put Waldron in his place. As long as he's aware of it."

"I think the Fairhaven twins being arrested is a start," Pepper said, no longer appearing quite so glum about Waldron giving her trouble.

Once Pepper was part of their extended family, so to speak, Lelandi had every intention of showing her that life with a mate could be good. Not that Eric would necessarily be the one for her, or that anyone in the Silver pack would be, but maybe if she saw how well it worked for Darien and her, Pepper would give having a mate again a chance. Lelandi couldn't help wanting to use her training to help others. She wished she could do the same for Eric. But maybe a little gathering like this could help to kindle the fire between the two wolves. She could only hope and help wherever she could.

Then Lelandi and Darien said good-bye to Pepper, Darien's arm around Lelandi. Just before Pepper pulled out of the drive, he kissed Lelandi. She smiled up at him, loving her mate.

Pepper had left with a real spring to her step, and Lelandi felt great about the whole situation.

Darien walked her back into the house. "It seemed to go well. But…I know you. What are you really up to?"

Lelandi snuggled against Darien. "Having some fun with another pack and ensuring that a network of extended friends can help her out at any time."

"And more?"

"Maybe. Only time will tell on that front."

Chapter 9

THE BIG DAY HAD COME FOR THE PACKS' GATHERING, AND everyone in Pepper's pack was in high spirits. The kids had been asking all along if there were kids their age in the other pack, while the adults wanted to ensure everything was perfect for the festivities. She hadn't seen her people this excited as a whole since Christmas, when everyone had a Christmas pack celebration and then their own small family get-togethers.

With everyone's arrival, the get-together was in full swing.

The bachelor males and single females were all spruced up for the occasion, as if they wanted to put on their best appearances in case they met a wolf they might like to court. Pepper hadn't really been thinking along those lines, because she wasn't thinking about finding a mate, but that could be an added benefit for the gathering. Then again, how would her pack be affected if suddenly several of her wolves wanted to mate wolves of Darien and Lelandi's pack? Would they stay with her or move over to the Silver pack? If they stayed with her pack, then all of a sudden it could really grow in size. What if some of them were alphas, and they started causing trouble for her? She wouldn't even need a mate to do it. Or what if they all moved to the Silver pack?

She sighed. She didn't need to worry about what-ifs.

"Need any help with anything?" Eric asked, startling her from her thoughts.

"Sure. We could use more ice for the coolers, and I need to grab more condiments."

"Looks like everyone's having fun already and we haven't even started," Eric said, walking with her on the long path to the house.

"For two weeks, this is all I've heard about. Half my single she-wolves went out and bought new clothes for the occasion."

Eric glanced down at what she was wearing. She could have worn jeans or capris, but it was hot and she was wearing shorts. Except the only kind she had were short shorts. She was also wearing a formfitting tank top. And instead of boots like she usually wore as a forester, she was wearing sparkly sandals. Okay, so she had to admit she had wanted to dress up a bit in a casual way.

"Not me. These are old clothes. I hate to shop."

"Looks nice." He glanced at her legs again, and she felt her body temp rise a whole lot. His comment wasn't just a casual one either, not when paired with his heated gaze.

"Thanks." She considered his blue jean shorts and his muscle shirt that showed off his beautiful biceps—not too bulky, but just right. "Yours too." Her gaze was just as heated, telling him he looked sexy to her. What the hell, life was too short and she was just as intrigued with him as he seemed to be with her.

When she was around him, she felt her palms sweat a little, her attention on him even when she was supposed to be doing something else. She was very much aware of his presence, his closeness.

She motioned to the freezer door up above and

opened the fridge door below it to grab the condiments. Having forgotten the freezer door was still open as he pulled out the ice, she clobbered herself when she stood, smacking her head against the freezer door.

"Ow," she said more to herself than to anyone else. She hadn't whacked her head hard; mainly she'd just startled herself.

"Are you all right?" Eric quickly set the bag of ice on the counter, closed the freezer door, and lightly touched her head where she'd hit it. She remembered his first-aid training and how he was always prepared to help someone.

"Yeah, thanks. No major gashes or anything, I take it?" she teased, trying to ignore how embarrassed she felt.

He was looking down at her with an expression that said he wanted to kiss her. And then he did, his hands framing her face as she leaned against the fridge. The kiss was sweet but quickly turned hotter as she fed into it, wanting this as much as he did. Her response escalated his, and before she knew it, he was rubbing her bare arms while she was running her hand over his gorgeous biceps.

Lips parted and their tongues tangled. Her body was on fire even before he ran his hands over her breasts, the sensation making her feel as though she wasn't wearing the tank top or a bra, that she was totally naked to his touch. And for an absurd moment, she wished she were. And that he was naked too.

"Hey," Richard said, coming into the house. "Did we have more ice?"

Eric pulled away from her, not jumping back like he hadn't wanted to get caught, but slowly, as if to say he didn't want this to end and that it was only the beginning.

Flushed to high heaven, Pepper told herself it couldn't be, or rather that it shouldn't be.

"Bringing a bag out now before it melts," Eric said as Richard looked from him to Pepper, judging everything that had gone on. "Though, as hot as it is in here, it might have melted just a bit."

The air conditioner was on, so it was nice and cool. She smiled at Eric, amused at his comment.

She imagined her eyes were as dilated as Eric's were. Her sub-leader could easily smell their pheromones. She was certain her nipples were fully erect, and her tank top would be showing them off to anyone who chanced to look at her top. So he *had* to know she and Eric were doing more than just talking.

She didn't know how to feel. After the momentary shock, she wasn't embarrassed to have nearly been caught in the act. It was her home. She was the pack leader. It was her choice to make. But on the other hand, she hadn't expected that getting the condiments and ice would have led to this.

"Here, let me take it out," Richard said, as if he wanted to ensure she had more time to visit alone with Eric and continue whatever they'd been doing.

Eric waited for Pepper's decision. She thought he looked eager to take Richard up on the offer. And they could go back to kissing.

"That's okay, Richard. We were just headed out." *After a big-time distraction.* Kissing Eric had turned her world upside down. She wanted more. How easily he made her forget not only what she had come in to do, but that her entire pack and many from his were gathering outside to play and eat and socialize.

Eric seized the bag of ice and gave Pepper a wink as Richard grabbed some of the condiments and headed outside with them. Now she was blushing again, as hot as her cheeks felt.

Richard looked like he was kicking himself for interrupting her time with Eric. But no one in her pack would have suspected that she was kissing a wolf in her kitchen during a pack gathering or otherwise.

She had thought her pack members might be a little apprehensive about meeting so many wolves from another pack, but everyone had been so thrilled at the prospect that she knew she'd made the right decision. They'd made the date for two weeks after the initial meeting so both Eric and Susan could heal up and enjoy the festivities along with everyone else. Pepper thought the timing was perfect, but she suspected Lelandi had really wanted to make sure that Eric could court her when he wasn't still feeling poorly.

Pepper thought that Eric would be interested in looking for a mate if he came across someone who intrigued him. Definitely after the interest he'd already shown in her. Especially after the kiss.

"Do you want to play volleyball?" Eric asked as he tore open the ice bag and poured the cubes into the cooler while she set her load of condiments on one of the tables. Richard hurried to do the same, then made himself scarce.

She shook her head. "I'll watch you play. Thanks though." She wasn't dressed for that—not in her short shorts and sparkly sandals.

"Not good at it, eh?" he asked, challenging her.

The men had set up the volleyball net in one of the

grassy areas, and the kids had gathered balls and other toys to play with. The ladies had decorated the covered pavilion with flowers where the picnic tables sat. A few of the picnic tables sat in the grass, but some of the wolves liked to sit under the shaded pavilion. Between setting up games and preparing the food, everyone had gone all out to make the Silver pack welcome.

Pepper was really glad she had offered for them to come here first. She thought her people, having the smaller pack, would feel more comfortable with the first pack gathering in their home territory. She envisioned joining the Silver pack in a gathering in Silver Town later and thought about how much fun that could be. It was like having a whole new world opened up to her and her pack members—a wolf world, which allowed them to let down their hair around other *lupus garous*.

Eric was still waiting for her to respond to his taunt about playing volleyball, the sparkle of the devil in his dark-brown eyes. Pepper hadn't been challenged by anyone in years. She couldn't ignore it. She was damn good at playing volleyball, especially at serving and making points. The taller guys usually hogged the ball, and she couldn't reach it while it was in play. But making points was the name of the game.

"You're right. I'm not very good at it," she said, smiling at him just a tad. She would *have* to play now.

"Well, if you're on my side, I can give you pointers," Eric said.

She could just imagine him missing the ball while he watched her jumping around in the short shorts. Or she could see him lifting her to hit the ball when she couldn't hit it otherwise, his hands on her hips, then sliding up her shirt and over her breasts as he let her back down.

She couldn't believe how his roughened voice gave her shivers, made her think wicked thoughts, and left her wanting more with him.

"I'll play with my pack. I wouldn't want you to lose on account of me."

He was looking at her like he wasn't sure if she was telling the truth or not, but was amused just the same.

Susan headed straight for them, and Pepper said to him, "I'll join you in a minute."

"Sounds good. Susan," he said in greeting, then took off to join the others at the volleyball net.

Four barbecue grills were already cooking the meats. The aroma of the beef, chicken, and hot dogs made Pepper's stomach rumble. She was ready to eat and visit with the new pack. The five kids they had in their pack—the twin five-year-olds, one ten-year-old, and two teens—were just as excited about meeting other kids their age who were wolves.

Now standing with Susan and observing all the fun to be had, Pepper was amazed how much things had changed for her and her pack in a matter of days. She hadn't seen any sign of Waldron and his pack members for the past two weeks. That made her wonder if they had heard of the gathering and were leaving her alone now that the Silver pack was watching her back.

She realized just how isolated her own pack had been. By necessity for the most part, because they'd never run into another wolf pack. A few stray *lupus garous*, yes, and Waldron and his pack of late. But this was the first time to really get acquainted with a pack that only wanted to help them, not use them for their own designs. Or, as in her great-grandparents' case, kill them off if they refused to leave the territory.

A couple of the teens and several adults, including Eric, were getting ready to play volleyball—the Silver pack against the Grayling pack. She was glad to see Eric wasn't running a fever and seemed to have full mobility in his shoulder as they tossed the ball back and forth, warming up before the game started.

"So Eric's looking as hot as usual," Susan said. She also was wearing short shorts and sparkly sandals, with a stretchy shirt that clung to her breasts, not her usual reserved look. "Really hot."

Pepper had just planned to oversee the activities, making sure no one got hurt. She hadn't really intended to play in any of the games. "He seems to have healed all right from the bite wounds," Pepper agreed. "Like you have from your injury."

"Oh. That's why you're studying him so intensely. Just to ensure he's feeling all right."

Pepper raised her brows at her cousin. "I was concerned about it as much as I would be with anyone."

"Uh-huh."

Pepper saw Lelandi and Darien watching the volleyball warm-ups. Lelandi wrapped her arm around Darien's waist, and he pulled her into a warm embrace and kissed her. Pepper noted that a few of her pack members and some of the Silver's saw, watched, and smiled.

"Wow," Susan said. "Now that's what you need. A pack leader mate like him."

Because of her own platonic relationship with her mate, and her own parents' disinterest in showing affection toward each other, though they had been affectionate with her, Pepper had grown up thinking that being a pack leader meant just choosing a compatible mate who would help lead the pack. Romance wasn't as important as good leadership. If a pack didn't have good leadership, it would dissolve and the pack members would move to other packs or start their own, if they were alpha enough and could manage. So she knew how important the leadership was, and she worked hard to keep her pack together.

Susan scanned the area. "Oh, would you look at that?"

"What?" Pepper turned to see what had caught Susan's eye.

Pauline was talking to a dark-haired man who was cooking some of the chicken on a grill. One of the Silver pack men.

"Will wonders never cease? But maybe that's a good thing," Susan said.

Susan didn't have to say what she was thinking. They both thought Pauline needed a mate to help her control her twin five-year-old boys. But neither thought she'd ever find another one. Then again, that was some of the problem with being an isolated pack. Pauline hadn't been interested in any of the men in the pack, but this connection with the Silver pack might open up some opportunities. The good thing was that if Pauline mated someone else and moved to the Silver pack, her boys wouldn't be living that far away, and Pepper could still visit her nephews.

"Well, if you're not going to play volleyball, I'm going to." Susan headed straight for the volleyball net.

Pepper folded her arms and watched as Susan joined

Eric's side instead of her own pack's. Now what was she up to? Susan kicked off her sandals and warmed up barefooted with the others.

Pepper smiled. If Susan thought she'd push Pepper into making a play for Eric, she was mistaken. Unless Susan really did have the hots for Eric.

Pepper headed over to the game, figuring they wouldn't start until she joined them and ready to show Eric she wasn't half bad at this. Like Susan had done, Pepper kicked off her sandals before she joined in on the fun.

Eric began the game with a serve that went right to her. Too easy, but she couldn't slam it down on the other side of the net like the tall guys could, so she set it up for one of her teammates. She noticed that Susan's mouth was gaping. Maybe because Pepper was playing. Or maybe because Eric had been trying to be nice, sending her the ball in a gentle way that assured her she couldn't miss returning it. It was more than being nice though. It was tantamount to saying he wanted her favor. He wanted this to go further between them.

Eric's brothers Brett and CJ were on his side too, both of them eyeing him with speculation. She suspected he usually played to win.

Then the game got into gear. When one of the men on her team slammed the ball onto Eric's side, the Silver team scrambled to get it and return it with just as much vigor. When she began serving, Pepper managed to make six points before the Silver team could return the ball and she lost her turn. Now Eric was smiling at her with a devilish look that meant payback. Not like he planned to squash her in the game of volleyball, but something more fun, more intimate.

She had never had this much fun playing volleyball, and it was all because of the underlying sexual tension heating up between the two of them. She made a kissing motion at him, hoping no one saw it, but wanting to distract him enough that he would miss the incoming ball—and he did. She laughed.

CJ joked, "Eric, are you trying to lose on purpose?"

Brett laughed. "Hell yeah," he said, "and for a damn good reason too."

She didn't think the kissing motion would distract Eric again, and she was afraid his team would be watching her to see what had stolen Eric's attention in the first place, so she just smiled and raised her brows a little while his wickedly intrigued gaze remained on her, his mouth curving up slightly.

"It's not winning the game that's so important," he said to his brothers, "but *how* you win."

"Ha!" CJ said. "You're playing an entirely different game than us. We have our names and reputation to uphold."

Everyone on both sides laughed.

She realized that a lot more wolves had moved around to see them play. Usually, everyone did their own thing while several activities were going on at the same time. But their game seemed to be drawing a lot of attention.

Even Sarandon was standing there, arms folded and smiling.

And of course Richard. He said he was too old to play vigorous games like this, and he usually manned a grill, but now he wanted to see what was going on. Or maybe to figure out if their leadership was going to be changing anytime soon.

Susan was smiling at Pepper from the other side of the net, and Pepper wondered if Susan had witnessed what she had done. She would hear about it soon enough.

Before long, Pepper's team won, but CJ and Brett were shaking their heads, saying next time Eric had to be on the other team.

Pepper laughed. "He played his best. You all did. It just wasn't good enough to match the Grayling pack."

Eric smiled, but his expression said he was thinking of having more fun with her.

After the game, Eric's brothers dragged him off to play tug-of-war against her pack, and Lelandi joined Pepper, motioning to all the activities going on. "This is so much fun. We get kind of stagnant when all we have to visit with are the same old people. Though the MacTyre sisters are new to our pack, and that's really helped to bring in fresh blood."

"I understand one of Eric's brothers already mated one," Pepper said. Sarandon had given her a rundown of his brothers during the Scout speeches.

"Yes. Well, they've been with us now for over a year, and CJ fell hard for Laurel."

"And she did for him," Pepper guessed.

Lelandi shook her head. "She was fighting it."

Like Pepper was fighting her attraction to Eric? That made her curious. That was the problem with her own mating. It had been inevitable. No one thought anything otherwise. No conflict. No other wolves showing up to woo her and sweep her off her feet. Everyone in the pack had thought it was just the way things were supposed to be. She couldn't imagine two wolves getting together when one wasn't interested. "Why?"

"She and her sisters were searching for their missing aunt," Lelandi explained. "That was why the sisters bought the hotel. That is their business though—renovating Victorian hotels, selling them for a profit, and then moving on. But once Laurel gave in to what she knew in her heart was true, she and her sisters decided to set down permanent roots. So they're running the hotel at full capacity, even turned the former maids' rooms into a suite of rooms to rent because the place has been so popular."

"Ah." So that was one isolated case of a wolf not wanting to mate. But they had loved each other. Pepper still thought that was atypical. What had her more than curious though was Lelandi's relationship with Darien. She had begun to think there didn't need to be any passion between the leaders of a pack, but Lelandi and Darien still acted like courting wolves. They had children already, and yet they seemed so passionate with each other. Their actions made her wonder how they had been when they *were* courting.

"Darien seems to be a good mate, giving you equal decision-making authority, but being all alpha male when it comes to taking care of threats. Yet he concedes to your psychology training and woman's intuition." Pepper wanted to mention how much she admired their obvious love for each another, but she didn't feel comfortable speaking about it when she and Lelandi had really just met.

"Yes, but I was as reluctant about Darien as Laurel was with CJ. And in truth, Darien had no intention of ever making me his mate either."

Shocked to the core at the revelation, Pepper couldn't

help also being amused. It was astonishing how much they appeared to treasure each other with a beginning like that. "Well, it's good it all worked out then, because you both seem perfectly suited to each other."

"I so agree. We're very happy together. You were mated before, I understand."

"Yes."

"For some, the grief process can take decades or even last forever. No one will ever measure up to the one we loved. I think if I ever lost Darien, I'd feel the same way. But time would tell. No two people are ever alike. So what we might love in one, we might not find in another. Yet, something else will make that person special to us. So even though I don't think I would ever find another mate I love the way I do Darien, I can't know that for a certainty."

Pepper was taken aback to hear Lelandi say so. She had believed Lelandi would remain mateless for the rest of her life if she lost Darien. "But it's different for us as pack leaders. We have our packs to consider. A new mate might want different things for the pack. You have your children to worry about too. What if a new mate didn't treat your children right?"

"I'd have a whole pack up in arms. Not to mention, he'd have me to deal with first."

Pepper laughed. She could just imagine Lelandi, although very sweet in her demeanor toward Pepper, could be a real wolf if anyone treated her children badly. "What if he didn't lead the pack like you were used to with Darien?"

"He wouldn't lead it the same way. That's the thing. Different wolf, different ways of doing things. We'd work it out. Life is taking chances."

"What if he wouldn't give you equal say?"

"It wouldn't happen."

Pepper wasn't sure. An alpha male could be terribly hardheaded. Waldron was. Her father had been. Even the wolves who had sought to court her were. She thought of Eric. "But what if it did?"

"Then as an alpha leader, you ensure you get equal say. Even if you mate with another wolf, it's still your pack. Your people. They will love you and side with you until your pack mate realizes you're vital to the rule of the pack."

Pepper could see that. Her people were loyal to her.

Darien sauntered over and smiled. "Great party. Everybody's enjoying it. Kids are having a blast. Adults are too."

Pepper hadn't realized the kids would have so much fun with the others. It was a great way for them to get to know other wolf kids. It was so hard to find them otherwise. And though the teens in her pack played with the little ones, it wasn't the same as having real teens to socialize with.

Darien watched the men playing tug-of-war. "So what were you ladies talking about that you got so quiet all of a sudden when I arrived?"

"You, dear," Lelandi said, patting his shoulder. "If anything should happen to you, how I would consider finding a new mate."

Pepper closed her gaping mouth. She hadn't figured Lelandi would ever say such a thing to Darien, not when they were so obviously in love. Then again, maybe that's why she could.

"Over my dead body." He smiled at her and kissed her lips. "You would never find anyone as great as me."

The ladies laughed and Pepper loved the way Lelandi and Darien were with each other.

She still worried about how a male wolf would impact her pack leadership, but now that she was involving her people with the Silver wolves, she could see that some change was for the best.

Someone started playing music and Darien said, "Do you mind excusing us? I want to take my mate for a dance if she's thinking of replacing me anytime soon."

Pepper smiled. "Have fun, you two." Then she went to get some fried chicken and potato salad. When she drew closer to where the food was being served, Pauline glanced at her, her cheeks reddening a bit. Because she was talking to a man? From another pack? If she found a new mate who made her happy, Pepper would be ecstatic for her.

Pepper motioned to the chicken. "Which is best?"

"Fried chicken, ma'am," the gentleman said, but this one wasn't the same one Pepper had seen Pauline talking to earlier. That one was younger and now playing tug-of-war with the others.

"This is Mason, president of the Silver Town Bank," Pauline said, "and, Mason, this is my pack leader, Pepper Grayling."

"My pleasure."

"Can you believe they run everything in town? The bank, hotel, bed and breakfast, newspaper office, just everything," Pauline said.

"I've heard great things about your pack," Pepper told Mason.

"They have some super interest rates on accounts. I'm going to switch my money over to their bank," Pauline said.

"Sounds like a great idea." Pepper wondered how many of her people were going to begin doing business with Silver Town now. She thought it was a wonderful idea—wolves helping each other, which, in a perfect world, would be the way it was. She couldn't imagine how complicated it would be to run a pack that large and a town that size. She could see why Lelandi would get another mate if she had to run things by herself. Yet, Lelandi wouldn't be alone in managing things. Not when Darien had two brothers who would continue to be her sub-leaders. They'd help ensure things ran as smoothly as before.

Pepper took her plate of food and headed for one of the picnic benches.

"Nice spread," Eric said, joining her, his plate piled high with barbecued brisket, corn on the cob, and potato salad.

"Who won?"

"Ah, the other side. More than half the team was made up of your people, and they must practice a lot."

She laughed. "I'm sure they didn't want to lose face if they lost the game to another wolf pack."

"The Silver pack too. We know so much about each other in our pack—everyone's moves and tactics—that fresh opponents made it fun. No one knew what the other side was going to do, what their weaknesses or strengths were. But all of your strongest players had to have been playing." He took a sip of his bottled water. "My brothers were giving me a hard time about you distracting me during the volleyball game."

She took a seat opposite him. "I really didn't think you could be that easily distracted."

"Hell, are you kidding? I thought you were trying to

tell me you wanted to return to the kitchen and finish what we started."

She smiled. "In your dreams."

He chuckled. "My brothers are still asking what you did to take my mind off the game. They said *they* were watching the ball."

She laughed again. "I like your brothers. I think it would have been fun if I'd had some siblings like that."

"No way. If you had brothers, I could just see them giving me grief for kissing you in the kitchen. Shotgun wedding. The whole business."

"True. And one of them might have been the leader."

"Your sub-leaders. I have no doubt you would have been in charge even then."

"Thanks, Eric. You look like your shoulder is doing better."

"Yeah, good as new. And with babying it for so long, I needed the exercise."

She doubted he'd spent a moment babying it.

"Did Lelandi invite your pack to our Victorian Days celebration in the fall?" he asked.

"Not yet. Sounds like fun. I'm sure everyone will want to attend."

Suddenly, Darien was stalking toward his brother Jake, his cell phone to his ear, his expression dark.

Eric got up at once. "I'll be right back."

She watched the men as Lelandi joined them. Pepper knew that the other deputy sheriff, the sheriff, and Darien's youngest brother, Tom, his other sub-leader, had stayed in Silver Town to protect and run it. Others had too, though Pepper assumed more than half their people were here, as big as the crowd was.

Eric spoke to Darien, then Darien nodded. When Eric returned to the picnic table, wearing a frown as big as Darien's, she knew something bad had happened.

"Someone set fire to three buildings in Silver Town. Darien and Jake are returning with some of our men. The women and children and the rest of our men are staying here. Including me. Until everyone's ready to end the party."

"You don't think this has to do with Waldron, do you?"

"Yeah, I do. But we're not discounting anything. The fires are contained, but Darien and Jake want to get back there in case any more are set, or if they can help catch the culprits." Eric finished his barbecued beef and corn on the cob.

"If they're human arsonists, you can catch them. But if they're wolves—"

"They'll be covering up their scent."

"I can't believe this." She finished her food and they dumped their trash.

"Well, the good news is we investigated the place where Waldron and his pack came from. Idaho. CJ is checking out there to learn what he can about their old pack."

"How did you learn that much?"

"The Fairhaven twins. When we told them they could be locked up for a very long time—considering we're wolves and run our own town, have a judge, the works—they decided to talk."

"Wow. Okay, so what have you discovered?"

"Nothing yet. They gave the name of the pack leader in Idaho. We thought that it was important to remind the boys that if they lied, it would go worse for them."

"But they still might have lied."

"We've located the pack and should have news soon about what went on. Darien hasn't been able to get hold of the pack leader yet. The boys were released late that afternoon the day after they were arrested. I'm thinking their incarceration—and possibly the boys spilling the information about their prior pack—caused Waldron to retaliate. I gave the boys a good talking-to that day, told them if they wanted to switch packs, we had a lot to offer them—stability, other teens to socialize with, job opportunities. Some of ours help run ski programs during the day and want to be on ski patrol during the ski season when they're older. During the summer, they help with the silver mine tours."

"I would have jumped at the chance if I were them." Pepper dug another couple of bottles of water out of the cooler and gave one to Eric.

"Thanks. It would be a great opportunity to steer them down the right path. I talked with your teens about the possibility too. They seemed to hit it off with ours. Anyway, as far as the Fairhaven boys go, they'd have to talk it over with their parents, who we said would be welcome to join us too. They're both teachers—one teaches English, and the other history. We homeschool all our kids, so the parents would be a great asset. We share duties on who has the most knowledge on certain subjects and teach the kids that way." He glanced down at the cooler. "Looks like it might need more ice."

"I'll send you in by yourself this time," Pepper said. "I could just see Richard watching us and making some excuse to visit the house if we both went inside. He's been like a father to me."

"Ahh, so then we'd have the shotgun scenario

anyway. Truly, I think he wished he *hadn't* intruded," Eric said and walked her back to the picnic tables.

"About the Fairhaven twins… Your pack taking them in sounds like a great idea. But the parents would have to deal with Waldron too."

"Right. But it's a great opportunity for them, and wolves can leave packs at any time. So hopefully they'll consider it favorably."

"What will you do now about the arsonists if they turn out to be Waldron and his pack members? If Waldron doesn't own anything, you can't confiscate it."

"We can let Waldron know his actions won't go unpunished. We just have to prove he had a hand in it. If he didn't, but his people did, they'll be punished. They will pay for the destruction and be incarcerated for a time, the stiffest punishment we can give."

"I'm so sorry. This could all have been because of me."

"Nonsense. It's because of Waldron, if he's done this. And I can't imagine who else would be responsible."

Although everyone still there was eating and talking, Pepper sensed that the overall mood had darkened. The adults were much more wary, not sure what was going on, but they appeared to understand that some trouble had befallen the Silver pack.

"Do you want me to stay the night?" Eric asked, and he seemed so sincere, Pepper scolded herself when she told him "no" vehemently.

"We'll be fine," she said, softening her tone. She didn't want him to think she was annoyed by his suggestion. But she didn't want him to believe she suddenly needed anyone from the Silver pack to watch their backs. Sure, some of it was fear of losing control of her pack. Was it that without her position as a leader, she felt she had no worth? She hoped that wasn't the reason she was so against mating another wolf. It seemed so materialistic, so driven for power.

Thankfully, Eric cast her an elusive smile, not bothered by her response. "You've got my number. Just call me if you need anyone's help."

She realized what he was saying. Not *his* help particularly. But that anyone would come to her aid. And at that moment, she thought she'd sounded afraid of him. Which she wasn't. Really.

"Thanks." The thing was, they lived four hours apart, so if she needed his help, or that of anyone from his pack, it would take some time for them to get here. Even so, she wasn't having him stay with her or with anyone else in the pack. That was plain silly and totally unnecessary.

The music started up again, and Susan began getting couples together to dance. When she came over to see Eric, Pepper gave her a stern pack-leader look that said she had better not suggest Pepper dance with Eric.

Instead, Susan grabbed his hand and tugged at him. "Do you know how to dance? If not, I'll teach you."

He laughed. "Guess I don't have a choice."

"Nope." Susan took him off to the grassy area where the others were dancing.

He smiled back at Pepper and said, "Talk to you later."

"Sure thing." Pepper didn't want to feel anything but happy that Susan was having fun, so why did it bug her that *she* wasn't dancing with him instead?

—◆—

Eric had really wanted to dance with Pepper, but she had given Susan such lethal looks—like she wasn't supposed to broach the subject—that Susan had taken Eric for a dance instead. The way Susan had been eyeing Pepper's reaction, he suspected she had thought of trying to push Pepper into dancing with him.

"How is your leg? It appears it's not giving you any more trouble," he asked.

Susan smiled brightly at him, and he thought that when she smiled, she looked a lot like Pepper. "It was a hairline fracture and seems to be perfectly healed now. But that's the trouble with seeing a human doctor. We can't do follow-up appointments because he'd realize something was wrong with us healing so quickly."

"Maybe you could see Dr. Weber, get another X-ray, and make sure it's perfectly healed."

"I think I will. He isn't at the party, is he?"

"No. He had a couple of babies to deliver, so he and his nurses are still at the clinic."

"I wondered about that. He must stay busy."

"Especially in the winter when the ski resort is open."

"Don't tell me you run your own ski resort."

"We sure do."

"Well, it sounds like I might need to take up skiing. I wanted to thank you for carrying me back to the cabin and offering to take me to your pack doctor. You were so gallant."

He could tell Susan liked him, but she also knew Pepper and he liked each other. He appreciated that Susan didn't try to come on to him. After the kiss he had shared with Pepper, he knew that was just the tip of the iceberg he meant to melt, and he didn't want to ruin things by showing anything but friendship toward Susan. "Just doing my job."

She shook her head. "You went *way* beyond the call of duty." Then she lowered her voice. "Pepper appreciated your help too, though she was trying hard not to show it that night. I heard what she said about you not staying to offer some protection to the pack. She has her reasons for worrying about...well, a man trying to take over. It's happened to her four times since she inherited the pack. And in every case, it got ugly. So she tries to avoid any entanglements in the first place."

"What about her first mate?"

"She knew him from childhood, and just so you know, he was a beta wolf."

Eric hadn't expected to hear that. He had thought she would want to be mated to a wolf who could share the responsibilities equally with her. Was she a control freak and didn't want an alpha mate making some of the decisions?

"So you see the problem? Even though *I* don't see you in any way but good and helpful, she sees you as a threat to her leadership." Susan sighed. "Even so, I want you to stay with me for the night. After what happened in Silver Town, I don't trust that Waldron wouldn't come here and make threats against Pepper. We don't have any real alpha males in the pack. They'd stand up to him, but he knows they don't have the bite to back their words."

Eric looked down at Susan, wondering if that was all she had in mind. He wasn't interested in courting her. Maybe she had only been sweet toward him while Pepper was watching.

Was his disinterest in Susan because she was only a sub-leader, and he was in denial that some of the reason he was so attracted to Pepper was her pack leader status? He didn't believe so, but even if he didn't have an underlying motive, Pepper was sure to think it was the basis of his interest in her.

"Won't she be upset with you when she said no to me staying?" Eric didn't want to cause friction between Pepper and Susan, or for Pepper to be angry with him. But he did want to stay to ensure Waldron didn't cause any trouble for Pepper's pack during the night.

"Not when I have the pack's best interests in mind. You'd stay at my house, and she has no say in it."

"I'd want her to know that I'm doing it." No way was he going to be sneaky about it. That was certainly not the way to build on a relationship with Pepper.

Susan smiled as she danced with him. "You're a nice guy, you know? You tell her, but it's still my house and anyone of my choosing can stay there. If she gives you guff, you just tell her I said so."

"You don't think she'll really mind?"

"Oh, she'll mind. But she also knows I would never do anything to intentionally hurt our friendship or our pack."

"What is Pepper so afraid of, if you don't mind my asking?"

"Falling in love again and losing the man she loves. That's the plain truth of it, but she'll never admit it. She cloaks her concern, saying she's afraid an alpha male will leave her out of the decision making, and she'll lose control of her pack. But if she was being honest with herself, she'd realize she's just afraid of falling in love again."

"What if she thinks me staying with you means a plot to take over her pack?"

Susan laughed. "I seriously doubt it."

"Well, just to be on the safe side, I don't want her to feel we're going behind her back on this. I want to make sure she's all right with it."

"I totally agree with you, but I know my cousin and she knows me, so she wouldn't think that of me. Are you going to tell Pepper about what happened tonight in Silver Town?"

"You heard?"

"I overheard Sarandon talking to one of your other pack members."

"I hadn't planned to." He shrugged. "We'll take care of it." He didn't want Pepper's sympathy, if she thought to give it.

Eric finished the dance with Susan and had every intention of dancing with Pepper while asking her if she minded if he stayed at Susan's place. He handed Susan off to one of his pack members, then headed to where Pepper was talking to a couple in her pack. He figured it was past time to do something about his interest in her, under the guise that they needed to talk about Susan's offer.

"I just want you to spread the word to be extra vigilant," Pepper said to the couple.

"We'll be that," the man said. They bowed their heads a little to Eric in greeting and then left Pepper alone to speak with him.

"I suppose you have to leave now," she said, and he swore she sounded a tad disappointed.

"You don't want to dance?" He hadn't meant it as a question, afraid she'd turn him down. He really wanted to dance with her, to get close and personal again. To show her in front of others that he was safe to be with. Though she had sure seemed all right with him when they were kissing earlier.

She hesitated.

He didn't. He took her hand with a warm grip and led her to where the others were dancing. He assumed her silence meant she was trying to quickly come up with an excuse. But he was going to try to talk her into dancing with him no matter what.

"Everyone's watching us," Pepper said, feeling so demure against him, so sweet and shy, that he thought Susan's words had merit.

He hadn't been sure that was the problem. He had suspected it had more to do with her worry about losing control of her pack. But now he wasn't so sure. And he was glad he'd brought her over to dance.

"Everyone's watching because you're their pack leader. It's probably been a while since you danced with anyone."

"Never."

He pulled her closer and they moved to the music—not as intimately as he would have liked, but it was a start. Though many of the wolves didn't wear much cologne or perfume, Pepper was wearing a subtle flower fragrance that made him lean down and nuzzle his nose behind her ear.

She chuckled a little, and he figured he'd tickled her. He breathed in deeply of her scent, of the wild wolf and woman. Before he realized what he was doing, he pulled her snug against his body and was moving with her to the strumming of the guitar, basking in the feel of her soft curves and the heat of her body setting his blood on fire. He would have to take a cold shower after this.

"You dance very well for never having done so," he said, trying to get his rampant need for her under control and his thoughts back to the issue at hand. "I wanted to ask you a question. I know you don't want me to stay with you and offer your pack protection, but Susan asked me to stay at her place. I wanted to ask if this is all right with you."

"No, it's not all right. She's an unmated wolf who lives alone." Even though Pepper sounded annoyed with him, she didn't pull away, continuing to slow dance with him nice and close, her breasts pressed against his chest, her thighs moving sensuously against his.

"We're not going to do anything. It's strictly a place to sleep in case you have any trouble. I'd be a stone's throw away instead of four hours away." Not that Eric wanted to stay with Susan. He knew some would speculate about their relationship. That he had rescued her. That he might be taking this further with her. When he was interested in Pepper. "If I'm going to watch out for you and your pack, it would be better if I were staying in the same area—close by." He slid his hands down her back, wanting to slide them underneath her shirt and feel her silky skin beneath his fingertips, but not with all the onlookers here today.

Her voice was breathy when she said, "I suppose if I say no—"

"Which you already did." He smiled, hoping she'd

concede that having him stay with her was the best option available, his hands still stroking her into submission.

"Susan will insist you stay there."

"I don't want to cause any problems for you, Susan, or your pack. I just want to be here in case something happens. I wouldn't be able to sleep a wink if I returned home. So I might as well be where I may be needed. If you're afraid I'll ruin Susan's reputation, I can stay with a couple, if any will put me up, or I can even run as a wolf. Which I'll probably be doing for some of the night anyway. And then I can sleep out here."

Hell, if he could, he'd guard her body all day and all night.

"Don't you have park duties?"

"I'll take leave for a couple of days after this latest incident, per Darien's order. He doesn't want me in the park for the time being while Waldron is looking to cause trouble for me. Of course, if I stay with you, it won't cause any speculation about us because everyone will know how alpha you are and that I'd be on my best behavior." Not that he wanted to be on his best behavior. He was already fully aroused. She had to feel what she was doing to him too, but he didn't want to let her go for anything.

She cracked a smile. "You can run as a wolf. I have a nice enclosed patio you can stay on and a wolf door. That way you can be the perfect guard wolf."

He grinned at her. *Hot damn!* "Ms. Grayling, you have a deal."

She smiled back but in a devious way, and then to his delight, she wrapped her arms around him, holding him tight. Dancing with her was like dancing with the goddess of his dreams. He thoroughly enjoyed this soft side of her. He swore that Mervin, Silver Town's barber who played music at every Silver Town event, was extending the song a bit. He'd have to thank Mervin later. Thankfully, Pepper didn't seem to notice, or she didn't mind.

"So who really wanted you to ask me first about staying with Susan? You or her?" Pepper asked, tilting her head up to look at him, her brown eyes soft and warm and aroused, her dark brows raised slightly.

"I did. But don't be mad at Susan. She was just worried about the pack."

"That's all right. I won't give her too big of a lecture."

"Wish me luck? In case I run into any trolls in the night?"

"Hmm," she said, sounding as though she wasn't sure what he had in mind, but she wasn't pulling away from him.

He leaned down and kissed her softly as a thank-you for the best dance he'd ever had. And he was thanking his lucky stars when she kissed him harder, but before he could match her enthusiasm, she pulled away. "I've got to tell everyone you're prowling the area as a wolf, so they won't worry if they see a stray wolf roaming around our homes in the middle of night."

He wanted to groan when she pulled away, yet he knew this wasn't the time or place. But he wasn't giving up on her for anything. "I'll let Darien know I'm staying the night too."

"On my back patio."

Eric chuckled. "I wasn't going to give him details, but I will."

"For Lelandi's sake."

Eric frowned. He didn't want Pepper believing he was eager to make a mating, even if he was certainly considering it. But that was the whole point in going slow with Pepper—so he wouldn't appear too willing and upset the proverbial apple cart. "What did Lelandi say to you?"

"Just that you're not looking for a mate, but I know something about psychology, and I know a matchmaker's ploy when I hear one."

He laughed. "As long as she's not saying I'm looking to settle down."

"Why not?"

"Let's just leave it at I've been unlucky in love." Which had nothing to do with his interest in Pepper and everything to do with not wanting to bare his soul to her about his past, not when he'd never told anyone but Sarandon. Though his father had known everything about it too.

But he figured it sounded good as a reason for not settling down, if she was worried about his intentions.

Chapter 10

AFTER ERIC AND PEPPER CONCLUDED THE DANCE, SOME OF the kids in Eric's pack asked him to play a game of tag with them, and as soon as he left Pepper, Susan joined her. "So, did he ask about staying with me?" Susan raised her brows and smiled, to Pepper's annoyance.

"I can't believe you'd offer when I said no," Pepper chastised her. "He's staying at my place, and he's going to check out the woods as a wolf some of the night. You're a single she-wolf. What would people think if he'd stayed with you?"

Susan was still smiling like a kid who had gotten the best toy ever. "Hey, there wasn't going to be any hanky-panky. The way he danced with you? Close? I can just imagine how turned on he was when you danced with him like that. Not like with me. He left lots of space between us. He's the perfect gentleman with anyone he's not interested in *that* way. And you might have noticed, if you were watching us dance—"

"I wasn't."

"Well, he didn't kiss *me*. I would have slapped his face had he done so, mind you."

Pepper shook her head. "No, you wouldn't have."

"I would have! If you'd been watching."

Pepper laughed. "You're still my favorite cousin."

"Your *only* cousin. You're not really going to send him out on his own to look for Waldron or his men, are you?"

"If I thought I needed Eric, I would have asked him to stay. I hadn't intended to have him or anyone else patrolling the woods for trouble. He just said he'd do it."

"Did he tell you which places they set fire to?"

"No. Which?"

"The jailhouse, the Silver Town Tow Truck Service, and Eric's house."

Pepper stared at Susan in disbelief. "Ohmigod. I can't believe it. Doesn't he want to see how bad it is? And take care of things there?"

"Apparently, he thinks our safety is more important."

Pepper was shocked that Eric had been so calm and seemed so unaffected about what had happened to his house. "But what if his staying here escalates the situation with Waldron?" Before Susan could answer, Pepper continued, "I can't believe it. He shouldn't be here. He needs to take care of matters at home. He must feel awful about it. Angry too."

Susan sighed. "If I were him, I'd feel that way. Which says a lot about his character, don't you think?"

"I wonder how bad it is." Pepper envisioned how his den had looked, with its butternut leather couches and plaid chairs. The dining room with its heavy wooden table and chairs. The view of the woods from the den window. It was a lovely house, and it suited him. She couldn't imagine anyone setting fire to it. She hoped they had stopped the fire in time and his place hadn't sustained too much damage.

She watched Eric playing tag with a bunch of the kids now, as if nothing bad had happened. He got a call on his phone, and rather than step out of the game, he

continued to chase after kids while several tried to grab
the tag at his belt.

"I wonder if his pack is telling him how bad the house is
damaged," Pepper said. "Maybe one of the other members
of his pack can stay here instead, if it makes him feel better
about us being protected, so he can go home to check on
his place."

Eric lost his tag to an older teen, then grabbed a smaller
child on his team and carried him on his shoulders.

"Hey, no fair," some of the older kids shouted, laughing, and took chase after him again.

"He's smaller than you," Eric said. "He needs a boost."

"He's *really* good with kids," Susan said.

Pepper had to agree. From seeing him with the Boy
Scouts and playing games with the children here, she
could tell he had a natural ability to play well with
them—any age too. Not just the more grown-up teens.
Just the fact that they had asked him to play, when
they'd only asked one other adult to do so, showed how
much they liked involving him.

Some of the adults were starting to pack up their
stuff, and Pepper realized she had felt safe with all
the Silver pack members being here. But once families began to leave, she did feel better that Eric was
staying, though she didn't want to admit it to him or
anyone else.

"I'm going to help clean up," Susan said before
walking off.

When they finished the game of tag and one of the
moms handed out chocolate bars to each of the players,
Eric got two for being the best sport. He smiled, thanking the mom, then stalked toward Pepper, still smiling.

When he reached her, she offered her most serious look. "That was cheating."

"What? Giving Robby a boost? He needed a little help." Eric gave her a devil of a smile and one of his candy bars.

"That was sweet of you." Then she folded her arms. "I just heard about your house. Why didn't you tell me?"

"Half my pack is taking care of it for me. They said I'd just be in the way."

Pepper didn't believe it.

"Why do you think I wanted to stay here?"

"That's not the reason. How bad is the fire damage?"

He sighed. "It'll take a couple of months to rebuild the damaged parts. I'll stay with Sarandon while the work is being done."

"You don't seem to be too upset with it."

"Oh, I am. Believe me. But there's nothing to be done about it right this instant. I just want to make sure Waldron doesn't do something like that to your homes. Or the forest. I wouldn't put that past him if he thinks he's lost the chance to be with you and wants to take revenge and then leave the area. Maybe that's what he did at his last location. Do you know where they're staying now?"

"No. I don't know if they're renting or have bought, or where they are staying exactly."

"Next time we catch sight of any of them, we'll follow them if we can. Trevor tried to follow the Fairhaven boys home, but they ended up going to a pizza place and another five places after that—video game archive, the park finally—and then hiked around for a couple of hours. Trevor couldn't stay with them the rest of the day and night and finally returned to Silver Town."

"What about learning the boys' home address when they were incarcerated?"

"All they had was the Idaho one. They hadn't updated their driver's licenses yet."

She thought maybe she or some of her people could track down Waldron's residence if they chanced to see any of his pack members. "I can't believe anyone would do that to your home and the other places. Are you sure you don't want someone else to stay with me while you go home and check out your place?"

"Are you kidding?"

She smiled at the inference. "All right. Well, if you're ready to go home, I'm ready." She said good night as everyone began loading the cars with games and food and kids. Then she led Eric to her back deck off the one-story house with views of the forest in all directions.

Eric was glad he'd been able to convince Pepper to allow him to stay with her, and not just because he wanted to protect her and her pack. He hoped this would help pave the way for a courtship. Before he'd met her, he couldn't imagine feeling about a woman the way he did about Pepper. Yet in the two weeks that he'd had to wait for the packs to gather for the festivities, he'd dreamed about kissing her, about getting to know her, about her getting to know him in return. And he had every intention of showing her he could give her some space, while at the same time letting her know how interested he truly was in her.

Once Eric had felt better, he and several other Silver pack members had tried to track down the wolves growing marijuana. They hadn't had any success yet. Eric had voiced his concern to Darien and Lelandi that the rogue wolves no doubt knew wolves had found their growing patches, and the rogues would now be wearing hunter's scents, making it impossible for another wolf to trace them. None of the Silver pack wolves had found any more sites where the plants were growing. But as many acres as there were, that didn't mean there weren't more.

Although they'd smelled the strong odor of the cannabis from a distance, he and the others hadn't found any of the trash that humans created in running illegal marijuana farms either. The wolves were sneakier. They probably assumed that if scent hounds were used to pick up their scents, they would find only wolves in the area. But now with wolves tracking them down? Whoever they were, they had to be angry Eric and his people were "stealing" their stash.

He just wished they could catch the culprits. He'd been on the lookout, scent-wise, while he was at the gathering, trying to learn if any of Pepper's wolves had been at any of the marijuana sites. He hadn't noticed any here, which relieved him. The wolf who had been at the campsite had probably been there after the pack left.

It was time to mention the situation to Pepper so she could ensure her people were careful if they visited the park and ran into the rogue wolves. "I wanted to talk to you about something I've been investigating off duty."

She frowned at him. "Sounds ominous."

"It's dangerous—for anyone who might run across the wolves. I discovered some were growing marijuana patches in hard-to-reach places."

Her eyes widened and her mouth gaped a bit. Then she frowned. "Not my wolves."

"No. I've smelled several wolves at the locations, but none match your wolves' scents."

She grabbed his arm and pulled him to a stop. "Wait, you thought they were some of mine?"

He swore if she'd been wearing her wolf coat, she would have growled and snapped her wickedly beautiful teeth at him.

"I smelled a wolf that had carried the scent of marijuana through your campsite. But since Waldron had been through there too, it might have been one of the men in his pack. Still, I have no hard evidence his pack is involved."

"Except we don't know if he has a job." Her lips parted and then she frowned again. "Ohmigod. This is really serious business. What if he wanted my land to grow the pot on?"

"I wondered the same thing. But I wanted to let you know in case any of your people encounter wolves that could be involved. I don't want anyone in your pack to get hurt."

"Maybe I should try to see Waldron and learn what I can."

Now Eric frowned at her. "No way."

She let out her breath. "All right. My people aren't involved in this, just for your information if you have any doubt. But thanks for telling me. I'll warn them."

He thought that went over well, considering he *had been* trying to determine if any of her people were involved. When her deck and stone patio came into view, what really got his attention was the hot tub built into the deck and the sun now setting, its pink-and-purple coloring reflecting in the blue water.

"Nice," he said, thinking he'd like to add something

like that to his place. "Must be great when you want to unwind."

"It is. And it's fun to sit out here when the snow is piled up around it."

He could just imagine how enjoyable that would be—especially if he got to join Pepper in the tub. "With the remodeling I'm going to have to do, I'll have to check into getting something like this."

"Feel free to use it while you're here tonight."

"I'm here to protect and serve."

"When you want to take a break. Just don't swim in it as a wolf."

"No fur allowed in the hot tub. Gotcha."

She smiled, took him inside the house, and showed him the spare bedroom and bathroom. She had said he was supposed to be sleeping on the enclosed porch. He didn't comment, glad she had changed her mind about that.

"Did you need anything? Spare toothbrush, toothpaste?"

"I always carry an overnight bag with me in my truck in case of emergencies. I'll just grab it and go for a patrol."

She looked a little surprised, but he meant what he said. His business here was to protect her and her pack.

"Let me know when you're ready to go. I'll join you."

"All right." It was her forest, her territory, but he didn't even want to think what would happen if they ran into some of Waldron's wolves in the area.

After he had stripped and shifted in the guest room, he found her waiting for him outside his door in her wolf form—her face framed with black and brown guard hairs, her muzzle ivory, a dark saddle on her back, and golden fur on her legs and chest. Beautiful.

She had the most intense look of any she-wolf he'd

ever met. If he hadn't been just as alpha as her, he believed he would have found her gaze intimidating.

He smiled, showing off his wolf canines, wanting her to know just how much he liked what he saw, and that he wasn't intimidated in the least.

She cocked her head to the side a little, as if trying to read his behavior. He couldn't help the way he saw her, and he wanted to show his attraction. He could tell himself he wasn't interested in her, but it wouldn't be true. It had nothing to do with her running a pack. And all to do with what he saw in her. Someone who genuinely cared about her people and others, about the natural habitat and its survival, about taking charge without being brutish. She had a quiet strength that made her all the more appealing. She didn't appear to be a wolf to challenge either. He wondered if her mate had appreciated her for it. He must have. She didn't seem to be the kind of wolf who would just mate with any wolf.

But it made him wonder what her mate had been like. How different Eric and her mate were, besides that he had been a beta. Eric realized he'd never thought in such terms before—wondering if a she-wolf would like him as well or better than another wolf.

In the case of his lost mate, he hadn't had any competition. But he had found himself comparing her to Pepper. His mate had been loving and vivacious, daring and fun to be with. A beta. She hadn't had a care in the world. Not like Pepper did. And that made her seem so much more serious, circumspect. Even when the packs were playing together, she watched everyone. If he hadn't commented about her lack of skills at playing volleyball and how he could help her, and if he hadn't taken her hand and led her in the dance, he knew she wouldn't have joined him. He was grateful she had.

As far as the kisses went, those were totally unplanned. But now when he dreamed about kissing her, it would be for real.

Even now as they explored the woods and searched for any sign of other wolves—other than his pack or hers—he noticed that though she was staying close by, which he was glad for, she was concentrating on the mission and not watching him like he was watching her.

He couldn't stop observing her because he was so enamored with her, but in addition, he was fascinated with her process—the way she was so focused and so thorough. At the same time, he was ensuring that he followed her lead and making sure he didn't lose sight of her. With their enhanced senses, wolves could easily multitask.

At that moment, he realized how nice it would be if she wasn't the leader of a pack but just a wolf he'd like to pursue. She wouldn't be worrying about him with her pack then.

Suddenly, she raised her head and perked her ears, her tail held out straight behind her. He looked in the direction she was watching, listening for any sound she might have heard, smelling the air for any scent she might have gotten a whiff of.

Another wolf, but it was from her pack. She barked and the wolf appeared from the woods, then headed for them. A big beige male, Richard, the same one who had taken charge when Eric carried Susan to the cabin. He was eyeing Eric warily, but then he must have smelled him and he relaxed considerably. Richard must have been out checking the forest, making sure that everything was all right without telling Pepper, or Eric was certain that she would have let him in on the situation.

Richard greeted her, head bowed a little.

The wolf waited, as if getting permission to continue what he'd been doing. Pepper woofed and nodded. He headed out and Eric continued searching her territory with her, ensuring no other wolves had been around. He was surprised none had been. He had expected to smell some sign of one or two investigating what was going on between the Silver pack and hers. Maybe Waldron's pack members were afraid some of the Silver wolves had stayed with Pepper's pack after the Silver Town buildings were burned.

Pepper, meanwhile, was trying hard to concentrate on searching for any sign of Waldron or his wolves, but she kept getting glimpses of Eric and catching him watching her. God, he was hot. The way he'd danced with her, up close and totally personal… She wanted more of his attention, to feel alive like that again. She didn't want to appear desperate, but ohmigod, he was one hunk of a wolf.

He seemed to be curious about her. He might think she was meek and mild-mannered from her behavior around her wolves and his, but her wolves knew better. If she was faced with real danger, she wouldn't hesitate to take care of it in the most ferocious way, if necessary.

She was glad he was running with her tonight. Though he was keeping an eye on her, it wasn't in a way that made her think he didn't believe she could manage on her own. She had been surprised to see Richard Oglesby checking out the area without mentioning it to her, but she was glad he was being vigilant too.

For two hours, she and Eric crisscrossed the area, looking for any sign of Waldron or his men. Yes, they'd been here, but not recently. Even so, it annoyed her to think they had been in her territory without her permission. She also smelled the Fairhaven boys' scent and hoped Darien would convince them to join the Silver pack so they could learn to be good wolf citizens and not get into trouble in the future.

When she and Eric returned to her house, he shifted and changed in the guest bedroom while she did the same in her room. Then he joined her in the kitchen.

"Would you like some wine?" she asked as a way to unwind after the nicest day she'd had in a long time.

"Love some."

She knew what she was doing. She was thanking him for staying to protect her pack, even when his own place was damaged. She was saying she was willing to consider seeing him further. She'd decided it once she learned he was more concerned about her pack's safety than the condition of his house. Well, and because of how he'd tilted her world on its axis twice at the gathering with the way he kissed and touched her, promising more.

She didn't want Waldron harming Eric if she started seeing him socially. On the other hand, she wasn't about to take any crap from Waldron and bow down to his need to control what she did. As long as Eric thought he could manage the repercussions, she would give him a chance.

She took two wineglasses and he brought the bottle of wine.

"At least none of his people were wandering around your place during the gathering," Eric said, following her outside to the patio.

"I agree. Maybe they were afraid, with the number of your people and mine, they wouldn't stand a chance of causing a scene." She lit a fire in the fire pit next to the deck of the hot tub, and as the night air cooled, they gazed at the stars dotting the black sky above.

"I've got to say, this is really nice." Eric poured them each a glass of wine and then they settled on chaise lounges. "I wasn't expecting this."

"It's really nice in the winter, and I love it on summer nights like this too. Sometimes I just sit out here and stargaze."

"As a wolf?"

"Sure. Sometimes. It's really peaceful, no sounds of people intruding. Just nature. I love it."

"Yet your pack members all have homes scattered throughout the woods. So no one's very far away."

"True, which is convenient, but the woods make it seem as though I'm all alone out here." Which in a way she was. "Do you ever wish things had turned out differently and you were the leader of Silver Town's wolf pack?" She still couldn't believe Eric would be truly happy unless he were running a pack. He wasn't even a sub-leader because Darien's own two brothers were.

"Nope."

She studied his serious expression and thought he was being honest with her. She sipped some of her wine. "Somehow I find that hard to believe."

"It's true. Just think of it. I get all the excitement and adventure I need being a park ranger. When I'm through with my shift, I can chill out. Unless the pack needs me for something. Otherwise, I can take off when I want to. Darien can deal with all the headaches of running a pack."

"True." But she still didn't believe that if given a choice, Eric wouldn't want to jump in and be the one to deal with all the "headaches."

Eric leaned back in the chair, relaxed, looking perfectly content and sexy in his shorts and muscle shirt, and studied the water in the tub. "What about you? Do you ever wish your life had been simpler? That you were just one of the followers, not the leader responsible for the safety and welfare of your pack?"

"Nope. I'm perfectly happy with what I do."

"When was the last time you took a real vacation away from here?"

Never, she realized, not that it bothered her. "If I wanted to take one, I would."

"Now to me, that's hard to believe."

She smiled. That was true. She didn't feel the need, but she also worried about her people. "When was the last time you took a vacation someplace you've always wanted to go?"

He shook his head.

"So where have you always dreamed of going?"

"Hawaii. Just once I'd like to run through a rain forest as a wolf, disappearing into a world that most can never see. What about you? If you weren't afraid of leaving your pack behind, where would your dream vacation be?"

"Scotland. I'd like to stay in a Scottish castle and run

all over the mountains as a wolf." Pepper leaned back on the chaise lounge. "Eric, are you sure you don't want to go home and guard your place? I really don't believe Waldron or his people are going to hassle us. We'll be fine."

"Sarandon and my other brothers are taking care of it. CJ, the sheriff, and the other deputy are taking turns watching over it in case someone tries something else. I really don't want to see it right now."

"You mean because you'd want to retaliate?" She would, if it had been her property.

"Yeah. I'd want to hunt down those responsible and make them pay for all the damage and give them a nice long stay in jail. Wolves don't like confinement. As long as no one's killed because of their actions, I think that would be enough punishment. But in truth, I really was concerned they'd strike here next."

"Or that they'd at least come to see me. Then you could catch Waldron and interrogate him."

"Yeah, I've considered that. I imagine if they did something to your property, you wouldn't be chasing them down. You'd be here for your people, ensuring everyone remained safe. Property can be replaced. People's lives can't be."

"I'd be chasing them down. But if I didn't catch them, I'd return to my people."

He smiled at her, and she wasn't sure whether he believed her or he admired her for it. Then his phone rang, and he checked the ID. "It's Darien."

"I can leave and let you take it in privacy."

"No, wait." Eric answered the phone. "Yeah, Darien, is this something Pepper should hear?" He nodded to her. "Putting it on speakerphone."

"I finally reached Waldron's former pack leader, and the news isn't anything that we really wanted to hear," Darien said. "The pack leader is his brother. He said Waldron and some of the pack left to start anew. Dispersing, like real wolves do so they can establish their own territory and find mates. He said Waldron's a great guy and never caused any trouble for anyone."

"If Waldron's responsible for setting the fires, in addition to stalking Pepper, I'd say that's all changed," Eric said. "What if the brother is lying to cover both their backs because he never set Waldron straight or couldn't control him? Maybe Waldron caused problems for the pack, so the leader made him leave—and several of his buddies too."

"It's possible. Or possibly he wasn't trouble under his brother's leadership, but once he got some power under his belt and some followers, he let it all go to his head. The problem is, without knowing of any crimes he committed where he's from, we really have no case against him."

"Unless we can prove he committed arson," Pepper said.

She knew they didn't expect her to be part of this. But the Silver pack had endured all this because of her reluctance to see Waldron. Now that they had pledged their support to her and her pack, she was pledging her support right back. She might not have the numbers or a bunch of alpha males like they did, but she and her pack members would offer all the support they could.

"If we can prove it," Darien said.

Pepper told Darien she and Eric hadn't found any evidence to indicate Waldron or any of his people had been there while the celebration was going on. "I really don't believe they'll bother us now. Thanks for the news, Darien. I'm calling it a night." She wanted to give Eric some privacy so he could speak to Darien if he needed to.

Eric said good night to her, staying on the patio to talk to Darien. She thought Eric looked a little disappointed that Darien had interrupted their visit and now she was going to bed. But she was tired and this was the perfect way to end the night before she did anything she would regret in the morning.

Chapter 11

ERIC TOOK A SHOWER IN THE GUEST BATHROOM, DRIED off, then started to shift, his muscles stretching and warmth filling every cell until his paws hit the floor. He headed out to the back deck and lay down beside the tub. For a long time, he just stared out at the woods, listening to the breeze ruffle the oak leaves and pine branches, searching for any sound that indicated wolves or humans might be moving about. Though he suspected that if Waldron and his people were around, they'd be running as wolves.

As a wolf, Eric was perfectly comfortable in his wolf coat during the cooler nighttime temperatures, and he'd rather be here like this, listening for sounds of trouble, than sleeping inside on Pepper's guest bed, which would require her to change the sheets after he went home. He only wanted to be here to help, not make more work for her.

He didn't get much sleep, because every sound made him raise his head to check it out. He took seven wolf runs during the night and was just coming in from the last one when he saw Pepper standing on the porch in jeans and a sweatshirt, her arms folded across her chest as she frowned at him.

"Did you get *any* sleep? You didn't even use the guest bed last night. I didn't mean for you to prowl the forest all night long. Come in and get dressed, and

I'll fix us some breakfast." She turned on her heel and went back inside, leaving the door open for him.

Eric woofed at her in greeting, amused she'd scold him. He was glad he could help and hoped that because of it, she'd had a good night's sleep. She looked tired though. He hoped she hadn't come looking for him half the night and worried he'd gotten himself into trouble.

When he joined her in the kitchen, she was making waffles and sausages, the smell of pork and maple syrup scenting the room. "Do you like waffles? I should have asked first."

"Anything is good. Thanks for making them. What can I do to help?"

"Nothing, really. Just sit down and relax. Thanks for taking care of things, but I really didn't mean for you to run all night long."

"Just checking out sounds." He frowned at her as he took a seat at the kitchen counter. "I didn't keep you up, did I?"

She pursed her mouth a bit.

"Sorry. I really had to check out anything I heard, or I wouldn't have been doing my job."

"Did you see any sign of Waldron or his wolves?"

"No. I can't understand it either."

"Maybe that's his ploy." Pepper served the waffles and sausages and brought over containers of maple syrup and butter.

"How so?"

"He's backing off with me. Maybe focusing his attention on you. Or maybe he realizes that attacking you—through the arson business and whatnot—has pushed me into making friends with you and your pack for protection. So he sees his actions are backfiring. He probably didn't realize you belong to a large pack and run a whole town. Or that your cousin is the pack leader."

"That's certainly possible." Eric cut into a waffle and took a bite. "I haven't had waffles in eons. And with chocolate chips? Even better. Just the way I like them. So thanks."

"After running most of the night, you need more than that. But I hadn't figured on having a guest for breakfast so I didn't have anything else to fix."

"These are great. And just for your information, I wasn't alone. I had company almost every time I went out."

"You're kidding."

"Nope. Susan ran with me once. Richard went out with me twice. A couple of other male wolves from your pack went with me at other times. And another she-wolf joined in on the fun one last time." He had wondered if they thought to get to know him, to show they supported his actions and let him know he was appreciated. He really hadn't expected all the camaraderie.

Pepper just laughed. "Well, good to know you had company. Even so, I imagine you didn't get much sleep."

"Sounds like you barely got any either." Eric's cell phone rang, and he answered the call.

"Have you had any trouble there?" Darien asked.

"No, it's been quiet here, Darien," Eric said to let Pepper know who was calling.

"Okay, well, you're not going to believe this, but Waldron called and said he'd heard about the trouble we'd had in town. He wanted to know if he could do anything to help us out."

"You're kidding. Mind if I put this on speakerphone so Pepper can listen in?"

"No, go ahead."

"Okay, thanks." Eric put the call on speakerphone.

Darien said, "Good morning, Pepper." He repeated what he had told Eric, and even hearing it twice, Eric couldn't believe it.

"You're kidding," she said, parroting Eric's response.

"We suspect he didn't realize we ran the whole town until *after* they set fire to a few places. Not a well-thought-out move on their part. Because the Fairhaven boys have been spying on you and Eric, I imagine someone would have informed Waldron of the get-together."

"And now he's backing off. Maybe he'll just leave," Pepper said.

"Hold on. My psychologist wife just finished feeding the kids and has something to say."

"Hi, Pepper? It's Lelandi. I've given it a great deal of thought, and I don't believe Waldron will leave. If he wanted to, he would have already left with his people. The fact he's sticking around and trying to make belated amends? That indicates to me he still intends to court you."

"So in your expert opinion, what would be the best course of action?" Pepper asked.

"Well, it's hard to say how he would respond, but if I were you, I'd begin courting another wolf."

Pepper's gaze immediately shot to Eric, who sure liked Lelandi's psychology training right about now.

"He can be one from another pack or even one within your own pack. Show Waldron he's already lost out. It might backfire though, and he might take the other wolf on. That's always a hazard of dealing with an alpha male who wants something others don't want him to have. But that's what I'd do," Lelandi continued.

"I wouldn't want to put any of my own wolves in jeopardy, since they're betas and couldn't deal with an aggressive wolf like him, and"—Pepper looked Eric in the eye—"I don't want to involve any wolf from another pack that would have to face the consequences either."

"All right. It was just an idea."

Still, Eric aimed to prove to Pepper he would do it, even if nothing came of a relationship between them, just to send Waldron the message he'd lost out. If it ended up in a wolf fight, Eric was ready for him.

"So if I don't court another wolf, do you think now that he's tried to make some amends, he'll leave Eric alone? Not try to drum up some scandal to make him lose his job?"

"There's really no telling. If Waldron thinks it will have a negative impact on how you view him, maybe not. But if he feels Eric still represents a threat to Waldron getting his own way, maybe."

Pepper tensed. "Well, I'm not courting any wolf."

"Then he will probably still try to win you over and leave us alone. At least, that's what I would do if I were him. But I'm not him, and like I said, there's really no telling. We were totally surprised when he came with a peace offering this morning."

"Did he offer to pay for all the damages?" Eric asked. He would love it if Waldron and his men got jail time too, but if they'd pay for the damages to the three buildings, he could live with it.

"He won't admit his people did any of it. But he did say he'd help us rebuild. Some of his people are carpenters,"

Darien answered. "There's no way in hell that he would offer to help out if his people didn't do it," Eric said.

"I agree. But he says because of the bad blood between you and him, he was certain we would automatically assume he had his people do it. He apologized for biting you too."

"And you said?" Eric was angry with the way Waldron was trying to make himself out to be the good guy when Eric knew damn well the wolf was responsible for the fires.

"I declined his help, saying we only wanted the persons responsible to pay for all the damages, and we wouldn't press charges if this ended here and now."

"That's agreeable to me."

"Did you want a personal apology from Waldron?" Darien asked.

"No. We both know why he attacked me. If he attacks me again, there won't be any need for an apology."

Pepper let out her breath, and Eric ran his hand over hers, telling her he wasn't stepping out of her life unless she really wanted him to. He certainly wouldn't do so, even if he believed Waldron would refrain from doing more to him or his property.

"Sarandon said you'd be staying with him while the renovations on your house are going on. Now that Waldron says there are no more issues between you and him, I'd say it's safe for you to go back to work if you want," Darien said.

"Yeah." Eric sighed. "I guess it's early enough that I can finish breakfast here, head to Sarandon's place, and then run in to do my job. At least I can save my leave days for something more important." Like if Pepper needed his assistance again.

"All right," Darien said. "If you have any inkling of trouble, you let us know."

"Will do."

Eric and Pepper said good-bye to Darien and Lelandi, then finished their breakfast.

"So what are your plans?" Eric asked Pepper as he helped clear the dishes.

"I hate to say."

He frowned at her.

She shrugged, smiling just a little. "All your running about kept *me* up. After cleaning up and seeing you off, I'm going back to bed."

He chuckled, then pulled her into his arms and said, "You know what Lelandi said had some merit."

"The part about me pretending to court a wolf? And then putting said wolf into a world of danger?"

"I like living dangerously. Why do you think I carried Susan to your campsite when she was injured, knowing your wolves weren't happy with me doing so? Or why I didn't kill the wolf who bit me when it would have been better for my own welfare to do so and not tuck tail and run."

"You didn't tuck tail and run. Your tail was alpha straight behind you. And this?" she said, her hands on his chest. "Must be some of how you like to live dangerously."

"Not that, but this." He leaned down to kiss her, her hands still between them, but nothing stopped his lips from claiming hers. Not in a soft and sweet way either, but in one that said he wanted to be courting her, pretend or otherwise. If he courted her for pretend, he was certain something more would develop between them. But this was definitely the first step.

Her hands never left his chest, and she seemed reluctant to go further, but her heartbeat, her mouth against his, and her scent said all he wanted to know.

She loved this, and if she could get over feeling like her world would end if she let an alpha male wolf into her life, maybe he could be the one to help her through it.

"Got to go," he said, wishing he could go to bed too—with her.

When Pepper said good-bye to Eric, she actually hated to see him go. She'd felt his heart beating rapidly beneath her palms, the heat singeing her, the way his mouth pressed against hers and asked for more. But she didn't want to make him late for work and get him in trouble, as much as she wished she could have had him stay.

She was tired and wanted to go back to bed, but she couldn't. Not when she needed to alert everyone to what was going on with Waldron and his pack. After she called everyone for a pack meeting to let them know the news, Susan and Richard hung around to talk with her further about it.

"Do you think he's going to honor his word?" Richard asked, taking a seat on the sofa in the den.

"Nope. I sure don't. Not after what they did. Well, maybe for a while, worried that the Silver pack will destroy them. They'd have the power and the reason to do so." Pepper served them fresh cups of coffee.

"I don't trust Waldron," Susan said. "And I think Lelandi's suggestion is a sound one. She's got the training to understand people better than anyone."

Richard agreed. "If Eric is willing to court you on a pretend basis, that will force Waldron to do something—either leave or show his true nature."

"Are you kidding? No way do I want a wolf from another pack to put himself in harm's way just so Waldron will leave us alone."

"Even if the wolf is willing? Eager?" Susan was practically sitting on the edge of her seat, ready to cheer Eric on.

"For what reason? To prove himself to the pack? To me? And for what benefit to him? There is absolutely no way I would do that to any wolf, even if he is alpha to the max and willing to take Waldron on."

Richard finished his cup of coffee and leaned back on the couch. "We could pay him to offer his protection."

"No."

"What good is there in having a trained psychologist offer advice if you're not going to take it?" Susan asked, throwing her hands up in exasperation.

"Lelandi might be a psychologist, but that doesn't mean she knows exactly how Waldron or his people would react if I pretended to court Eric. It doesn't mean they'll go away. And it could mean they'd kill him. So no."

"Pepper," Susan said, "for seven years you've allowed yourself to believe it was your fault Harold died."

Richard nodded, looking sympathetic.

"And whose fault was it, if not mine?"

"The wolf who killed him," both Susan and Richard said vehemently, only Susan added, "Damn it! And you can't keep taking the blame for it. Harold loved you. You loved him. An alpha wolf wanted what Harold had and killed him for it. And you killed the wolf. But you can't believe it was your fault. Any of it."

"If I hadn't mated Harold…"

"And the alpha male had tried to take over the pack?" Susan asked. "Then what? Do you think Harold would have stood by and watched? He would have fought the wolf. And that would have resulted in the same ending."

"And if the same thing happened to Eric? Only I wasn't going to mate him and he ended up getting himself killed for me? We have no idea how he would fare against Waldron. We've only seen Waldron injuring Eric. Maybe Eric couldn't fight off the wolf enough to make him leave. I don't want his blood on my hands."

Susan looked at Richard as if waiting for him to convince Pepper to see to reason.

"All right," Richard said, sounding determined. "I'll court you. But we can pretty well figure out how that will end for me. A faux courting, of course. I don't want anyone to think I'm trying to rob the cradle and take over your pack. Except for Waldron, of course."

With tears in her eyes, Pepper rose from her seat and pulled Richard into a hug. "You're too important as my sub-leader." She hugged Susan next. "I know you mean well, but I can't do it. We'll wait and see how this all plays out. If Eric is back to work and nobody bothers him and I continue to say no to Waldron if he pushes it with me, I'm sure he will finally tire of me not giving in to his wishes and move on."

"Right," Susan said. "Like there are a ton of unmated she-wolves out there running their own packs with businesses and prime real estate in their name, just waiting for Mister Macho Alpha Waldron to show up on their doorsteps and take over."

Pepper hated to admit Susan was right. Then she glanced at her calendar and read her handwritten note on today's date. "Shoot, I've got a presentation I forgot about. We can talk more about this later. If you come up with any other solutions, let me know." Pepper rushed them out the door and hurried to get ready for a talk at a businesswomen's luncheon. She wasn't sure what they would think of her lecture on the importance of trees. The month before, a lady did a talk on makeup, and the month before that, travel. So she really didn't know if tree studies, growing trees, Christmas trees, or keeping deer numbers down in the national parks were going to be hot topics.

She headed out to the country club hosting the affair. At least she'd get a free steak lunch out of it. But as soon as she began the long drive into town, she swore a truck was following her. She hoped it was just one of the Silver pack members. Not taking a chance, she got on her cell and called Darien, because if anyone would have ordered someone to protect her, it would be Darien and Lelandi.

"Hi, Pepper? How can I help you?" Darien asked. "Lelandi's in a counseling session, but she can talk to you in a little while if you'd prefer."

"Someone's tailing me. Is it one of your people?"

Chapter 12

ERIC *KNEW* WALDRON WASN'T GOING TO LET PEPPER LIVE IN peace. Since Eric worked at the park halfway between Silver Town and Pepper's lands, Darien called him immediately after ending the call with Pepper.

"I'm sending CJ as backup because he can use his badge and weapon," Darien added.

"All right. Did you let Pepper know I'm the one coming to take care of this?"

"Yeah. She wasn't happy about it."

"I don't know how I can convince her I have no intention of taking over her pack. That my helping out doesn't mean courtship, mating, and the rest."

"She said she didn't want you to have to keep taking leave from your position on account of her."

Eric would have to call his boss to let him know he was taking an early lunch break and made sure he was covered for the time he would be gone. But he believed Pepper's concern was for more than that. She felt threatened by his helping her any further.

"Lelandi said not to worry over her. Just show her you're only doing this as a wolf, a friend, and don't expect anything more of it. She wanted to know how last night worked out though."

"I told you—nothing happened. No sign of Waldron and his people at all."

"She meant between you and Pepper."

"Nothing happened there either. I did end up running with some of her pack members on various trips out to check on her lands. She even ran with me the first time."

Darien told Lelandi.

"Perfect," she said in the background.

Eric sighed. He could see Lelandi was reading way more into this than was going on. Which is why he didn't mention anything about the wine he and Pepper had shared before she went to bed. "Anything more on the search for the pot-growing wolves?"

"No sign of them. We haven't located any more marijuana plants either," Darien said.

Eric's phone beeped. "Hey, listen, I've got a call coming in. I'll call you when I learn anything."

"Watch your back, Eric. I don't trust Waldron or the members of his pack."

"I agree with you there." Eric took the other call, surprised to see it was Susan. He worried the pack was having trouble beyond that Pepper was being tailed. "Yeah, Susan, what's wrong?"

"You know when I said she's afraid to lose her heart to someone again?"

"Pepper?"

"Yeah. There's a lot more to it. An alpha male tried to take over our pack. But to do that, he had to kill Harold, the male pack leader and Pepper's mate. Which he did. Then he thought he was going to force Pepper into submission, and she'd give in and mate him."

Eric was ready to kill the wolf. "Where is he? Is he alive?"

"Pepper killed him."

Eric didn't say anything for a moment, stunned the she-wolf could kill an alpha male.

"Don't tell her I told you, but you see why she's afraid to have another mate? Afraid of any alpha male getting near her pack?"

"Her mate was a beta."

"Yeah. That's what I keep telling her. She feels it's her fault because she took him for her mate. But if she hadn't, the alpha male would have killed him anyway because Harold would have tried to protect her. Anyway, Richard and I told her she should date you…for pretend. But she doesn't want to because she's afraid you'd get yourself killed for no good reason."

"I'd say it was for a very good reason. But I don't aim to get myself killed over it."

"That's what we said. But she doesn't think you should have to do something like that when there's no incentive. Richard said we could pay you for protection, but she said no to that too."

"Well, she just called Darien for help, and he sent me because I'm the one closest to her location."

"What? What's happened?" Susan sounded alarmed.

"She's got a tail. My brother, CJ, the deputy, is meeting up with us when he can. We'll take care of it. No problem."

"See? We knew Waldron wouldn't give it a rest. Will you let me know what happens? She didn't tell me about this latest development."

"She thought maybe it was one of us watching out for her. I'm sure she'll let you know about it herself, but I'll give you a call once I know more." He wasn't sure what he was going to do when he caught up with Pepper and her tail. He would hang around the country club, watching out for her, but as to the tail?

He'd have to play it by ear.

———※———

All Pepper had wanted to do was ensure her tail wasn't one of Darien's men. But she could see now that calling him had been a mistake. She understood Eric was the closest to her location, but she seriously believed that sending him was a ploy on Darien's part, and Lelandi's, to ensure that Eric was her knight. She would have taken care of the matter herself. Although she was wearing a skirt and heels and would be at the posh country club, so she didn't want to draw attention to herself in a negative way. She had hoped some of the women might be interested in her Christmas tree farm or tree nursery. But if she acted like an ogre in the parking lot, they'd stay clear of her and her businesses.

She was already angry because Waldron wouldn't leave her alone. And now she was certain Eric would think that he had to be her protector. She didn't want him to take more leave just because of her either. She wanted him to have his leave time to do what he wanted to do. Something fun, like take his trip to Hawaii.

She called Susan and said, "Just so you know, be watchful today. More of Waldron's people may be observing us. I picked up a tail at the house."

"Oh. Did you want me to get hold of Richard and—"

"No. I called Darien, and he's sending Eric and his brother CJ."

"Oh. Good. They both have guns."

Pepper let out her breath. "It just causes more problems for us. For all of us."

"No…it…doesn't. The Silver pack is a sister pack to us now. If they need our help with anything, they can call on us, right? And you would jump to come to their assistance."

"True."

"All right. So you asked for help from their pack leader, and he sent the men he thought could handle this best. Especially since Eric is closest to your location."

"No, I didn't ask for help. I just called to see if Darien had sent one of his men to follow me. Anyway, there was no talking him out of it." Then again, maybe Darien wouldn't have sent Eric if he had been on a job farther away than other pack members. Pepper had to quit being so suspicious of everyone's motives. "I just arrived at the country club, and I see Eric's truck pulling up behind the tail and him flashing his lights. Got to go. Update you after I give my talk."

"Okay, got to get to work. Talk to you later."

Pepper got out of her mini-SUV and walked toward Eric and the guy he'd pulled over. She wanted to know what was going on before she headed in to her luncheon and lecture. She wished she could invite Eric to join them for lunch after all the trouble he'd gone to. CJ too. But it was a women's business affair.

The "man" driving the truck was Leroy Fairhaven, and his brother, Jonathan, was sitting in the passenger seat. She folded her arms as Eric made them get out of the truck and then searched them for weapons. He glanced in Pepper's direction and said, "Hey. I'll turn them over to CJ when he gets here. If you need to get to your luncheon…"

"In a few minutes."

Eric nodded, then said to the boys, "Okay, you know she can get a judge to issue a stalking protective order and—"

"Your own judge?" Jonathan asked.

Eric raised his brows. "Yeah. So we won't have any trouble taking care of it. What is your business at the country club? Have a lunch date? Membership? Golfing? Jobs here?"

"We were going to apply for jobs," Jonathan said with a smart-ass smirk.

The other boy nodded.

"Okay, well, here's the trouble with that. You followed Ms. Grayling from her house. You weren't home when you left to come here to 'apply' for jobs. You've been caught two other times, once by our sheriff's department, and once by me and another Silver wolf pack member. So it's not a case of maybe, but it's a fact. Now, since you're under eighteen, we're taking you both into custody, impounding the truck that isn't even yours, and—"

"It's mine," Leroy said morosely.

"Okay, so we're impounding the truck because we can't leave it here on private club property while you're in Silver Town sorting out your lives again. Did Waldron put you up to this?"

Jonathan looked at the ground and nodded. "We don't do anything without his say-so."

"So you lied about that the other day when we asked you the same question."

Jonathan glowered at Eric. "What were we supposed to do? He's the pack leader. What he says goes."

"And you're getting in trouble for it."

Jonathan shrugged. "Gotta do what you're told to do."

"Not when it's illegal and can land you in jail. I offered you a chance to join the Silver pack so we can work with you and keep you *out* of trouble."

"What if we want to join hers?" Jonathan asked, motioning to Pepper.

CJ drove up, got out of his police SUV, and sauntered over, looking stern and ready to take the boys to jail. "Looks like you boys liked your stay in our jail."

"No jail to stay in now," Jonathan said, smarting off.

CJ smiled. "Oh, we've taken care of it. Might be a little smoky for a while, but you can live with it."

"What about joining her pack?" Jonathan asked again.

Eric shook his head. "She doesn't need the headache, and what's to say you wouldn't still spy for Waldron if you joined her pack?"

"I'll take them in," Pepper interjected. "I'll call Richard and let him know he's got two new charges, if the boys' parents agree to either join our pack or let us foster the boys."

Eric and CJ looked at her like they thought she was making a mistake.

"Richard will make sure they're working or helping the pack in some way," Pepper continued. "If it doesn't work out, they can return to Waldron's pack with a stalking protection order, and that will be the end of that. Good deal for you boys. Richard can talk with your parents and see which way they want to go on this." Pepper got on her phone and called Richard. "I have a couple of boys who will work under your tutelage, if their parents agree. The boys have already said they'd rather be your charges than work for the Silver pack."

"Do you want me to talk to the parents?" Richard asked.

"Yes. I've got to go into the luncheon now. After I'm through with it, I'll call you and speak with them too. As to the boys…" She glanced at CJ and Eric, hoping one of them wouldn't mind taking the boys to see Richard.

"I'll make sure they drive straight to your place. Or Richard's. Wherever you need me to escort them," CJ offered.

She relayed the information to Richard and gave CJ Richard's location. When she ended the call, she said to the boys, "If you stay with us, I expect you to be on your best behavior. Any problems, and you're out of there. If we have any more trouble with you, it's the Silver pack's call, since they have a wolf-run jail."

"All right," Jonathan said, sounding mopey about it.

"Yes, ma'am," Eric said with a stern voice and even sterner look.

"Yes, ma'am," Jonathan said.

They all looked at Leroy. "Yes, ma'am," he finally said, looking as sour about the whole affair as his brother did.

"Okay, well, now that that's resolved, I have to get on with my lecture. Thanks, Eric and CJ, for coming to help out."

Eric nodded.

"You're welcome," CJ said. "Anytime."

Then she turned and headed toward the front doors of the country club, hoping that taking the boys into her pack wasn't a colossal mistake. But her pack could use a couple of teens working with them and making friends with her teens. She thought if the boys behaved, they could turn their lives around before they got into real trouble. She figured that once they realized they had a good home with her pack, they wouldn't feel loyalty to Waldron's. And if it didn't work out that way, she'd send them packing. Three chances and they were out of there and could live with the consequences of their actions.

She knew Eric and CJ thought she was crazy for offering to take the boys in, considering why they might want that arrangement—thinking that she didn't have a bunch of alpha males in her pack to make them mind, maybe planning to keep Waldron informed about her everyday activities. But her people were great with the teens already in the pack. They kept them busy and out of trouble. If the Fairhaven boys abused their privileges, they'd lose them for a time, and if that didn't set them on the right path after a few attempts? No problem. She'd just turn them over to the Silver pack.

Having mixed feelings, she entered the clubhouse and headed for the room where the meal would be served before she gave her talk. She hoped she wouldn't sound as annoyed as she felt about this whole business: Waldron's continued harassment, the Silver pack's involvement, and taking two teenage boys into the pack and maybe their parents too.

CJ said good-bye to Eric and then followed the teens out of the parking lot. To an extent, Eric understood why Pepper had decided to take the boys in—to show Waldron he wasn't going to have his way in this and that the Silver pack wasn't going to decide this either, since the stalking business had all to do with her. Eric did worry that the boys would cause her more trouble than she and her pack could handle because of the pack's small size and lack of alpha males.

As soon as Pepper walked into the building, Eric called Susan to give her an update as he had promised.

"Oh wow, okay. So what are you going to do now? Go back to work?"

"No. I'm here now. I'll just hang around in case something more happens when Waldron gets word that two of his pack members probably won't be coming home. But you're Pepper's sub-leader. So I'll let her tell you what's going on from now on."

"Totally understand. Thanks so much, Eric. If I were in the market for a mate, I'd choose you."

He smiled. "But you're not?"

"Oh, I am. Only I'm aiming for someone who doesn't need to take over our pack."

"Not me."

"Yeah, well, we all know it. We just have to convince Pepper."

"I really don't see that happening. And who says I'm interested in taking over the pack?"

Susan laughed. "It comes with the territory."

"You better not let Pepper hear you say that. I'll let you go and talk to you later." Eric and she said good-bye, but he really had no intention of getting between her and Pepper. Letting Susan know what was going on with Pepper would be sure to rebound. Still, he was glad to know what Pepper's issues were.

He called for a pizza delivery, despite the fact that he was parked at a fancy country club, the likes of which he'd never belong to. He hoped no one would ask him to leave. When the pizza guy drove up, he was grinning.

"I thought you were a crank call. The boss said it was for real."

"I'm acting as a bodyguard for a VIP, high-roller type," Eric said. Pepper might not be a high roller as far as being filthy rich, but he really thought the world of her, and that made her richer than any billionaire out there.

"Wow." The guy took the money and handed over the pizza. "So who is she?"

"Top secret. Let's just say she's a high-class act and I was lucky to get the contract for the job."

"Too cool. I'll tell the boss it was legit." Then the guy drove off.

Eric pulled out a slice of extra cheese and hamburger pizza, leaned his back against the truck, and watched everyone coming and going. He was dying to know what Waldron would do next. What the Fairhaven boys would end up doing next. What their parents decided to do. He called Darien to give him a heads-up. "Hey, I know CJ probably told you what happened. But I wanted to let you know I'm just hanging around here in case Waldron gets mad about the whole situation and confronts her."

"Good show. I'm not sure about her taking those boys in."

"I'm sure she'll do fine with them." Eric finished the last of his pizza and saw a group of women exiting the country club. Then he saw Pepper coming out and was impressed with how she was dressed in a skirt and jacket and high heels. She looked smart and sexy at the same time.

Just then, a black pickup truck pulled up to the front of the building and parked. A blond-haired guy got out, wearing blue jeans and a dress shirt. He was parking in a no-parking zone, not that Eric could do anything about it, but the way he was zeroing in on Pepper got Eric's attention. "Hey, listen, I've got to go."

"Gotcha."

Eric stuck his pizza trash in his truck, then headed toward the guy.

"Hi, Pepper," the blond man said and closed his truck door.

Was it Waldron? Son of a gun.

He was rugged looking—like he lived half the time in the mountains cutting trees by handsaw—and muscled, with stubble covering his jawline. His amber eyes appealed to Pepper to give him a chance, but his mouth remained serious, as if it was too difficult to even approach offering her a smile. Which made Eric think the man was truly irritated with her for all that she'd done with the Silver Pack.

Pepper stopped and crossed her arms. "I want you to pay damages for the buildings you had burned in Silver Town, Waldron."

"We didn't have anything to do with that. Sorry for the trouble they've had. I offered to send some of my carpenters to help out though, just as a way to assist another pack in the vicinity."

"But you knew about it and had motive, so I don't believe you when you say you had nothing to do with it. Worse, you went after places that all had to do with the Fairhaven boys being taken in—the jailhouse, the tow truck place, and Eric's house—because you have some notion he's interested in courting me."

"Hell, he is."

"All right, and so what if he is? That's my business, not yours."

"If he is, he'd better watch his back."

"And you think this is supposed to intimidate me? Make me give him up? I don't understand how you think this will make me change my mind about you. You have nothing to offer me."

"Protection from other alpha wolves wanting what you have. Not only that, but all wolves want offspring. And since you don't have any of your own…" He raised a brow. "I can give them to you."

Halfway to the building, Eric stopped walking and stood next to an SUV, listening to the conversation. As long as Pepper was handling this to her satisfaction, Eric didn't want to butt in. Surefire way to make her feel he was trying to take over. Although it was killing him not to have his say over the burning of the buildings in Silver Town. He figured that after she left, he'd have a private word with Waldron.

"If you harm anyone, set any more fires, anything else like that—"

"What? Are you going to make me pay?" Waldron gave her a smart-ass smirk, reminiscent of Jonathan's action, and Eric guessed the kid was copying the pack leader.

Eric bristled. *He'd* make him pay for it.

"Oh, and by the way, the Fairhaven boys? They've been nothing but trouble since they grew old enough to be trouble," Waldron said. "Their parents are well rid of them. If the Silvers want to charge the boys for the arsons, they have my blessing."

"So your pack members *did* do the damage. Thanks. I'll let Darien know."

"No. I'm just saying if anyone has a real gripe with the town, it would be the teens. The tow-truck business, jailhouse—"

"And Eric? How does he figure into all this as far as the boys are concerned? He wasn't involved in their arrest."

"He lectured them at the park when he had no right to."

"He's a law-enforcement park ranger working in that park, and the teens were stalking us. So yeah, he had every right and the badge to go along with it."

Eric wondered how the boys would view their pack leader now that he was laying the blame on them, especially since Waldron had to have put them up to it. If he left them to deal with the repercussions, the boys might even reveal the truth this time and not take the bum rap.

"I've got business to take care of," Pepper said and turned to leave.

"You wanted the Fairhaven twins, and I'm giving them to you without any fuss. So what do I get in return?" Waldron asked, smiling.

She faced him again, her expression composed. "Peace of mind now that the teens who are nothing but trouble are no longer giving you grief in the pack? You owe *me* for taking them off your hands." She turned then and stalked off to her vehicle.

Eric smiled. Pepper handled that like a she-wolf with real class.

As soon as she was out of hearing, Waldron got on his phone. "Hey, we're going to have trouble with this Eric Silver. Yeah, she's seeing him. So we'll have to do something about it."

Eric strode across the parking lot to have a word. He heard Pepper's mini-SUV's engine start up. He ignored it when Pepper pulled out of her parking space, driving toward them.

"If you want to do something about it, go right ahead," Eric said, coming up behind Waldron, his attention fully focused on him.

Waldron whipped around, his jaw dropping, but he quickly clamped his mouth shut, his eyes narrowing.

"Let's do it now. Between you and me. No sending your teens to do your dirty work. I mean, how low can you get?" Eric said.

"For your information—"

"Unless that's the only way you can deal with rejection," Eric said, cutting him off.

Pepper pulled her vehicle to a stop right next to them. "Eric, can I speak with you?" Her question was more of a command than a query.

Eric was sticking up for himself as much as he was for her. If someone was threatening to do something to him behind his back, he had every right to confront the one giving the orders. He made one final comment. "The lady isn't interested in you. Back off." Then he turned to Pepper. "Yes, ma'am. I'm parked over there." He motioned to the next aisle, intending to walk to his truck and speak in private with her there.

"Get in," she ordered, sounding exasperated...with *him*!

He smiled at Waldron, rubbing it in that she had requested his presence, even though she sounded annoyed with him. He couldn't help himself. After all Waldron had pulled, Eric was itching for a fight to take him down a peg or two. Ever since the day Waldron had bitten him, Eric had felt he'd led the man to believe he was a coward. That he would always run away in the face of danger. And Eric wanted him—and Pepper—to know he had the strength to prove that wasn't so.

Eric climbed into Pepper's car, and Waldron started talking on his phone again. Eric gave him one last glower as she pulled down the aisle where he was parked.

"What do you think you are doing?" she asked, her voice sharp.

"Protecting myself. He was telling one of his people I was seeing you and they'd have to do something about it. Now if that's not a threat, I don't know what is. But the whole point of the matter is that I wanted to meet him face-to-face—as a human this time—and let him know I won't be running off next time."

She didn't say anything for a moment, then sighed. "I thought you had already left."

"No. Not after you took the teens on as your responsibility. I was afraid once Waldron got word, he might show up to hassle you further."

"You were watching us the whole time?"

"Yeah."

"You didn't come over and say anything while I was talking to Waldron." She looked incredulous, as though she couldn't believe Eric would just let her deal with it on her own.

"Nope."

She let out her breath. "Okay…I don't want you to take this the wrong way, but I really do owe you my thanks for Susan and for all the rest of your help. I'd like to invite you to dinner." Before he could say a word, she quickly added, "I'll invite Richard, Susan, and the Fairhaven boys. We'll have a nice dinner and talk sociably. I'll tell the boys what I expect from them and what they can expect from me. I'll let them know what Waldron said about them setting the fires, and that since they torched your home as well as other Silver properties, you will be sitting in on the dinner to give your input. You can have a conference call with Darien and Lelandi on the matter before then."

"Sounds good to me." It wasn't quite what he had expected as a thank-you dinner with her, but more time spent with the she-wolf was, well, more time spent with the she-wolf. He would prove he had no intention of taking over whenever she had to deal with her people or others, like Waldron. He would sit back, learn her approach, and be happy to provide any input she wanted, if it made her happy.

Later, he hoped a dinner with her would be less crowded, and he looked forward to that.

Chapter 13

THE FAIRHAVEN BOYS APPEARED APPREHENSIVE WHEN Richard brought them to Pepper's house for dinner that evening. Leroy had his hands shoved in his pockets, glancing at his brother. Jonathan was trying to look tough and unafraid, his thumbs hooked in his belt loops.

"Jonathan, Leroy, glad you could have dinner with us," Pepper said. As if the kids had a choice.

"Why?" Jonathan asked.

Pepper knew from the start the kid wasn't going to be easy to win over. "We're going to talk. And have a nice dinner." She turned to Richard. "Why don't you take the boys and Eric outside? You can prepare the ribs on the grill."

"Sure thing," Richard said.

Eric smiled a little at her as if he'd just been relegated to being one of the troublesome boys. She hadn't meant it that way, but she smiled back.

When they went outside, she and Susan began preparing everything else for the meal while the guys were out on the back patio, talking about life in general. She figured it was a good start for the teens to learn what the males in her pack loved to do during social gatherings—which wasn't plotting to take over another pack or whatever else Waldron was scheming to do. Did Waldron ever have fun social times for his pack? Did he include the teens in adult activities or only have them do his dirty work? Someday, she figured she'd learn the truth.

"What do you think will happen with the boys?" Susan asked, sounding apprehensive as she shucked corn on the cob.

"They'll be fine. Oh sure, we might have some trouble with them because of the way they've been raised, but I'm certain they'll find their place with the pack before long. Richard said he was showing them which trees were diseased and too far gone to save today. They cut down a number of trees and have the blisters to show for it. Good hard work never hurt anyone. They'll be tired tonight for certain. And that's how we'll handle this. The more work they do to show they're eager to be good citizens in the pack, the more privileges they'll earn."

"Richard and I believe Waldron gave them up so willingly because he figures they'll spy on us. Did you confiscate their cell phones?" Susan grabbed another ear of corn.

"No. It's true they might be keeping him informed, but if they want to keep in touch with their parents, I want them to have every opportunity to do so. I want them to be here of their own free will. They can leave anytime. But I want to make sure they understand what the consequences will be if they leave us and continue stalking me or do anything else to create trouble for either of our packs. And that they'll still need to pay for the damage to the buildings in Silver Town no matter what, if they were the ones who set fire to them. Even though they might inform on us for a while, I truly believe they'll come to realize we're the good guys and have great things to offer them."

"Richard's been great with them all afternoon. I took lunch to them and we all ate together. They seem like they could be good kids if given half a chance. We'll have to see how they are with the rest of the pack." Susan broke the corn cob in half and began shucking another.

"We just have to let them know that being with us is not a punishment, but a way to learn a job skill and be able to get along with others in a working pack."

"What about Eric?"

"What about him?" Pepper asked, turning on the heat under the pot of water for the corn.

"Why is *he* here?"

"No reason other than that I wanted to discuss the arson. Since Eric's home and two other buildings were burned in the Silver territory, I figured he could represent his pack and…" Pepper shrugged. "We'll see what happens from there."

Susan sighed. "You really need to get with the program with him."

Pepper frowned at her. Susan gave her a bright smile back.

Half an hour later when they all sat down to eat, Pepper asked what the boys liked to do best of all. They both loved hiking and fishing, but when Eric reminded them about the skiing near Silver Town and how he and his brothers and cousins could show them how to do it this winter, both boys listened quietly and nodded.

Pepper thought that they were afraid to try it out— which she really didn't think was the case—that they were afraid of the Silver pack, or that they had no intention of staying around that long if their short-term goal was just to spy on her pack. The worst-case scenario was that they were certain they would be part of her pack by then with Waldron as the leader, so they knew they wouldn't have anything to do with the Silver pack.

After having a delightful dinner and good conversation about things they thought the boys might like to do and what they were expected to do, Pepper finally brought up the serious issue of arson and Waldron's claims that the boys had always been problem wolves.

"Now, we don't really believe you're troublemakers for his pack. We think Waldron's making it up to lay the blame on you both," Pepper said, judging their reactions.

"He actually said we set fire to the buildings?" Jonathan asked, his voice dark.

"Yes. And he said we could turn you over to the Silver pack so they could press charges."

"So does that mean we're going to jail?" Jonathan asked, looking like they'd led him to the slaughterhouse.

"We can work something out," Eric said. "But we have to know if you acted on your own or Waldron told you to do it. Or if you're covering for someone else."

Jonathan let out his breath. "He really said we did it?"

"He did," Pepper said, getting the distinct feeling Waldron had lied.

"We didn't cause any trouble for the pack," Leroy said. "Waldron told us to follow you. And when he learned you were eating out with Eric, he got really angry. He told us what to do after that. We were to follow you back to the park and see what you were doing. He said if we got caught, we wouldn't get into too much trouble because we are underage."

"You mean about setting the fires?" Pepper asked.

Jonathan was scowling. "No, about following you around."

"So you didn't set the fires? Or you had help?" Pepper asked. She didn't think the boys could have set all the fires in the same night.

Leroy looked at Jonathan.

Jonathan swallowed hard. "We didn't set fire to anything."

Leroy shook his head, agreeing with his brother.

Pepper was beginning to believe it. "So, in truth, he wanted you to take the blame because he believed you wouldn't get as much punishment as an adult would. But when you said you wanted to join my pack, he figured you could take the blame no matter the consequences." Pepper was shocked at how rotten Waldron could be. He'd been charming with her, trying to win her over before she'd met Eric, but now she could see just how devious he was.

Jonathan frowned. "He really said we caused trouble for the pack?"

"Yeah, he did. And he said I should give him something for taking you boys off his hands. But I told him if you were so much trouble, he ought to pay me for including you in my pack," Pepper said to the boys, then turned to Susan. "Did you want to bring in the dessert?"

"Yeah, sure."

Richard and Susan began clearing away the dishes.

"It's not right that your pack leader would set you up to take the blame for something he dictated." Pepper set her napkin on the table. "Or blame you for something you didn't even do. Pack leaders are meant to take care of their people. Make sure they abide by pack rules, which means also abiding by human laws. It's too dangerous for our kind to get caught and go to a human jail for any length of time. Your pack leader is supposed to set the example of what to do, showing how to protect yourself from other wolves and live among humans in a way that doesn't bring unnecessary negative attention to yourself. What he's doing is wrong."

Jonathan looked sheepishly at Eric. "He"—Jonathan motioned to Eric—"came by the jail with our dinner after we got pulled over for following you in Silver Town. He brought us a pizza just like we said we'd like, sodas, and chocolate milk shakes too. He wanted to know the truth about why we were stalking you. We wouldn't have torched his house. He was nice to us. Everyone was. The sheriff let us come out of the cells to watch TV. One of the deputies, CJ, brought in some movies for us to watch that he thought we'd like."

"Yeah," Leroy said.

"We didn't let Waldron know how well we were treated while we were in jail because he might have thought the Silver pack members were trying to bribe us into telling the truth. But we never got into trouble in our pack. Unless someone else started something. Or we did something by accident," Jonathan said.

She thought it was interesting that Jonathan seemed to be angriest about Waldron accusing him and his brother of being troublemakers. "Why did Waldron leave his pack in Idaho?" she asked.

"Benjamin, the pack leader, said if his brother didn't leave with those who sided with him, he would kill him."

"Why?"

"Waldron wanted to run the pack. He was trying to

create a mutiny. Only Benjamin caught him at it and expelled him right away. He told Waldron if he saw him in Idaho anywhere near his territory, he'd kill Waldron outright and any of his followers too."

"Why did your parents go with him?" Pepper asked, shocked to hear it.

"He promised our dad a sub-leader position. Dad wouldn't have had one otherwise." Jonathan sat back in his chair. "Waldron made a lot of promises to the pack."

"What made him come here?" Eric asked, his tone suspicious. "How would he know that Pepper was a single she-wolf running a pack?"

"She wasn't a single she-wolf when Waldron first found out about her. She killed his cousin when he murdered her mate and tried to take over her pack," Jonathan said, pointing at Pepper. "Not only was Obie Waldron's favorite cousin, but he always said he wouldn't fail where his cousin had. But still, Waldron was trying to take over his brother's pack first. It's bigger and would give him more power, and Waldron knew everyone. He thought he'd have an easier time of it than trying to win over a new pack. Of course, he didn't tell us that, but Leroy and I overheard him talking to his sub-leaders, our dad included."

"Hell," Eric said.

Pepper felt her whole world spin. She was stunned that Waldron could be related to the animal who had killed her mate.

Seeing Pepper's face turn ice-white, Eric didn't know what to do. He wanted to talk to her in private, but he didn't know what to say to make her feel better.

Susan and Richard had remained in the kitchen,

cleaning up, which Eric thought was a ploy to stay out of the way and let Pepper and the boys have this discussion without so many adults listening in on the conversation. To help them to open up more.

Then, as if on cue, Susan and Richard started serving dessert—chocolate mousse pie. Everyone ate it while the subject switched to what needed to be done tomorrow, and the boys seemed a little lighter-hearted after giving up their secrets.

Pepper was quiet while Susan and Richard and the boys dominated the conversation with talk of what they had planned for the pack for the rest of the year. As the adults finished their desserts, the boys had a second helping.

Then Richard looked to Pepper and she nodded. "It's time to say good night. I had a nice visit with everyone," she said.

"Thanks," Jonathan said, and his brother echoed his thanks.

"I'll take them home," Richard said. "Come on, boys. We have to get up early to go to work tomorrow."

They both groaned, and then they all left.

Susan hurried to take care of the dessert dishes.

"I'm sorry about what happened to your mate," Eric said to Pepper.

"I had no idea Waldron's relation had anything to do with it. If I had, I would have viewed him being here a lot more warily. Sounds to me like revenge could be at the root of it. Explains why he is so persistent." She joined Susan in the kitchen. "Thanks, Susan. I'll take care of the rest of this."

"The dinner seemed to go over well with the boys.

They loved the food, and I think they realize how rotten Waldron is," Susan said, putting the last of the dishes in the dishwasher. "Um, about him being Obie's cousin—"

"We'll talk about it later. I'm tired and not in the mood to speak of it right now."

"Sure," Susan said and cast Eric a look that indicated she hoped he'd stay and visit with Pepper a bit to ensure she was going to be all right.

He hoped to, but it was really Pepper's call.

When Susan said good night and left, Eric asked Pepper, "Do you mind if I have a cup of coffee before I leave? After being up most of the night, I don't want to drift off on the drive home." He figured she'd be glad to send him on his way too. She'd most likely be thinking about what had transpired tonight, maybe wanting to sort it all out on her own. But if she needed to have someone to talk to, he wanted to be that someone.

She let out her breath, looking tired but beautiful. "About that. It's a four-hour drive home for you. Stay the night. You can leave for work tomorrow from here. It's about the same distance to your job as going from your…" She suddenly stopped speaking. "I'm sorry. I forgot about your home."

"It's all right. And you're correct. The distance from Sarandon's place is about the same too. And thanks. I'll take you up on the offer." If Waldron pulled anything tonight, Eric would be here to protect her.

"Sure. Let's have some coffee then. Decaf if you'd like. That's what I'll have, or I won't be able to sleep tonight."

"Same for me since I won't have to drive." Eric eyed the second mousse pie in the fridge as she reached in to get cream for their coffee. "I didn't want to ask in front of everyone else and give the boys the idea they could finish the pie, but…"

Pepper smiled. "You want another slice?"

"If you don't mind."

"No. I'll have another too."

He brought out dishes and forks. "Sorry about using up more plates."

"No problem. That's what dishwashers are for." She poured them both cups of coffee, adding cream and sugar, but this time instead of going back to the dining room, she led him into the den. They took their seats on the faux suede sofas where it was a lot more relaxed and cozier. "I might as well tell you about my mate. All of it."

Eric hadn't expected this, but he was glad she felt comfortable discussing her mate with him now. She'd changed from her business skirt, jacket, and heels into a pair of soft jeans and a sleeveless blouse and looked a little more relaxed now that the boys had gone.

"Have you ever known a couple who have been friends so long that everyone assumes they'll be mated?"

Eric set his empty coffee cup down on the table and ate his pie. "Kind of. Sam, who owns the tavern in Silver Town, and Silva, who now runs a tearoom, were destined to be mated, even if they couldn't see it for the longest time. But to see all that passion between them… The rest of us knew it had to happen sooner or later."

"Oh, well, not exactly the same with us. Because of that, I waited years before I agreed. I think some part of me felt like I needed someone who was more than just a best friend. I think you need both. Some spark of passion and the friendship that shows you care about each other every day of your mated life. Not just during courtship or the first years of the mating. But forever."

"I agree. So you were best friends, but you felt something was missing."

"Yeah. Maybe that he should have been more alpha." She finished her pie and set her plate on the table, then drank the rest of her coffee.

He noted she quickly dropped the issue of needing more passion in her life. "Because the alpha wolf killed him."

"Yeah, I always wondered if it would have made a difference. Obie was coming on to me and trying to get my mate to react, but Harold was following my lead, although I know he was embarrassed about not doing anything about it. But he was a real beta wolf. I didn't want him to fight Obie, and I knew Harold didn't want to fight him either."

"So you've always led the pack on your own."

"Yes. I never thought we'd have trouble with an alpha male like that. Harold had gone off on a run after we'd had a big fight. He'd said he wanted an equal role in the leadership, which would have been fine if he'd been a leader. But he wasn't. He sat back and let me deal with everything. He was a hard worker, loved by all, good with the kids, but he was not a leader. While Harold was running as a wolf by the creek, Obie jumped him. He had been waiting for Harold to be off on his own. I heard the wolves fighting, stripped, and shifted. I was sick with worry. I knew in a confrontation between Harold and Obie, Harold would lose. Among the beta wolves in our pack, Harold managed fine. But matching him with an aggressive alpha wolf? No way.

"When I saw Harold lying on his side, gasping for breath, I tore into Obie. He was just standing there, gloating over his success. He didn't see me coming, which gave me the advantage because he was so much larger than me. I sank my teeth into his neck and held on with such tenacity that I killed the beast. When I released him, I finally saw three males of his pack watching me, but none moving closer. I growled and snarled at them, and then I howled for my pack, but we were too late. Harold died in my arms. If we hadn't had a fight that night—" She wiped away tears. "If I hadn't made him my mate..." She shook her head.

Eric wasn't sure Pepper would appreciate it if he moved closer to comfort her, but he slipped his arm around her shoulders and gave her a tender hug. "Who's to say the same thing wouldn't have happened if you had taken a different mate? Or that if you hadn't taken Harold as your mate, he might still have been provoked into an attack with the same result?"

She swallowed hard. "I keep reminding myself of that. For the past seven years, I've had trouble with alpha males thinking my pack would be an easy takeover. Just mate me and they'd be in charge. But none of the wolves would have been good for the pack or for me."

"And then Waldron comes along."

"Right. I should have known he was related to Obie. Now that I know, I can see he has some of the same mannerisms, both as a wolf and as a human."

"He must have thought you wouldn't learn the truth before it was too late. Then here I come along, causing you more anxiety." Eric wanted her to acknowledge that she was unsure of him in the same way. And he wanted to talk about it. To straighten out her misconception of him.

"I don't want you to get killed over me or over my pack."

Eric raised his brows. "I don't intend for him to kill me for *any* reason."

She let out her breath in annoyance. "He brutally attacked you already and—"

"And I didn't fight back. I ran off. It won't happen again. Believe me, over the years, I've been in enough wolf fights—and lived to tell about them. You don't have to worry about me. What bothers me is you thinking I'd be like the other alpha males you've had difficulty with."

"I've never met a bachelor alpha male who wasn't thinking of taking over my pack. So you have been an enigma to me. I keep thinking you'll suddenly begin to behave like the others did." She shook her head. "But you're nothing like them. Oh, sure, you have all the alpha wolf posturing. But whenever I've had to deal with anything pack-related around you, you stay back and watch how it plays out. You wait for an invitation to step in.

"Not like Waldron. A few weeks back, Waldron paid me a visit when I was speaking to Richard about some pack matter. Waldron told Richard what to do, as if he were already the leader of the pack. I asked Richard to leave and then tore into Waldron. He only seemed semi-amused. I knew then if I ever mated him or another wolf like him, I'd have a devil of a time protecting my pack—from him."

Right then, Eric wanted to kiss her and make her feel better. He wanted her to see that some alpha males were all right. He wanted to court her, to learn if they had enough common ground that they thought it might work out.

Ultraserious, Eric rose from the couch. He knew this was one hell of a gamble, but she'd allowed him to have a guest room last night. And he felt like dinner tonight had been a test to see how he handled the boys. To see how he spoke to Susan and Richard, her loyal sub-leaders. He felt she wouldn't have said he could stay tonight if she wasn't reaching out to him, wanting to learn more about him, to see if he truly was different from the others she had known.

Pepper stood, but before she could start grabbing dishes, he took her hand and pulled her tentatively into his arms. She was still unsure of him and what this might lead to. Yet she didn't fight it, didn't pull away or say no. She allowed herself to be drawn into his arms, and he gave her a light hug—at first. He didn't want her seeing him as some alpha who couldn't control his libido around her, despite the way his pheromones were spiking and triggering hers to react. He could hear her heart beating pell-mell with intrigue.

He lifted her chin and looked into her eyes. They were filled with curiosity and interest. He leaned down and kissed her mouth. She slid her arms around him, which gave him permission to slide his arms around her back. To gently rub her back with a soothing caress. To hold her closer and show her he was interested in her in a way that had nothing to do with pack leadership and everything to do with the way a man hungered for a woman.

Their kiss was gentle at first, and then she pressed him for more like she'd done before, but this time neither work nor pack members would intrude. His blood sizzled as he touched her lips with his tongue, but she hesitated to open up to him. He backed off just a little, unwilling to let it go. He felt the hesitation in her whole body—the desire there, but the concern too. Then, as if she was ready to throw caution to the wind, she parted her lips and touched her tongue to his. But there was nothing tentative about it.

She kissed him as if she'd die if she didn't taste him, feel his mouth and tongue against hers, and experience the passion ignite between them. For the moment, he forgot about everything else. He didn't remember that he was trying to go easy with her or that he wanted to prove he was one of the good alpha wolves. All he wanted to do was breathe in her she-wolf scent, the fragrance of pines and firs she'd worked with today, and absorb the taste of the sweet coffee and chocolate mocha flavoring her mouth. He luxuriated in the feel of her soft body pressed against his, the way she was kissing him, making him hard and wanting more.

She pulled away with obvious reluctance, and he sure as hell was reluctant to let her go. But he had to, if he was going to prove he really was different from the alpha males she'd encountered in her life. He wondered now if her mate had been that passionate with her. Maybe he had been, but it had been a long time ago.

"We'd better go to bed if you're going to wake in time for work," she said.

"I'll manage." He wished they could just keep this up. But he knew it was best if they ended it like this, on a positive note. And he hoped she wouldn't regret it in the morning and put distance between them again.

"Thank you…for everything," she said. Then she took the plates and silverware into the kitchen while he carried in the coffee mugs.

"I'll just grab my bag." He was going to have to pack more clothes if he kept staying overnight. Luckily, while he was at work, CJ had dropped by the park and brought him a change of clothes for the day and an extra set for emergencies like Eric always liked to carry. This time, he wasn't calling Darien to let him know he'd be here again tonight. But he did have to call Sarandon, since he was supposed to be sleeping there now that his place had to be rebuilt.

When he went out to get his bag out of the truck, he called his brother. "I should have gotten in touch with you earlier, but I was invited to dinner at Pepper's house after the incident at the clubhouse, if CJ mentioned it to you."

"He did."

"Well, I'm staying the night again."

"Expecting trouble?"

"Maybe." In the silence that ensued, Eric could just imagine the conclusion his brother was drawing. "I didn't get much sleep last night. She wanted me to stay over, and I'll go to work from here. It's the same distance as it is from your place."

"Do you need me to bring another change of clothes to the park tomorrow? Maybe enough for a few nights?"

"No, it's just for tonight. I'll be at your house tomorrow night."

"Okay." Sarandon sounded like he didn't believe Eric.

But Eric had no intention of pushing anything further with Pepper. It had to be her call. "I'll talk to you later."

"Okay. Let me know if you change your mind about

the clothes. I'll be taking a group hiking and will be stopping by the ranger station anyway."

"All right. Night, Sarandon."

"Night."

Eric headed into the house and found that Pepper had already gone into her bedroom and shut the door. He said, "I had to tell Sarandon I wasn't coming home tonight. I'll see you in the morning."

"Night," she called out.

"Night, Pepper." He headed for bed and stripped out of his clothes. He never slept in anything so that if he was needed for a spur-of-the moment wolf mission, he'd be ready.

Chapter 14

PEPPER COULDN'T BELIEVE HOW HOT ERIC WAS. SHE DIDN'T think all alpha males were like that. Somehow she was connecting with him on several different levels, which made this feel so right. She'd been fighting the attraction she had for him, trying to see him as just another alpha male who could be real trouble. But he wasn't like that. She would never have known about his treatment of the Fairhaven teens if they hadn't told her, so he hadn't done it to earn points with her.

But she was still worried he might be like the other wolves. It often happened in human relations. The guy would be nice to the woman, or vice versa, until the couple married, and then maybe a year or two down the road, the newlywed game was over. Since wolves signed up for a lifetime, that wouldn't work for them. Yet the way Eric kissed her, the way he became so aroused around her… She had to admit she'd never had that kind of passion with her first mating, and she loved the way Eric made her feel sexy, passionate, and adored. Harold had been too much of a long-term friend before-hand and hadn't been comfortable with even kissing her. Tongues? Forget it. He was more for a small peck on the lips. Sure, they'd consummated the mating, but he had never wanted to have sex with her for pleasure. It had been more a matter of duty, and she'd felt all along that he regarded her more as a sister than his mate and lover.

She'd had passionate, short-term relationships with humans, which were allowed until she had selected a mate. So she knew a lack of passion on her part wasn't the trouble. But of course, the other guys she had dated hadn't been wolves, and she hadn't been willing to take it any further than just a few nights of fun. Now she wanted to prove to herself that she was a passionate person with another wolf. That she wasn't lacking in that part of her life.

As much as she'd wanted more with Harold, trying to get it had been exhausting. She'd tried all methods of seduction—candlelight and wine, moonlit runs before slipping into the hot tub. Even wearing sexy clothes or no clothes, watching sexy movies, just anything to help get him in the mood. What did he do? Act embarrassed.

She didn't have to do anything to rev up Eric's engine. Even a smile seemed to encourage him to draw closer, to want to touch her, to smile back and look wickedly intrigued. Even her invite to dinner tonight had made him appear to want to take her up on the proposal and much more. Whenever she'd offered Harold dinner before they had mated, he'd said sure because he loved her cooking. But there hadn't been the hopeful looks that she'd want more than just dinner.

She had to confess she was feeling the same way toward Eric that he seemed to feel toward her. The sensation of being drawn to him. The physical need to take this further. Which was why, when she reluctantly pulled away from kissing him, she'd retired to her bedroom before he returned to the house with his bag.

Despite her lack of sleep last night, she tossed and turned most of this night too, her thoughts on tall, dark, and wolfish next door—remembering how passionate he was with her and wishing they could take it further.

When she woke early that morning, she intended to do what she always did first thing: take a run on the wolf side. Some of her pack members would be out too, and they'd greet one another. Often, she felt like a pied piper, with her pack hooking up with her and running with her through their woods. She loved her pack, her people, but she was beginning to believe she was missing out on something more. Something only a mate, a wolf more like Eric, could give her. As quiet as the house was, she presumed Eric was still sleeping after having been up most of the night before.

She slipped out of her slinky, short nightie and tossed it on the chest at the foot of her bed. Then she stalked to the bedroom door and opened it. And got a shock. Naked also, Eric was standing in the hall, apparently doing the same thing as she was—shifting and taking a run. He was stretching to the ceiling, his glorious body on display, taut, muscled, and gorgeous.

They had an awkward moment—both standing naked outside their bedrooms so they could shift and run to the wolf door built into her den door that led out to the patio.

Shifters were used to seeing their own pack members naked. It was no big deal, just a way of life for them, and they lived long lives so they really were used to one another. But seeing someone not of the pack and who looked like Eric did? And when both of them were interested in each other?

He was tanned all over. Did he lie out somewhere naked? He was hot and wolfishly toned, his muscles perfectly formed, not an ounce of extra flesh, dark curly hairs surrounding an impressive, half-aroused cock. Seeing his perusal of her made her own nipples tingle, her body awakening and responding to his interest in her.

"Morning run?" Eric asked, shaking her from her gawking, though he appeared to be trying not to drink her up with just as thirsty a gaze.

"Uh, yeah."

"Mind if I run with you, or do you like to go alone?"

She loved just breathing in the woodland scents and enjoying the solitude. Insects, birds, squirrels, and other animals were stirring at this morning hour, so she wouldn't be completely alone. But it was different when she was running with a pack member, that wolf taking some of her concentration as she watched to see if he or she caught anything interesting in the wild that she missed.

She appreciated that Eric would ask and not just assume she'd want to run with him. "Since you're up and ready…"

"Mostly up and ready," he said, and she couldn't miss the double entendre.

From some other wolf, she wouldn't have appreciated it. But from Eric, she did, and she smiled a little. That was something the other alphas who were bothering her hadn't done, teased her in a fun-loving way. They were all business in trying to get her interest. "Well, before it gets too hard for you to run…do you want to lead or follow?"

He chuckled. "I'll follow. You can show me the area where you like to run."

They shifted, and in a flash, she was sprinting through the house and into the den, then bolting through the wolf door as if she were in a race with the male wolf behind her. Whenever she went on her wolf outings in the morning and the evening after work, she spent the time exploring and ensuring no other wolves had intruded on her property. She didn't race through the land as a wolf, but with Eric, she ran full out, just for fun. She felt him chasing after her, not just keeping up with her or following her, but chasing her.

Her heart rate sped up, and he made her sprint faster than she normally did. She was having a blast, though she'd be tired later since she hadn't slept well for two nights.

She thought he'd keep his distance and continue to follow her, but he suddenly was loping beside her. She felt good having him there, enjoying this time with her, his tongue already hanging out, his eyes sparkling with delight as he cast her a look that said he loved being with her like this.

Then, uncharacteristically for her, she headed for the small lake on the property, reached its shore and, without hesitation, dove in.

He stood on the bank watching her. She yipped at him to join her. Then she saw a couple of her pack members heading that way from the woods, probably because they'd heard her. When they saw her in the water and Eric on the bank, they quickly disappeared back into the woods.

She sighed. They'd tell the rest of the pack they had seen her encouraging Eric to swim with her. She often did so with her pack members on a hot summer day, but not before work in the morning. For her to do it with an alpha male who might be interested in courting her? Never.

Eric watched as her pack members disappeared into the pine trees, then he bounded into the water after her.

She wanted to laugh. He looked prepared to tackle

her, but he just swam up to her and licked her face in greeting, and she licked his in return. Then he waited until she began to swim across the lake, paddling next to her as if he were her equal, like a mate would, not like one of her beta followers.

She liked having him by her side and she liked how he gave her a thrill of the chase, though she had every intention of chasing him home. They got out on the other side and shook off, then she began to explore the area like she should have been doing, instead of playing with the male wolf. Though she could envision them going out earlier for a morning run, playing, and then getting down to the business of protecting the pack.

When she found no recent sign of Waldron or his people on her land, she assumed he was lying low or knew that Eric was still on her property. Maybe—though she thought it was way too much to hope for—he was giving up on her. Or maybe he was just wearing hunter's spray to mask his scent.

She chased Eric back to the house, and though she knew he could run faster, he kept just out of her reach to tantalize her. And he *was* tantalizing with his wolfish scent and his keen interest in her. She was already falling for the wolf.

By the time they reached the patio, they had dried off. She pushed her way through the wolf door, then headed for her bedroom to shower and dress before fixing a quick breakfast. She didn't remember a time when she'd had so much fun checking out the property in the morning. It was just one of those things she did daily, unless she were sick. She took different paths to make it more interesting. The environment and wildlife were always changing, which helped. But she'd never played with another wolf before work, and she had never raced out the door, encouraging a male wolf to take chase. Not even with Harold.

As soon as she was ready for work, she called out to Eric's closed door. "Anything in particular you want for breakfast?"

"Yeah," he said, heading for the door. "But I don't think it's on the menu."

She smiled. Harold had never talked to her like that.

He opened the door and smiled at her. "Anything works for me. Then I have to run. I'll be working a double shift tonight. Forgot all about it. Do you want me to ask one of my brothers to drop by your place this evening?"

"No, we'll be fine." She really believed they didn't need the Silver pack's help to the extent the pack's members were providing it. In truth, she wanted to see Eric in a courtship way and not in a manner that said he was her protector. Just admitting that much was a big change for her.

"Okay, sounds good."

She liked that he didn't insist she have someone check on her.

She looked in the fridge at her meager offerings. No eggs. No ham or sausages. She was nearly out of milk. No bread. "I really need to go grocery shopping today. Would more waffles be all right?"

"I *love* your waffles."

She hoped he was being honest with her. By the way he was helping, he really seemed eager to have more waffles for breakfast. Usually when she worked in the kitchen, she liked some space, and she had to really concentrate on not burning the waffles as she added extra chocolate chips. Eric brushed against her to reach into the cabinets to get the plates and breathed in her scent. When she looked up at him to see what he was really up to, he gave her a little smile that said he was eager for more than just waffles. She realized that with him around, work was no longer work, but fun and sexy. Harold would have been checking emails on his phone while she cooked, not even conversing with her. But Eric? He never looked at his phone except when he had a call that couldn't wait.

And helping in the kitchen? Eric definitely added a sexy spin to it.

"I have tomorrow off," he said as he helped her prepare breakfast. "If you had any free time, we could go out for a meal."

"I'll be busy all day, and I have a birthday party to go to that night." She was already regretting that she couldn't take the day off too to see where things might go between them.

"Some other time then." Eric sounded upbeat about it, but she thought he believed she was just making excuses. It probably was best to put some distance between them anyway.

She needed to run her pack, take care of her day job, and deal with Waldron. Fitting in a romance seemed too complicated right now. Besides, Eric had his own work schedule, the problems with the pot-growing wolves, and the mess concerning his house.

"Okay. Works for me," she said.

After they had eaten and locked up the place, and Eric was hauling his bag to his truck, she thought this was good-bye. That he wasn't sure about her needs or wants and wanted to give her space. But she didn't know his history. Maybe *he* was the one who was reluctant and needed space.

Yet she wanted a good-bye kiss. Needed it to hint there might be more. She realized how much she wanted something more in her life. Someone like him. No, not someone like him, but him, if he turned out to always be like this—sexy, fun, protective—and gave her the lead on making her own decisions for the pack. At least for now.

Would he be shocked if she seized his hand, pulled him into a hug, and kissed him? Probably almost as much as she would shock herself if she gave in to such a notion.

He hesitated to leave, as if unsure how to say good-bye, and she finally did just want she wanted to do. She took his hand and pulled him close, looked into his dark eyes filled with intrigue, and that's all it took. He wrapped his arms around her, pulled her in tight, and kissed her on the lips with such passion, she felt the earth tilting on edge. She knew then that Harold had definitely been the reason for the lack of ardor in their relationship—the difference between him and Eric was night and day. Pepper kissed Eric back, her heart beating triple time, her pheromones kicking in to boost the interest.

Eric's tongue stroked her lips and he said, "Hmm," in such a sexy way, she thought he was ready to sweep her up in his arms and carry her back into the house for more private time. And she wanted him to—not to mate, but she wanted to see just how sexy he was in bed.

She parted her lips for him, inviting him in, then stroked his tongue with hers. She felt his growing arousal pressed against her, and she cherished that she could do that to him. With her mate, she'd had to work extra hard to get him to this point. She'd begun to wonder if all male wolves were like that, because the humans she had dated never had an issue. Or maybe being a beta wolf, Harold had felt intimidated by her. And she felt bad about that.

"About the…birthday party," Eric said, his words drenched with longing. "Do you think you could get me an invitation?"

She smiled up at him. "It's for five-year-old twins."

"I like kids," he said.

Her smile broadened. She knew he did. He'd shown it over and over in the way he treated them. "All right."

"And we could have dinner after the party."

"We're having hot dogs at the party."

"Drinks then."

Yeah, he wanted more with her. "I'll let Pauline, their mother, know to prepare for another adult to attend."

"I'll be there. Or come here first, and then we can go over together. Whichever you prefer."

"You can come here and we'll go over together."

He kissed her one last time, his thumbs rubbing her face gently, his kiss just as hot, his body pressed just as close, and then he parted from her, his eyes darkened with desire. She imagined hers looked the same.

Certainly, their pheromones were stirring each other's up, and their hearts were beating as if they were in a wolf race all over again.

"Tomorrow night," he promised, and then he got in his truck and took off.

She felt like she'd won the gold. What a way to start her day. What if she could always start it in such a way?

If he was like this now, what would he be like if she tried the wine, candlelight, and hot tub on him? The sexy movies? The sexy nightwear? No nightwear? She saw the rise that had gotten out of him this morning.

She was definitely adding wine and candles to her grocery list.

Chapter 15

ERIC WISHED HE HADN'T AGREED TO TAKE A DOUBLE SHIFT. He had done it in part to make up for another park ranger having taken his shift when he was injured, but now he really wished he could have stayed with Pepper tonight. She'd opened up to him, and, hell, he hadn't even really talked about himself yet. Would that change the way she felt about him?

He'd sure had a good time with her this morning: the run, the swim, and the way she had kissed him.

He sighed. When they got together after the birthday party, they'd talk.

After he arrived at the park, he was hiking to the first of the campsites he needed to check when he got a call.

"Sarandon?" Eric answered.

"One last chance, Brother. Did you need me to bring you another change of clothes?"

"Yeah, go ahead. I'll be staying at the park on a double shift."

"Okay, you got it. What about tomorrow?"

Eric smiled. "I have a birthday party to attend, but I have the day off, so I'll be dropping by your place for a while, getting some sleep, then taking care of some other business."

"Any trouble with Waldron?"

"No. He's playing it cool…or he's making plans for more trouble."

"Watch yourself at the park."

"Will do."

"I'll be up on the mountain all day with the climbers, so if you need anything, just let me know, but I probably won't be able to get to it until this evening."

"Thanks, Sarandon. I appreciate it."

They ended the call, and when Eric arrived at the campsite, he was immediately called out on a rescue mission. A couple of fishermen had found a canoe resting in the rocks with no sign of the occupant. After hours of searching through the woods along the river-bank, Eric finally located the canoeist by using his wolf scenting ability. The man had a nasty gash on his fore-head from where he'd hit his head on the rocks when his canoe flipped. He'd become disoriented and wandered off into the woods. Eric quickly called the other search-ers to let them know he had located the canoeist. Eric told them about the man's condition while cleaning and bandaging the wound. Once medical personnel arrived and took care of the man, Eric returned to the campsite he needed to inspect.

Afterward, he made a trip back to one of the mari-juana patches. He didn't believe anyone would be growing a new crop there now—it was too late in the season to start one—but he wanted to see if he'd find any evidence he'd missed before.

He was surprised to see that some of the seeds had sprouted late and a few stragglers were growing there. But because of it, Eric also found a new wolf scent. Just a hint, which made him wonder if the wolf was wearing hunter's spray and hadn't applied enough to cover his own scent. It was one of the same wolves he'd smelled before. The rogue wolves must have realized some late-blooming seeds might have sprouted.

As much as Eric wanted to confiscate the plants, he couldn't while he was working the job. Irritated to the max that wolves would be involved in the illegal venture, he called CJ. "Hey, I found ten more plants in Patch 5."

"Got it. Be out there in a bit. Can you hang around to watch it in case the wolves return? Surreptitiously though?"

"I will for a while, but if I get an emergency call, I'll have to go." Plus, Eric had jobs to do. He couldn't go missing for long without someone wondering where he'd disappeared to and worrying he was in trouble.

A flash of a tail whipped about in the brush several feet away. Hell. A gray wolf with a black-tipped tail. He must have believed Eric was a hiker who had found the plants, and the wolf thought he could scare him off. Until he smelled Eric's wolf scent and took off instead.

"See one. Shifting and taking chase."

"Eric—"

Knowing his little brother was going to warn him to wait for backup, Eric turned off his cell, stripped, and hid his clothes in brush farther away from the plantings. If a wolf was snooping about though, he'd find Eric's clothes and gun and phone in a heartbeat. But this was only the second time they'd gotten this close to learning who the rogue wolves were. And Eric wasn't going to let this go. Even if it meant an ambush.

He shifted, his muscles warming with the change, his body turning from his human form to his wolf's in a flash, and then he tore after the wolf. Hunter's spray made the rogue wolf harder to follow, but he was leaving just enough of a scent for Eric to keep after him.

The wolf reached a creek filled with rapids and hesitated to cross. That hesitation was all Eric needed to reach him and tackle him. He wanted to injure the rogue wolf enough that he couldn't escape and could be taken into custody. But Eric would need his pack's help to do that.

What a mess it would be if he accidentally killed the rogue wolf, Eric thought as he lunged at the wolf. He hoped no one was in the area to witness the two wolves fighting or, worse, videotape it and share it with the world.

As soon as Eric tackled the wolf, he smelled the cannabis on him, probably from him moving around in the plants as a wolf. The wolf was a big gray that matched Eric in size and was just as ferocious when Eric attacked him. The wolf swung around and bit at Eric, his snout wrinkling as he bared his canines. Their teeth clashed as they stood on hind legs, both trying to get the best of the other. Both were snarling and growling. As soon as they dropped to the stony ground, Eric went for one of the wolf's hind legs. Eric was so quick, he managed to grab the leg and chomp down hard enough to break the bone.

Eric heard a crack, and the wolf howled in pain. Eric hoped to God none of the wolf's pack members were nearby to come to his rescue. Though he was prepared to fight every last one of them.

But what to do with the injured wolf now? If Eric shifted and any humans saw him, that would be a nightmare. Even if he shifted to carry the wolf out, he was certain the injured wolf wouldn't be docile. Eric would be fighting him every step of the way, trying to avoid his lethal teeth. And they were too far into the park for Eric to howl for any of his Silver pack members.

Though he knew his last words had warned CJ that his oldest brother could be in the middle of a real mess. CJ would have contacted the sheriff and everyone by now to help Eric out. But they would still need an hour or more to arrive.

What about Sarandon? But then Eric remembered his brother was climbing on a mountain and wouldn't be able to just leave his charges and come to Eric's rescue.

Eric watched the wolf panting and sitting, his eyes narrowed and his whole expression filled with hatred. Not that Eric blamed him, but the wolves had to know they might get caught sooner or later.

He hoped he didn't get an emergency call when he wasn't monitoring his phone. He didn't want to put a visitor to the park at risk.

Hell. He snapped at the wolf to get him to move toward the woods.

The wolf snapped back at him and didn't budge. Eric knew the wolf could walk on three legs, but he also knew the wolf didn't want to be taken in. Eric thought briefly that the wolf might be all wolf, but he quickly dismissed the idea. A wolf would have run off on three legs, not remain there growling at him.

Eric bit him in the shoulder—not hard, but enough to get his attention and make him move.

This time the wolf stood without putting any weight on his broken hind leg and limped toward the woods. Since he hadn't howled, Eric assumed the rogue wolf was up here alone, maybe figuring no one would catch him if he wasn't running with a pack.

Eric snapped at him again, forcing the wolf to return to the marijuana patch. Though it had only taken them about fifteen minutes to run to the creek, it took them forty minutes to return to the plants.

Again, Eric hoped no humans were trying to follow them. He'd been listening intently enough to ensure no one was. The whole way back, he was sweating it out, praying he hadn't gotten a ranger call. Then in the woods near the open area where the patch was growing in full sun, Eric shifted. He was far enough away that he didn't think the wolf would try to attack him. Besides, he had his gun and he'd use it in a nonlethal way on the wolf if necessary.

Eric grabbed his phone. No one had called him about anything urgent, thank God. He got dressed, eyeing the wolf the whole time. Eric called to let the park staff know he'd been chasing a cougar away from a campsite and gave false coordinates about where he was, but close enough so that if he were needed, he could get to that location soon enough.

The wolf had lain down, as if his fate was already sealed and he could do nothing about it. Eric had half expected the wolf to fight him further. Eric would have, in his place. But since he was armed with a gun, he assumed the wolf figured things could get even worse if he tried to attack now.

Eric immediately updated CJ. "Got the wolf. He has a broken leg. I'm back at Site 5. How long before your ETA?"

"Fifteen minutes. We have a whole team of Silver pack members headed your way. A couple of them in wolf form should see you in just a few minutes and can provide backup if the wolf has buddies in the area. I'll notify both docs and let them know we're bringing in an injured wolf. What about you?"

"I'm fine. A couple of minor scratches. Nothing that won't heal quickly."

Then he heard something running through the brush.

"Someone's coming." Eric readied his gun. When he saw Darien and Tom, Darien's youngest brother, Eric smiled. "We're good," Eric said to CJ. "Darien and Tom are here."

"Okay, they'll relieve you. This is good news. Now we'll get him to talk." CJ sounded darkly satisfied with Eric's efforts.

Eric was glad he'd had the chance to finally catch the bastard. CJ would take the wolf—or if he shifted, man—out of the woods, and the Silver Town sheriff and deputies could deal with him next.

CJ talked to Eric the rest of the time CJ was hiking through the woods along with Trevor, the other deputy, and Peter, the sheriff.

"Good job," Peter said, sounding damned impressed, when they reached Eric.

"Thanks. Really only came up here to look for more clues. I didn't realize more plants would be growing or that I'd catch one of the men involved."

Then Eric's phone rang, and he answered it. Dispatch told him about a case of mushroom poisoning. "Be right there," he responded. To his pack members, he said, "I've got to run." He really wished he could help question the rogue wolf, but he had to get his mind on his job.

"Talk to you when we know more," Peter said.

Eric nodded and took off, making his way through the woods to where his truck was parked two miles away. He would continue to work his double shift, anticipating a real breakthrough on the case in a matter of hours. He hoped.

Then he sped to the campsite to see to the case of food poisoning, a kid who'd eaten mushrooms not meant for human consumption.

"He loves mushrooms," his teary-eyed mother explained. "We didn't think he'd see any in the forest. But this one looks just like the ones we buy in the grocery store. But he started throwing up and..." She choked on her words and stopped.

The mushrooms looked so similar to the ones Eric bought in the store that he could see the mistake at once. And they could be fatal. They tasted really good too, according to people who had eaten them by mistake. He had the boy and his mom picked up and transported to the nearest hospital, where they would put the boy on an IV with a solution that would counteract the poison. Early treatment was important to prevent kidney or liver failure. Hoping the boy would be all right, Eric continued to take care of park business, but he didn't hear from Peter about what the man had revealed.

Later that day, Eric received word that a family dog had gone missing at one of the campsites while chasing after a rabbit. Eric had the lead on that case because he was closest to the location and had a great reputation for finding lost pets and people. Locating the dog was easy. But trying to get it to come to him was harder. Animals loved him, once they got over the fact that Eric smelled like a wolf. *Lupus garous* had no trouble raising animals because the animals knew their scent, associated it with food and kindness, and realized the *lupus garous* weren't a danger. But in a case like this?

He had to gain the dog's trust.

Eric kept downwind of the dog, carrying some of its favorite treats and one of the chew bones the owners had passed out to the searchers. They had only brought a couple of chew bones, but the other rangers knew to give Eric one of them because he had the best tracking rate for animals. They swore he was a bloodhound in another life. If they only knew he was a wolf in this one.

"Come, Rascal," Eric said. If he'd had some hunter's spray, he could have sprayed some on himself and hoped that would hide his wolf scent. Eric crouched in a non-threatening manner to get the shih tzu to come to him. He coaxed and offered the treats and the dog's bone to him, hoping he could get Rascal to come close enough to be scooped up and carried back to his campsite. The dog had run four miles from his home away from home and was a matted mess, with leaves and twigs tangled in his long, silky hair and pine needles sticking out of his beard. That indicated he'd had his nose to the ground, smelling the scents. Eric was glad he didn't have to be the one to clean him up.

The dog finally came to him, and Eric gave him a treat, then lifted the pooch into his arms and told him what a good boy he was, praising him to high heaven. He and the dog became best buddies on the way back as he fed Rascal treats and called in that he'd found the dog. The owners were ecstatic. They'd been upset with him for running off, mad at themselves for losing him, and afraid he'd be cougar food when night fell.

Eric was glad to bring Rascal back into camp safe and sound, and to see the happy owners. Hikers and other campers were snapping pictures of the dog's return to his grateful owners. So far, the day had been busy, which was how Eric liked it. Helping others was what he enjoyed most about the job. A family erecting a new tent that was giving them fits as tempers flared and darkness approached, a couple changing a tire, or campers with a truck stuck in mud were all par for the course. Keeping the peace and ensuring that troublemakers didn't ruin it for anyone else was another important mission. But what Eric loved most were rescues and saving lives.

He slept through most of his lunch and dinner breaks, and then got ready for the night shift. He still hadn't heard back from Peter, so he called him. "Did the man give up who he is? Is he running with Waldron's pack?"

"No. He refuses to shift into his human form. I'm half tempted to kill him to force him to change, but then I couldn't question him," Peter said.

Eric chuckled. "Well, let me know if he comes clean."

"Yeah, we'll call you if we get anywhere with this. He's in a crate right now, and we've got round-the-clock guards on him."

"Okay, talk later."

After Eric ended his call with Peter, a call came in requesting Eric's help in scaring a grizzly bear out of a campground. That had him rushing to get there pronto. Not that he believed it was actually anything more than a black bear, but they could be dangerous too.

When he arrived at the camp, he saw a large cinnamon-colored bear scrounging around a campsite, looking for scraps of food. With his enhanced sense of smell, Eric smelled beans, bacon, hamburger, and more food left on used paper plates all over the area around the campfire, which was still burning.

The park rangers were supposed to scare bears off
so that they would have a natural fear of humans. But
visitors to the park sometimes wanted to feed a bear if
they saw one or get pictures taken of themselves close to
a bear, selfies even. The more risks people took getting
close to wildlife, the more dangerous it became for them
and the wildlife. If a bear was provoked into injuring a
visitor, that could mean putting the bear down. Visitors
to the park had to realize they were just that—visitors.
The wildlife lived here twenty-four seven.

Eric didn't plan to harm the bear, only to yell and
chase it off. Sometimes he'd have to use clear paintballs
from a paintball gun. In this case, the campers had gone
to bed for the night after having consumed a hell of a
lot of beer and hadn't taken care of their food or trash
properly. One of the men had left the camp to pee in the
woods, he said, and run across the "grizzly bear," *his
words*, and called in the frantic message.

When Eric arrived, all he had to do was yell and shoot
a noisemaker and the bear ran off. Then he lectured the
four men on the proper storage and disposal of their food
and trash, and supervised them until it was done. As
inebriated as they were, they wouldn't have managed
without him being there to make sure they complied.

After he finished with that, he made his rounds to
the other campsites, checking for bears and making sure
food was stored properly everywhere. Then he smelled
cooking in one of the cabins that didn't allow it and
evicted the residents on the spot. No cooking meant
no cooking. Other cabins allowed it, but some at the
national park were not equipped for it. The rules were
well spelled out, and the reservationist always reminded

the cabin renter what the rules and regulations were and the consequences if the visitor violated them.

This was the part of the job Eric didn't like. But if he let one group get away with it, then others could try to pull the same thing—and rules were rules.

The visitors were so angry that he thought one of them might get physical. Eric had a Taser, just in case, and he would use it if necessary. But one of the guys talked the other into just "packing up their shit" and going, and then they left. Not trusting them, Eric followed them out of the park.

At the end of his second shift early that morning, Eric had planned to head to Sarandon's house for some much-needed sleep. But then he got a call from Pepper that made his heart kick up a notch.

"Eric, Waldron and some of his men were here last night. I just took my morning run and—"

"I'm on my way. I just finished my shift."

"I'll be at the Christmas tree farm for most of the day. You don't have to rush to get here or anything, just come before the party starts. I just wanted to let you know they were here again."

Despite her words, she was reaching out to him, wanting his help or some reassurance that everything would be okay if he was there. "I'll head to your home and take a run around the place."

"You need to sleep. Unless you got to sleep half the night."

He smiled at that. She had to know enough park rangers to realize sleeping wasn't part of the job duties. He was glad she had called on him to help. He really thought they might be making some progress.

When he had a chance, he'd tell her about the wolf they'd taken into custody—still not knowing if Waldron and his wolves were really involved.

Pepper really appreciated that Eric didn't mind staying at her place while she was away. She didn't think she would have any trouble, but having Eric there would ease her mind.

"All right," she said on the phone to Eric. "I've locked the wolf door to ensure no other wolves enter the house while I'm gone." Pepper normally never locked it, but of late, with the problem with Waldron and his men, she'd started to. "You can run by Susan's house first. She has a key to my place, and I'll give her a call to let her know you're on your way there. You can get some sleep and protect the house in the meantime." Not that she really thought he'd need to protect the house. She hoped he'd just get a good sleep. If anyone saw his park ranger truck out front, they'd be sure to leave the place alone anyway.

What would her pack make of it if they learned he was staying there again? Susan would know and would let Richard know, just to be on the safe side. Maybe the rest of the pack too.

Pepper realized she was all right with that. Word about them being together on the run and swimming in the lake had probably spread anyway. This was a lot less intimate: she was at work and he was going to be at her home sleeping. Besides, he would have been coming over later to go to the kids' birthday party.

Now she was glad she had invited him and he had accepted. But she really would have to get more groceries.

"Be there in a couple of hours." Eric hated to hear that Waldron was encroaching on her land without permission, but he was glad she felt comfortable asking him to help out, which seemed to be a major change in her thinking. He called Peter again.

"Has the wolf shifted and told us anything yet?"

"No. He still refuses to shift. So he can stay in the cage until he does. Or not. He can just live like that until he can't remain as a wolf any longer. New moon coming up."

Damn. The new moon was still three days away. Eric hoped the wolf wasn't a royal and the new moon would force him to shift into a human. Royals had the oldest *lupus garous* roots and could control their shifting.

"Okay, thanks for the heads-up," Eric said. "Waldron and some of his men have been at Pepper's property again. I'm headed over there and will sleep for part of the day at her place."

"I won't call unless we have some real breaking news."

"All right."

Then Eric called Sarandon. "Hey, I'm all right with clothes, but Waldron and some of his people were wandering around Pepper's property while I was working at the park last night. I'm sure they've been watching her lands to see when I leave. I'm going to stay at her place and get some sleep while she's at work. I just wanted you to know I might not be coming home tonight."

Sarandon said, "I hate to hear she's having more trouble with them, but I'm glad she's asked you for your assistance. If you need any of us to help you out, let us know. At some point, you may need to come home and tell the men working on your place if you want anything changed. I've been talking to them and sent you all the pictures I took yesterday, but I'd feel better if you checked in with them."

"I did. I looked over the pictures of the damage and okayed all that you had already agreed on. Brett set up a webcam so I can monitor the progress, and either he or CJ will be there supervising things, so we're good."

"Why didn't I think of that? Okay, well, I'm on my way to lead a group on a hike to identify flowers. Congrats on catching that guy, by the way. The whole pack is abuzz about it. Wish I hadn't been busy climbing the mountain at the time. Call me if you have any trouble."

"Will do."

Thinking Pepper might not have had time to shop for groceries since yesterday morning, Eric figured he'd drop by and get a few things. If she didn't need or want them, he'd take them to Sarandon's. He thought this was a nice way to pay her back for her kindness to him. He hoped she didn't mind or feel like he was overstepping his bounds, because he was past ready to court the she-wolf.

Chapter 16

PEPPER CALLED SUSAN TO TELL HER ERIC WAS COMING OVER to stay for the day. She wasn't sure about the night, although she had every intention of saying he could, if he wanted to. But she didn't need to tell Susan that. "So Eric will be by for the extra key to my place in a couple of hours. I just wanted to give you a heads-up. He's worked a double shift at the park, so he'll most likely be sleeping for a good part of the day. If you see anything troublesome, call me as usual. If I think we need his help, I'll call him. But I don't want to disturb him otherwise."

Pepper began inspecting the Christmas trees on their farm. Thankfully, today was Susan's day off, so she was home just chilling out. Pepper didn't want Eric to have to make a special trip to the tree farm to pick up the key from her.

"Sure thing. Do you want me to run by your place and fix him breakfast? Or, actually, I could just fix breakfast for him here."

"I don't have anything but waffles. I'm sure he's sick of them. So I'm sure he'll appreciate the offer."

"I've got everything he might want for a hearty breakfast. When he comes by for the key, I'll feed him."

"Thanks. I've got to grocery shop. But I'll have to do it after work this evening. Call you later." Pepper was glad Susan was better stocked than she was. She hated running errands. Pack members often said they'd shop for her if she liked, but she hadn't wanted to impose. They were her pack members, not her hired help.

A couple of hours later, Susan called Pepper. "You are not going to believe this. You have to mate him, Pepper, or I will."

"What did he do now?" Pepper assumed it was something positive, as excited as Susan sounded.

"He picked up groceries for you! I know I shouldn't have, but I was curious and I asked to see what he had gotten for you and wow, some of the choicest cuts of steaks, more chocolate mousse pie, everything you'd want for breakfast, and a couple of bottles of wine. He even got you fixings for a lobster bisque he's going to make. Sounds to me like he's planning to stay for a while. Which would be a totally good thing, as far as I'm concerned. If he becomes a burden at your place, just send him over to mine. He can bring the groceries too."

Lobster bisque? No wonder Susan was ready to grab the wolf and mate him.

"Anyway, he declined breakfast and said he'd throw something together at your place."

Pepper was surprised to hear he had turned down breakfast at Susan's place. Was she afraid Pepper would view it as Susan making a play for him? If so, he was a lot more intuitive than most guys she knew who, even if they hadn't wanted anything to do with Susan romantically, would have at least enjoyed a home-cooked breakfast.

"Oh, and he said not to worry. He'd clean up afterward. He asked if you had a Crock-Pot. He said he was going to make his special lobster bisque, but the steaks? Another night maybe? I loaned him my Crock-Pot, in case yours wasn't easy to find. Please tell me you don't want him. I'll let him down gently, and then I'll do whatever I need to do to claim him."

Pepper laughed. "Are you sure you could handle him?"

"Seriously? I'd definitely give it a shot. If you don't want him for a pack leader mate, he'd still be a great addition to the pack—for protection, at the very least—if he were my mate."

Pepper didn't believe Eric would be happy as just a follower if he had the opportunity to be a leader. Even if he became a sub-leader, she was afraid that wouldn't be enough. "He's a leader at heart."

"Right. So mate with him so I don't have to embarrass myself."

"How would you embarrass yourself?"

"He's only got eyes for you. And I'd get turned down. You know how it is. A woman is just as hurt by rejection as a man. But I'd feel so much better about it if you caught him. You know we all loved Harold like a brother, but I've seen the way Eric is interested in you. And it's not in the least bit brotherly. With me?" Susan sighed dramatically. "He's just like Harold was with me. So tell me this business of Eric staying over is becoming a steady habit you don't want to break."

"Okay, Susan, part of me says he's a good bet. That he would be the right one for me and for the pack."

"Hot—"

"It's forever you know."

"Absolutely."

"Not just for me, but for the whole pack. With Harold, everyone knew him from the time we were children. He was a known quantity. With Eric—"

"Yeah, yeah, so everyone knew Harold would do everything you said he'd do."

Pepper let out her breath. "Harold didn't ever want to take charge or suggest anything, even as much as I encouraged him to do so. He just wasn't a leader. Even when he said he wanted to lead, he didn't have the personality to make it happen. If I take a new mate, it means change. I won't control everything with the pack."

"You don't think Eric could bring some fresh, new ideas to the pack that would improve things?"

"What if you or others in the pack don't like his ideas?" What if he turned their whole pack upside down with his different notions?

"We'll voice our opinion like we always do."

"What if he doesn't want to help lead the pack?"

"Fine, then he can just be your hot lover and mate and be part of the pack like the rest of us."

A hot lover sure had its appeal. And if he could colead without taking over completely, Pepper would sure rethink having a mate. "I've got to go, Susan."

"But you're seriously considering it, right?"

"I'm…considering it."

"Hot damn! I thought we would have to call for a pack rallying cry. Talk to you later."

Pepper smiled as she ended the call with her subleader. She'd had mixed feelings about telling anyone, but she felt Susan knew her best, and if anyone understood the pack dynamics and what Pepper really needed in her life, it was Susan.

Pepper felt more and more that this was the right move for her to make. That Eric was right. The situation with their longevity changing had also made her consider taking a mate. She might not have had children with Harold, but what if it wasn't her fault? What if she was with a wolf like Eric and able to have children? She'd love it. Love them. Love him for it.

But would he feel the same way as she did about coleading a pack? He had said a pack could be a lot of trouble. Maybe he really *didn't* want to lead one. She knew park rangers could have a lot of concerns on their jobs. Maybe he didn't want the additional burden that leading a pack could mean.

Then again, she thought they could make this work, if they both wanted it enough. Hell, what she wanted more than anything was more of his passion, his kisses, and well…more.

She called him before he had a chance to retire to bed.

"Hey," he said.

His voice was groggy and sleepy. He sounded charming, like she'd just woken her lover who was in her bed, waiting for her to come home and join him. That made her wish she was. What if she told him she was considering courting him? She couldn't wait until he was more awake and she was home to see his reaction.

"Oh, Eric, I'm so sorry if I woke you. Susan said you picked up some groceries, and I just wanted to make sure I didn't duplicate what you got. I thought I'd catch you before you fell asleep. I want to thank you. You really shouldn't have gone to the trouble when you've already done so much for me."

"No trouble at all. I hope that you don't mind."

"I hate grocery shopping. I buy everything I shouldn't and forget everything I should buy. And yes, I make lists and forget them at home."

He chuckled. "I normally don't make lists, so I thought that was the only trouble. Here's what I picked up for you though." He emailed the list to her and then said, "I wasn't sure if you'd like it, but I'm making lobster bisque for us for dinner—before the children's birthday party and hot dogs. If it doesn't appeal, I can make something else for us."

"It sounds wonderful. I've never had it, but I do love lobster." Unable to wait until she got home, she slipped in, "Um, we can court." And then before he had time to say anything in response, she quickly added, "I'll be home around six. And, Eric, thanks so much. I'll pay you for the groceries when I get home."

"Nothing doing. It's my treat, as much time as I've spent at your place for the past few days."

"All right. Well, get some sleep and I'll see you later. You can tell me about all of the excitement you've had during your double shift."

"Be glad to. You can tell me what you found out about Waldron's visit. Have a good day, Pepper."

"Sleep tight." He hadn't responded to her courting comment. Maybe he didn't hear her mention it. Maybe he didn't want to discuss something like that over the phone. She sighed.

She'd never expected to have a bachelor male wolf staying at her place like this. Not that she hadn't thought about it, but more as a fantasy with no real expectations. She wondered what Pauline would think about Eric and a courtship with Pepper. Hopefully, she wouldn't be annoyed with Pepper because she might be interested in another mate. But it had been seven years since she lost Harold, and only three for Pauline's loss.

———∿∿∿———

Eric settled back against the soft blue sheets and closed his eyes, glad Pepper was okay with him buying groceries and fixing her dinner… Wait! Did she say she wanted to court him? He sat up in bed and stared at the painting of Bear Creek Falls cascading down from the mountains near Telluride. She *did* say she wanted to court him!

He frowned. Didn't she?

Chapter 17

IT WAS KILLING PEPPER TO NOT BE ABLE TO LEAVE WORK early to help Eric with the meal, or just be there because he was doing something special for her. Not to mention that she wanted to spend more alone time with him if they were going to court. She sure hoped his nonresponse was only because he was so tired that he hadn't heard her and not that he wasn't interested.

When she finally arrived home, she was later than she'd hoped.

As soon as she walked in the door, she smelled the lovely scent of tea roses and strode toward the dining room, eager to see what Eric had done. A gold box of Godiva chocolates graced the table, along with at least two dozen velvety red roses in a Waterford crystal vase of blended colors of burgundy and blue. Two champagne glasses were sitting next to each other like a dating couple, and a bottle of champagne was chilling in a crystal ice bucket.

Wow. He was a keeper. If he didn't know she'd said she was interested in courting him and this was his way of saying he wanted to court her, she was telling him again.

He walked into the dining room wearing her purple apron with the motto in hot pink letters: *I keep the best snacks UNDER my apron*, catching her full attention. The apron just didn't have the same connotation when she wore it.

She smiled at him, wanting to see more of his snacks,

then saw the scratches on his face and arms and frowned. "You look like…" She paused as he pulled her into his arms. "You were in a wolf fight. Weren't you?"

"Yeah. At the park, but I don't know if it was one of Waldron's wolves. The wolf was definitely involved in the weed growing." Eric was looking down at her so seriously, she was worried there was more to it, though the way his "snacks" were pressing against her belly, at least his body was interested in something else. "About what you said earlier… If I think you said what I hope you did when I was half-asleep, I want you to know the lobster bisque is just one of the special meals I make." Then he frowned, still holding her close, pressing his delicious heat and his burgeoning arousal against her. "Did you say what I think you said?"

"That we should court?" She smiled up at him. "Yeah. I think we might be just right for each other. So when do I get to sample some of your…snacks?"

He gave her such a wicked grin, she knew he didn't want to court her for long before he mated her. Which was usually the way it was with wolves, once they decided to court.

"Thank you for all of this," she said, motioning with her head, because she had wrapped her arms securely around him. She wanted this closeness, this tenderness between them. She wished that her nephews' birthday party wasn't tonight.

She kissed Eric then, not only to thank him for everything, but to seal the deal as far as a courtship went. He kissed her right back, his tongue spearing her mouth and stroking her tongue, and she felt her panties dampen. Man, was she past ready to enjoy even more of him than this.

He pulled his hot mouth free from hers and kissed her forehead. "I hate to break up a great beginning, but I don't want to make you late to the birthday party." He started to lead her to her seat, which she thought was so gallant.

"Wait," she said, pulling out her phone. "I have to get a picture of this." She took a picture of the table setting and one of Eric wearing her apron.

He laughed. "I hope you're keeping the picture of me just for yourself."

"For Susan. She gave me the apron as a gift last Christmas. I want to show her how you put it to really good use."

Smiling, he shook his head. "I was envisioning what the apron's message would mean when *you* wore it."

She chuckled. "Completely different snacks."

"That *I* can't wait to sample." He escorted her to her seat, then served the bisque. He poured them each a glass of champagne, removed the apron, and joined her.

They toasted each other, then after she sipped hers, she ate some of the bisque—creamy, a little buttery, with lots of big chunks of lobster and a hint of garlic. It was so good that she asked him for the recipe.

He gave it to her and added, "But I'll fix it for you anytime."

"I'm going to have to take you up on that."

"You should have seen me in the store, fretting over what I'd make for dinner tonight to convince you what a perfect wolf I am."

She laughed. But then she turned the conversation back to the situation with the rogue wolf. "So what happened with the wolf fight?" She wanted to hear that Eric had gotten the best of him and the wolf hadn't gotten away.

"I broke his leg and had him arrested. He won't shift, so we can't question him."

"The new moon's out in three days."

"Right. So as long as he's not a royal, he won't be able to hold his wolf form. That's what we're hoping for."

She shook her head. "I'm so glad you caught up with one of the wolves. Let me know if he's from Waldron's pack. I've let my pack know about the situation with the other wolves." Then she told Eric what she had done today at the Christmas tree farm, because it was one of the pack's businesses. If she took him for her mate, he'd need to be just as vested in the properties as Harold had been. In fact, Harold had been so busy with them, he used his tiredness as an excuse when they retired at night. She certainly didn't want that with a new mate. But she did want Eric to see the businesses as important to the pack.

He asked her a million questions about the process of cultivating the trees and replenishing them. She had a million answers to give him. She was glad he was interested in the Christmas tree farm and tree nursery. He seemed impressed with the operation, which she loved. She reminded herself that he loved his national park duties, so that was in line with what she did—as far as protecting and cultivating trees.

She glanced at the clock and sighed. "It's time to go to the party. Are you sure that you want to go? You could just stay here and chill out, and we could have the rest of the champagne later." She hurried to clean up the dishes while he rummaged through a sack, then pulled out two balls, one red, built sturdy for wolf cubs, and another blue one for human kids.

She smiled. "You didn't have to bring them gifts."

"Always. Kids expect it, and I wouldn't have wanted to disappoint them."

"I got them puzzles." She suspected as active as the boys were, they'd love the balls more.

"Perfect. You've given them something to stimulate their brains, and me—"

"Their brawn." Speaking of brawn, she wouldn't mind seeing more of Eric's brawny side again, and with that in mind, she was planning a trip to the hot tub after the party.

Then they were off to Pauline's birthday party for the boys.

"They're my nephews," Pepper explained on the way over. "They're good kids, but they can be a handful sometimes. We have a number of pack members who take them in to help with schooling or playdates at various times of the week so everyone can get a break and play with and teach the kids."

"I take it Pauline lost her mate?"

"Yes. Three years ago. She's…an alpha. So sometimes I have to remind her that she's one of my pack members, not a sub-leader and not the leader. I do it in a subtle way. She's so not like her brother was. I love her, but I just have to be firm with her. I could never have given her the role of being a sub-leader, or she would have thought anything she said was the law."

"Do you feel that she wouldn't like it if you took another mate?"

"I've considered it, yes. She was close to her brother and glad I had mated him. I think it filled a need for her to be able to say she was connected to the leaders in a family way. She was just as upset as the rest of us when the wolf killed him. If I hadn't taken the wolf down, she would have. I'm really close to my nephews, so I would love it if they grew up in the pack. But I really think she needs a mate of her own."

"Was her mate an alpha or beta?"

"Beta. She needed someone to boss around."

Eric cleared his throat. "If my observations were correct, she's looking at prospects in the Silver pack. Which could be a good thing. We have a lot of bachelor males, and it's not that far away from your pack. If one of our males mates her and moves here, he'll still be close enough to family in Silver Town. Same if she moved to be with him."

"I have to admit that troubles me a little. It's inevitable and it shouldn't bother me, but I have had some concerns about that."

"About her moving?"

"About several of my people finding mates among your pack and all moving away."

He smiled. "I don't think you'd find that happening. At least with me, I'd be moving right in. If the wolf were agreeable."

She smiled back at him but didn't comment as she parked the car and hurried to get her gifts for the boys. She was still thinking about Eric wearing her apron, only she envisioned him not wearing anything else.

The birthday party was a great success. Pepper couldn't help but notice that the adults seemed curious about Eric staying with her. They asked him many more questions about his job and listened to some of the exciting stuff he'd had to deal with as a park ranger, while keeping an eye on the kids and making sure everyone was playing nicely. She thought her pack members figured they should get to know him better in case he ended up being a permanent member of the pack—as their alpha male leader.

She normally didn't hesitate when deciding she needed to move forward on something. But this was different. Mating with him would change her life, her pack's life, and his. She couldn't be too impulsive in determining this. Yet she was sure leaning in that direction.

One of the boys, Matthew, the redhead, talked Pauline into turning into a wolf so he could test out the wolf ball. And then the other boy, Adair, his towheaded brother, shifted, just as eager to see if he could get the ball away from his brother. They were always doing that: Matthew, the more alpha, always took the lead to try things out.

During the party, Pepper hadn't acted like she was courting Eric, but she noticed everyone watching the two of them whenever they moved together, spoke with each other, or interacted with each other. Her people could guess from their verbal and physical actions and reactions just where this was headed. Unless something big happened to change their minds.

Eric acted like she did, not possessively toward her, just sociable and casual. And yet everyone knew there wasn't anything casual about their interest in each other. Wolf scents would prove it. And the way she and he smiled at each other said much more. Or the way they touched when she handed him a plate of cake, or he brushed his hand against hers when he offered her a cup of punch. Just the fact that they were serving each other showed a mutual respect and a hint of something more.

Yet they hadn't declared anything officially yet.

The Fairhaven boys were there too, and Pepper was pleased to see them shift into wolves and play in a way that showed they knew how to interact with younger kids. She thought the boys would do all right with the pack. It really was important that the pack members supported one another.

When it was time for everyone to leave, they said their good-byes. Pauline went out of her way to thank Eric for coming and giving the boys gifts for their birthday. "The wolf balls really drew all the kids together, more than any other gift. To me, that was pure genius."

Eric smiled. "Sometimes the simplest toys can be the best. When my brothers and I were that age, that's what we had the most fun with. And got the most exercise out of too. I'm glad they enjoyed playing with the other kids, and they all joined in on the fun. Thank you for inviting me at the last minute."

"We all benefitted from you coming." Pauline glanced at Pepper. "Thanks for asking if Eric could come. I think you've found a real winner there." And her genuine smile made all the difference in the world to Pepper.

With tears in both their eyes, Pepper hugged Pauline. Both had been devastated when their mates died. Pauline's husband had been killed in a car accident while driving on an icy road through the mountains. He'd been perfect for her, and she'd been shattered. Pepper wondered if Pauline would really look closely at some of the Silver pack members and find a mate of her own.

Most of all, she was glad that Pauline didn't seem to harbor any hard feelings about Pepper being interested in Eric. She wanted to tell Pauline that if she found a mate, Pepper hoped the two of them would stay with her pack.

When Pepper and Eric returned to her house that night for champagne and a dip in the hot tub, she knew he was ready for this, the grown-up part of the night, every bit as much as she was. She dressed in her shimmering blue bathing suit that showed off the swell of her breasts and was cut high on the thigh—super tantalizing for a she-wolf who wanted to catch a he-wolf's attention. She suspected anything she wore would prove sexy to him. He wore black briefs, since he hadn't known he'd be enjoying a hot tub night with her, looking perfectly hot as she grabbed a couple of beach towels and tossed them on a cushioned bench chest.

With their glasses sitting on the drink tables next to the tub, Pepper settled back into the hot bubbles and finally relaxed. Even though she'd picked up candles, she didn't use them, afraid it might seem a little overboard at this point. Later, she could use them, if she felt she needed the extra romantic touch.

"About the courting..." He raised his brows a little, a smile settling on his lips. He looked like he was ready for more than just talking about it.

"Right. I was considering what you said—about running a pack and all the trouble that could entail. Do you really feel that way?" She had decided if she did take another mate, he wouldn't be a follower like Harold. She wanted someone who would help in the decision making. Not take charge and leave her out of the plans either, but someone who was more of an equal partner.

Eric sighed. "Sometimes. But you must feel that way sometimes too."

"I do." A pack was a lot of work, and so were the businesses they ran. Sometimes she wondered what it would be like if she were free to do her own thing. But then she'd be working for others, and she really did love being in charge.

He studied her as a couple of solar lamps cast a soft glow over them and the water, and she couldn't think of a more perfect setting.

"Just think," Eric said, "if you and I could simply see each other like this. You wouldn't be worried about an alpha male taking over the pack, and I wouldn't be worried about how you'd view me because of it."

She let out her breath on a heavy sigh, knowing this discussion was important, but wanting to have a romantic night. "You're a leader at heart. Every time I see the way you act and react to situations, I know you are. Even tonight with something as simple as picking up balls for the kids' birthday party. I think part of the reason they loved them so much is not because of the toy, but because you picked it out for them. They loved you when you were playing tag with them at the social gathering. You have a real knack with kids of all ages." And with her.

"True, I do seem to have leadership ability and I won't deny it. But when I returned with my brothers to the Silver pack, I realized being a follower wasn't so bad."

"Even if you're not the leader of a wolf pack, you still tell park visitors what to do. When you go to rescue people or find them, you take charge."

He smiled. "When I met you, I realized how much more there is to life than leading a pack. I like the way you run your pack. You do a great job with it. You really don't need a mate to help."

"You're right. But I would want my mate to be just as active in running things as I am. If you had a say in the way things are accomplished with the pack, you might want them done differently."

"If I can see something might be better by doing it a different way, I'd certainly mention it. That's how Darien and Lelandi run the Silver pack. I think pack members are happiest when they have some say. I don't have any trouble with listening to others, taking orders, or taking charge if necessary."

"What if…" Pepper said, moving closer so she was sitting beside Eric, her leg brushing against his. The intensity of his gaze deepened, a small smile playing on his lips. "I had my heart set on something and you didn't agree."

He pondered this as they finished their glasses of champagne and set them aside.

He wrapped his arm around her shoulders and pulled her closer, settling her against his hot body, his skin smooth, his muscles powerful. "It depends on what you had your heart set on. If it endangered you?" He shook his head.

That's what she wanted to hear. That he wouldn't be a beta follower and just let her have her way because she was used to it. That he would want to ensure it was the best thing for her and the pack.

She slid her hand over his thigh. "If you're interested—"

"Oh yeah." He pressed a kiss to her forehead, then each cheek. "I'm way more than interested. But I want to make it clear that what exists between us has nothing to do with your pack."

Because he didn't want her to think he was anything like Waldron.

Eric leaned down to kiss her mouth, his hands cradling her face as she hungrily gave in to the kiss. This was so right, so good. She'd missed being thought of in a sexier, more intimate way. Eric made her feel alive, sexy, and much more like a she-wolf who had appeal, not based on the land she owned and the pack she ran, but for herself.

His mouth was on hers, the champagne flavoring his tongue and lips, his sexy scent reaching her over the warm, bubbling water. She stroked his arms, loving the feel of his mouth against hers, hot and hungry. Just like hers was, unable to get enough, not wanting to give this up, wanting to kiss him until the sun rose in the morning.

He pulled her bathing suit straps off her shoulders, lowering her top until her breasts were exposed, making her feel decadently wicked. Her breasts ached for his touch, her nipples sensitive and aroused. He leaned down and kissed her breasts almost reverently before he began to nuzzle his cheek against one rigid tip, and she wanted to cry out in pure ecstasy. She loved the way Eric took charge of the seduction, not waiting for her to initiate anything. She put her hand on his thigh, telling him she was ready for this. She did appreciate that he was willing to let her decide how far to take this.

He licked the nipple he had nuzzled, then latched on and sucked and licked it tenderly, hotly, rousingly. She felt as though she was melting into the hot water as Eric began to lick the other nipple. He took it in his mouth and swirled his tongue around it, making her tingle all over. He moved to kiss her mouth again, his fingers stroking her nipples as she ran her hand over his briefs, his arousal full blown. She loved feeling him like that, knowing that she had done this to him, that he seemed to love her touching him as much as she loved him touching her. As soon as she began to rub his erection, he paused in kissing her. She pulled down his waistband, wanting to see his gorgeous cock, and it sprang free in the water. He was already large, but the water made his erection appear even larger.

She began to stroke him, and he shook his head. "You first." He pulled her bathing suit down in the silky water. He stroked between her legs, touching her most erotic spot, giving her the ride of her life, and making her reach for the sliver of a moon. The stars twinkled in the midnight-blue sky like tiny candles, perfect for a night like this. She knew beyond a doubt she didn't want to give him up for anything.

She practically climbed onto his lap, wanting to howl at the moon when she felt the orgasm coming. "Harder," she whispered against his whiskery cheek, and he obliged, stroking her tenderly, faster, harder, until she hit the pinnacle and cried out into the night.

She felt boneless, afraid she couldn't do him justice. She began to stroke him, but instead of melting under her touch like she did his, he tensed with the pleasure and caressed her breasts, making her want to take him to bed with her and never let him go. "Would it be too impulsive of us," she said breathlessly, "to go for a full mating?"

His mouth curved up appreciably. "I love you." And Eric meant it with all his heart.

"Let's take this inside."

He helped her out of the tub. What a hell of a wonderful way to begin a mated relationship.

"I never thought I'd be saying this to another mate, but I love you, Eric. You complete me, make me feel alive again," she said. Before she could grab a towel, he wrapped one around her and pulled her into his arms for a warm embrace and kissed her again.

"You mean everything in the world to me."

Then he released her long enough to wrap a towel around his waist. As she grabbed her bathing suit and snagged his briefs, he grabbed the champagne glasses and empty bottle. She left the wet clothes in the laundry room off the kitchen while he dumped the champagne bottle in the trash and set the glasses on the kitchen counter.

As soon as she came out of the laundry room, still wearing the towel, he stalked toward her. She smiled, tilting her head to the side a little in question, right before he scooped her into his arms, whipped around, and carried her to the bedroom. "Guest room or—"

"Master bedroom. We're going to be coleaders of the pack now, right?" She lifted one beautiful brow and he smiled.

"I never thought I'd be coleading a pack. But with you, it feels just right."

"I should have warned you… I didn't have any children with Harold. I might not be able to have them. And you're so good with children—"

He realized then that might have been another reason for her reluctance to have another mate: the worry that she couldn't have offspring. "A pack always has children of varying ages. Either my birth pack, or yours. I love kids, it's true, but I work with them on the job and with the packs. I won't feel I'm missing out if I don't have a couple of rug rats to call my very own."

He set her on her feet next to the bed. He knew it would take time to get used to each other leading the pack, but loving her—no difficulty at all. "I love everything about you, Pepper Grayling. You can't imagine all the dreams I've had about you, but believe me, dreams just don't hack it."

She laughed. "Even if we continue to call it the Grayling pack, in honor of my parents and my father's father and grandfather before them?"

"Yes. And I will even be a Grayling if you wish it."

She gave him a heartfelt hug, which made his cock swell even more as her lithe body pressed against it. "I would love it. But I want you to truly colead with me. If you can think of a better way to do something, please share it."

"And if I sound too bossy, just tell me."

"It's a deal."

They climbed into bed and she pressed her body against his, and he loved how wickedly sexy she felt as she moved against him.

Pepper was amazed how intensely she wanted Eric, needed him, needed this—his tenderness, his passion, the raw and sensual smell of him, the feel of his hand exploring her body, the feel of his skin and muscles beneath her fingertips. Exploring. Enjoying. Energizing.

Kissing him, she felt her concentration on his masculine lips slipping as he pressed his rigid erection against her mound, not entering her, but rubbing against her in a way that said he wanted in.

His gaze on her was just as hot as the rest of him.

Searing into her soul, claiming her for his own. As she claimed him.

She surrendered to him, something she'd never done with anyone in her life. It felt good to roll over on her back and soak in the feel of Eric's touch, to focus on the way his tongue caressed her taut nipples.

His tongue was touching the tip of hers, teasing and solicitous. She matched his actions, move for move. She knew this was right—the passion between them igniting every time they kissed. She knew that's what she'd been missing before.

He rubbed his wickedly intriguing scent over her body as she moved against him, doing the same with her scent on him—claiming the wolf as her own. His mouth covered hers, kissing her, alternating between soft and hard.

He moved his scorching mouth over her cheek, down her throat, lower still over her collarbone in a sweet slide. His fingers glided down her body, garnering most of her attention as he worked his way down her abdomen.

Her hands swept over his taut muscles and smooth skin as he touched her sweet spot, rubbed, stroked, and made her groan with escalating need.

He plunged a finger between her parted legs, made her wetter, needier, and she begged for more.

"I need…you," Eric said, barely breathing out the words.

Her blood raced through her veins as his strokes brought her closer to the sun's hottest flames. She was near the peak when he drew her over, sending her heart soaring, his name on her lips.

"Ready?" he asked. One last chance for waiting on a mating, but she was ready for this, wanting it, feeling as though if she didn't, she would wake him in the middle of the night and mate him anyway. She wasn't changing her mind about this.

"Yes." The word was said with such need, he gave her a wicked smile back.

He pushed in, slowly at first. She was so tight, and he wanted this with her, the mating, a companion for life, his partner. Life was too short, and he wasn't about to waste it in waiting.

His pulse and hers were pounding hard. He began to thrust deep inside her, loving her silky, warm body wrapped around his cock, the way her inner muscles clenched him tightly in her grasp.

It was more than sex between *lupus garous*; it was a lifetime promise to be lovers, friends, and companions. She overwhelmed his senses, tilted his world on edge, made him aware of nothing around him but her. He hadn't believed he'd ever find a woman to love again.

Her body moved against his as if they'd already had a lifetime together, in perfect sync, knowing how to push this to the edge and back. She bent her knees, giving him deeper access. He took advantage of her offering, thrusting home until he felt the end coming. He nipped at her chin and her lips, and sank his length deep between her legs until he released on a groan.

"Hot damn, woman," he said, rolling over onto his back and pulling her on top of him.

She smiled and snuggled against him. "This. Was. Perfect."

"Don't get too settled in," he warned. "I've got lots more where that came from."

"Bragging or—"

"Promising."

"Good. Wonderful. I will hold you to it."

He was sleepy and normally would have just dropped off for a bit before he ravaged the she-wolf again, but he began to think of everything he needed to talk to Pepper about—his deceased mate, his father. A mate should know those things.

"I love you," he said, wanting her to know it with all his heart.

"Eric"—she sighed his name against his chest—"you have made me so happy and gone way beyond any expectations I had. I love you for that and everything else about you."

"I had no doubt you would be perfect."

She laughed. "No one is perfect."

"In bed? Hell yeah you are."

"Hmmm, you are too."

She was truly a wonder, and he felt he was one lucky wolf to have run into her in the park that one day, even if he was injured for having done so.

"This is truly a wondrous way to end the day."

"This is only the beginning." He snuggled with her, her soft curvy body fitting just right against him as the night cooled down. This couldn't get any better.

But they still needed to deal with Waldron. The bastard might think Eric was as easy to kill as Harold had been. If Waldron truly believed that, Eric would set him straight in a heartbeat.

Chapter 18

EARLY THE NEXT MORNING, PEPPER STIRRED IN ERIC'S ARMS and kissed him on the cheek. He smiled and kissed her right back.

"We need to check out the area, get some breakfast, and go to work. Ready to run as a wolf?"

"Hmmm, do you always wake up thinking about work? I had other notions in mind."

"Ha! You are a wild man. Other notions? We made love four times last night. Which I loved." She nipped his chin, then slid out of his arms while he watched her leave the bed and shift.

He yawned. "I'm going to have to sleep during my lunch hour. All right. I'm coming." He climbed out of bed and shifted too, then she tore off for the wolf door, and he raced after her. She slid on the tile floor, trying to make the corner, and he wanted to laugh. But he slid on the same corner and grinned at her as she gave him a fun-loving wolf smile, then dove through the door. He chased her for a good quarter of an hour, and then she chased him. It sure shook off some of the grogginess of sleep, better than a stiff cup of coffee. He could do this for hours with her.

Every moment spent with her clinched his belief that she was the right one for him, and he really longed for a couple of days enjoying each other when nothing else could intrude.

———∿∿∿———

Pepper had planned to be more serious: get the job done, have breakfast, and then get to work. Yet, she loved this aspect of their mated relationship. It had made the routine more of an adventure. She could definitely get used to the added benefit of having the wolfish hunk for her mate.

Her heart skittered when he was hunting her. She hadn't had anyone chase her in years. Even when she was little, she was the alpha, so she often did the hunting. She enjoyed pursuing another alpha. As she chased him, his tail straight out behind him waved at her like a flag saying, "Catch me if you can." She loved how fast he ran, but then slowed a bit so she could catch up to him, and then raced off again. He had longer legs, but she was a good sprinter. He had such a devilish look in his eyes, enjoying teasing her, loving being both the hunter and the hunted. This was just too much fun.

Then out of the corner of her eye, she saw a wolf headed straight for Eric's right flank, like an arrow ready to slam into him. Eric had seen the big gray male—not Waldron, but one of his pack—and quickly turned to fight him. Pepper worried there were more of them out there this morning.

Eric whipped around so fast, he caught the wolf off-guard, when the wolf probably thought he was about to do that to Eric. The wolf yipped and fled. Eric could have run after him, but he didn't. He stayed with Pepper.

She was furious with Waldron and his pack. These were her woods. Waldron and his wolves were encroaching on her lands, and she wouldn't allow it. She couldn't, or it would be tantamount to saying she didn't have control over them. Yes, she owned the property rights, but wolves needed more than that. They needed to know they owned the territory.

Pepper flew past Eric in wolf-hunting mode with one large, gray wolf on the menu.

Eric was astonished at her tenacity, though he understood why she was chasing after the wolf. It was her property and she wanted to make it clear no wolf would attack her, her pack, or her guests and get away with it. He wondered if this wolf had anything to do with the one he'd taken down in the park.

For a fraction of a moment, he had waited to pursue the wolf. But now he could hunt it without reservation.

He bolted after her, fearing the wolf could be leading them into an ambush, and he didn't want Pepper injured.

She was so incredibly fast, she managed to bite the wolf's tail. The wolf yelped and sprang forward with a renewed burst of energy. He leaped over a fallen tree, but as soon as Pepper had cleared it and Eric reached it, he smelled fresh wolf scents. One was Waldron's. Eric barked at Pepper to get her to stop.

She immediately did, but she looked like she hadn't wanted to for anything. She was panting, watchful, sniffing the air. For the longest time, she stood watching the retreating wolf race through the forest until he disappeared from sight.

Eric joined her and nuzzled her face, encouraging her to return with him. She growled a little, but then with reluctance, she finally went with him. After loping together for a little bit, she continued to search for any other signs of Waldron or his wolves. Her scent said she was angry, and she was no longer playing. Eric hated Waldron for making her feel her lands weren't safe for her or her people. He assumed that's just why the wolf did it too. Or payback. Or both.

When they didn't find any more scents and no other wolves lurking about, they returned to her house. Once inside, she shifted right away and scowled at Eric. He thought she was mad the wolf had tried to attack him, but he wasn't expecting her to be angry with him.

"Why didn't you go after the wolf?"

Eric shifted, and instead of going on the defensive, he pulled her naked body into his arms, held her close, and kissed her forehead. "I thought he might lead us into an ambush. I didn't want to leave you alone if the wolf's intent was to draw me away from you so Waldron could hassle you."

Pepper was so tense in his arms that he began caressing her silky back, wanting her to realize they really could do this. They might think differently about how to deal with situations that arose, but they could work things out for the best. "Did you smell Waldron and some of his other wolves by that fallen tree?" he asked.

"Yes." She relaxed a little.

"I think they intended to ambush me like his cousin did your mate. Except you were the one chasing their wolf down—"

"We both were."

"Only because I didn't want you embroiled in a fight by yourself."

She relaxed against him even more then, and he thought how wonderful she felt pressed against him, wrapped in his arms. "I'm not a beta wolf when it comes to fighting other wolves. I do consider every scenario before I rush into a situation like this," Eric said.

"I'm sorry, Eric. It's going to take time for me to get used to the way you do things so we can lead the pack as more of a unified force."

He was still stroking her soft, naked skin, loving the feel of her and wanting to return to bed with her. "Do you know who the wolf was?"

"Yes. They call him Turbo because he's so fast."

"Hell, you were just as fast. I need to pay Waldron a visit. CJ and Trevor are still trying to track him down. I thought the bastard was supposed to be so alpha, but he sends his teens to do his dirty work, and now this."

She took a deep breath. "I'm so sorry."

"Don't be. I've dealt with his kind more than once over the years. There's no dealing with them in a concili-atory manner. They're hardheaded and insist they have their way."

"Other than the attempted wolf attack, I really had a great time this morning."

"Before we got up or after we took our run?"

She laughed. "All of it."

"The best part is it's only the beginning." Though he knew the only way to really concentrate on their new life together was to take care of Waldron and his pack. All he cared to think about for now was being with his mate, and no one would ruin that for them.

She pulled him through the house to the master bath. "Want to take a quick shower?"

"Hell yeah." He smiled, loving his wickedly sexy mate.

As soon as they were in the shower, the warm water sluicing over them, he began soaping her up and rubbing all the right spots to make her feel like she was going to heaven and wouldn't return in a million years.

"Good?" he whispered against her ear.

"Oh yeah," she mouthed against his shoulder as he stroked her nub, his other hand sliding down her back as she ran soap over his torso. He was already fully aroused. She loved the way he turned her on and more than satisfied her need for sexual fulfilment.

His fingers deftly stroking her, she gave in to the state of bliss, soaking up the raw passion until she was ready to burst. She knew she'd been missing something in her life. She just hadn't realized it could be this powerfully good. She slid her hands down his wet back, caught up in the rapture of the moment. The climax hit, and she cried out his name, grateful they had agreed to mate. She never thought she'd experience sex, not like this. Once wouldn't be enough.

He moved her hand down to stroke him, and she encircled her fingers around his velvety hardness. He was already primed from bringing her to completion, their pheromones sending their senses reeling, but her stroking him was sending him over the edge. When he began to tense, to thrust harder into her hand, he was ready to come. But then he did the unexpected—he lifted her so her back was against the wall, her legs around his hips, and he penetrated her wet sheath. He drove into her hard, with passion and resolution, mouth nuzzling her face and kissing her before he thrust his tongue into her mouth.

And then he groaned with release, filling her with his warmth and love. For a long time, he just held her close like that. Then he kissed her again, a sweet and searing kiss, and she kissed him back with just as much eagerness.

Then he sighed. "Better finish this so we can get a bite to eat and then head out."

She moaned softly. "I think we need to schedule a week off so we can enjoy each other without interruption."

"Absolutely my thought too."

They soaped each other up again, and she was glad she had a tankless hot water heater so they could linger a while longer while sudsing each other up. They massaged each other's scalps, and she felt like she could melt into the tile floor. Sliding her soapy hands all over his body proved a tactile delight, but more so when he was soaping up her breasts, her nipples, and between her legs. Though judging by his arousal, he was enjoying this a hell of a lot too. Then they rinsed each other off in a playful way. When they were through, they dried each other off and it was time to dress, then fix a quick breakfast. She really wanted to go to bed with him, cuddle, and maybe do this again. But it would have to wait.

As for Turbo's attack on Eric, she already had some concerns about her coleader mate that she wanted to address.

Chapter 19

WHILE BAGELS WERE TOASTING, PEPPER BROUGHT OUT SOME cantaloupe and honeydew melon. "When you didn't go after the wolf, I was afraid history was repeating itself," she said to Eric in the kitchen, the morning sun peeking through the window.

Eric fixed them both a cup of coffee. "He could have led me into an ambush where Waldron or some of his wolves waited, and Waldron or others might have hassled you. Two of us together were a safer bet. That part of our relationship will take some getting used to, learning each other's strengths and building on them."

She sighed. "That's what my beta mate would have done. Stayed with me. I thought since you were an alpha you would have reacted differently."

"No. He would have been right to stay by your side. Even if I'd been alone, it would depend on the circumstances. Were others waiting for me somewhere else if I had chased the attacking wolf down? If I were him, I'd have howled for wolf backup."

"I'm glad the wolf didn't bite you."

"He wouldn't have had the chance. If he'd actually bitten at me, I would have killed him."

"Do you think he was really going to bite you? When he ran off so suddenly, I had the impression it was a ploy to get you to take chase."

"I agree. I wondered if he thought I'd run off because

of his aggression, like I had done when Waldron attacked me. What if they're testing me to see how I react to other wolves?"

"Then do you think Waldron or someone else was watching us? Or Turbo reported back to him?"

"Yeah. To them, it might still look like I'm afraid to take any of them down. You bit him instead. I'm still an unknown entity." Eric thought Waldron and his pack might not even realize the Silver pack had taken the other wolf and incarcerated him. No one had contacted Darien, and they had seen no signs of any unknown wolves in Silver Town. To them, he was probably just missing, and that could mean any number of things.

Eric stroked her back and kissed her cheek, and then they took their seats at the breakfast table. "Tell me about your land. What would he gain by attempting to force you to mate him?"

"A profitable Christmas tree farm, a tree nursery, and forested land for hunting and fishing and running as wolves. All of our adult pack members have incomes, so we're a self-sustained pack. We might not run a whole town, but we do well financially. As a dispersing wolf with a pack with no home now, he probably sees this as a perfect place to settle down. He would just need to win over the she-wolf who owns the land and runs the pack."

"He's been doing a lousy job of it, and now it's too late. But I still believe there's a good chance he's involved in the marijuana business."

"I've never smelled weed on him."

"He might be supervising the operation, but letting his other wolves handle the goods."

"Even if he isn't doing anything criminal like that,

from the first moment I saw him, I wasn't interested in him. There was something about him that didn't appeal. The way you and I met was a natural consequence of you working at the park. No hidden agenda. You didn't know I was there, that I had a pack, that I was unmated. But with Waldron, I met him in the grocery store. It just seemed odd at the time to me.

"Now that I know his cousin had already been here and had killed my mate, I can see how meeting Waldron wasn't purely by chance. He wasn't able to oust his brother and take over his pack, so Waldron decided to come here and attempt to win me over. He seemed like a salesman trying to sell himself to me. That's what I like about you. You're just yourself. You just make yourself available to me and the pack without any hidden agenda." She served up the bagels, butter, honey, and jams.

"Oh, I have a hidden agenda."

She smiled up at him. "Yeah, but it wasn't to gain control of the pack. I've had so much trouble with alpha males. As soon as they learned I ran a pack, they became rabidly interested. No longer was there a need to get to know me, but a real push to get my consent for a mating. It really turned me off."

"I understand. If I had run a pack and some she-wolf started chasing after me because she wanted to be a pack leader…"

Pepper chuckled. "There are more male wolves than she-wolves, and a lot more male wolves running packs alone than she-wolves, I imagine."

"True, but if you had said you were walking away and letting someone else be in charge of the pack, like Susan or any number of other she-wolves, I wouldn't have been hanging around for her or anyone else. I would have been chasing after you. I don't understand how Waldron's cousin thought killing your mate would make you give in to him."

"I believe he intended to make it look like someone else had killed Harold, and then he would comfort me and protect me from the big, bad wolf. Only *he* was the big, bad wolf. He really hadn't expected me to arrive on the scene, which gave me the advantage." She let out a heavy breath. "Enough about me. What about you? You said everyone has a past. Were you mated before?"

"Yeah, once. My father hated red wolves with a passion. I learned later it all had to do with him being rejected by a red she-wolf and her family before he met my mother, who was a gray like him. Anyway, I fell in love with a red wolf, but her family didn't want me mating her because I was a gray, and my dad was furious with me."

"Darien's mated to a red wolf," Pepper observed. "Your father must have been Darien's uncle."

"He was. And he murdered Darien's first mate, a red. So there's a history there. So when Darien took a red mate, Dad was just as angry with him over it."

"How did your mate die?"

"I…mated her in secret. I thought eventually I could take her home to the Silver pack, but her own pack learned of it and ambushed us. Her father nearly killed me, and when she got in the way to protect me, one of her uncles killed her. I don't think he meant to. The fighting abruptly stopped. They left me for dead and carried her body home. Sarandon found me and brought me home, where he cared for me until I was able to manage on my own. My father was still angry with me, said I deserved what I got, and that was the last time we ever spoke.

"I was angry with my father about his feelings toward the woman I loved. I grieved for four years over her death. I left home but returned every once in a while to see how my brothers were faring. On one of the return visits, I stayed longer with Sarandon than I had in a long time, missing the pack and the camaraderie. I learned of my father's hand in Darien's mate's death. Darien killed my father for it, which was his right as pack leader. And my brothers and I left the pack."

"Oh, Eric. That must have been awful for you. All of it."

"Yeah. It was. CJ was homesick and wanted to return to the pack. I felt what my father had done was all my fault. I felt that the pack would see us as our father's sons, like him, not to be trusted. But we couldn't stay away and finally returned to the pack."

"No one treats you ill for what your father did, do they?"

"No. Despite how much my father angered me, he was still our father. And if my mother hadn't died early on, maybe my father would have been all right. At least I always believed he would have been."

"How do you feel about it now?"

"I thought I'd never mate again. As soon as I met you, it was different. When I saw you that first night and you didn't want me to help out, I was instantly attracted to you." He smiled. "Probably because of the challenge in your eyes. Well, before that even. When I was carrying Susan to the cabin and saw you playing in the creek with the other women, I thought you looked like a goddess."

She laughed. "No."

"Hell yeah. You were wearing that beautiful, pale-blue silky creation in the water and were half wet and, well, yeah, you looked like a goddess—totally seductive and desirable. I worried you were human and would see me carrying an injured wolf in my arms, surrounded by wolves. Then I figured you had to be part of the pack. Even though my priority was getting Susan some help for her injured leg, I sure wanted to meet the she-wolf of my dreams."

Smiling, Pepper shook her head, then finished eating and carried their plates into the kitchen while Eric poured them each another cup of coffee.

"It's true. I even dreamed about you that night. I wanted in the worst way to meet you and let you know I was a good guy. All of you packed up the campsite so quickly, and with what I thought was one of your pack members staying behind and attacking me, I felt I'd left a bad first impression with you and your pack. I wanted to meet you again and do it properly this time."

"Did you, in your dream?"

"No. Waldron attacked me again, only I was in human form. Then my brother knocked at the door and woke me from the dream completely, and I realized I was just having a nightmare. You were the dream. Waldron put a bite into it. Probably because my shoulder was still hurting."

"And you were burning up. I can't believe you wanted to make the right impression on me. You were an angel to have carried Susan all that way. She was annoyed with me for not thanking you more."

"No problem. Because of all the trouble you've had with alpha males, I totally understand."

"We were making so much noise, we didn't even see

you step on the beach for a moment before you disappeared back into the woods on the path to our camp. But one of the wolves running with you came and told me Susan had been injured. He didn't tell me a perfect stranger had carried Susan into camp. I thought one of our people had brought her back. So I was shocked to see you standing there, all six-foot-one of you."

"Like a god, right?"

She laughed.

"Well, just so you know, I couldn't fight the attraction I have for you. I couldn't quit thinking about you. When I had to inspect one of the campgrounds on my double shift, I took the same footpath as your people had. If me seeing you, meeting you—"

"And getting horribly bitten."

"Yeah, I have to say that did cross my mind. That Waldron was out there stalking me, especially after the threat he made about my job."

"I still worry about that."

Eric tightened his hold on her. "Don't. I'm not a beta wolf, Pepper. I'll never be like Harold in that regard. But I'm good at standing back and letting others take charge. When I'm needed, I'm capable and willing to step right in and take care of the situation."

"I like that about you. And I like how passionate you are with me. I was beginning to think something was wrong with me."

"Are you kidding?"

"No."

He frowned.

"Harold was like a brother to me."

"You mean…"

"There wasn't any passion. If you wonder why we didn't have any kids, that probably had a lot to do with it."

"I can't even imagine being around you and not feel hotly attracted."

"Thanks. You don't know how much that means to me. Harold and I had known each other for so long, we were way too much like brother and sister."

"I don't feel brotherly toward you in the least."

She smiled and nipped at his chin. "Goddess, huh?"

He smiled and began to kiss her again to show her just how desirable she was.

She sighed. "I guess next we have to tell everyone."

"Next is work, then tonight more loving—lots more loving—and then the day after tomorrow I'm off and you'll have to take the day off, and we'll do more of this, and…"

She laughed. "I knew you would take over."

And she loved him for it as he began kissing her again. But she also suspected that as soon as Waldron learned of their mating, he would cause more trouble for them, just like his cousin had.

Chapter 20

THEY HAD SO MUCH TO DISCUSS YET. PEPPER HATED THAT they had to go off in different directions and work. At least she could talk on her phone while she was conducting business today. Eric had a two-hour drive to the park, and since he could receive calls on his truck panel, he could drive safely and talk to her.

Hating to let him go, she kissed his lips once more, gave him another warm hug, and sighed. "I'll call you as soon as I get to work."

"Okay, sounds good."

A few minutes later, she was on the phone, feeling like it had been forever since she had talked to him.

"Are you ready to tell everyone we're mated?" Pepper asked.

"Hell yeah. Lelandi will want to throw a big celebration with the Silver pack."

"That would be nice. What will your brothers think? Your cousins?" She sounded a little worried.

"I don't believe they'll be surprised in the least. What about your pack?"

"I think they figured it was coming. What are you going to do about your house?"

"*Our* house. Fix it up and sell it, unless you think we should rent it out or keep it as our ski resort home."

"Then I'd have to take up skiing. I've never thought of doing anything like that."

"Hey, Susan already said she wanted to, and a pack leader's got to lead, so…"

Pepper laughed. "All right. How about if we keep the place for anyone from the pack who wants to use it for visits into Silver Town? Doctor visits, ski trips, or anything else they might need."

"Works for me."

"What about our honeymoon?"

He chuckled. "Do you really think you could leave your pack alone for a week or two?"

"Yeah, I do. Once we resolve the issue with Waldron and learn if he's responsible for the marijuana."

"Knowing my brothers and my cousins, any one of them would be more than happy to look in on the pack while we're gone."

"I can… We can talk to Richard and Susan about it. So when are we going? And where?"

"You have your heart set on Scotland. This is our busy season for visitors to the park, so after Labor Day? Scotland? I've heard that a couple of Highland wolf packs even own castles. Maybe we could see if they would allow us to rent a room."

She sighed. "I knew there was a reason I mated you."

He chuckled. "You mated me because you love me."

"True. What about your trip to Hawaii?"

"Next year. How about we go there to celebrate our first anniversary? But we'll go after the busy season."

"We should have waited to mate until it wasn't the busy season for the park."

"Not on your life. I sure wish we could be snuggling in bed while we're having this conversation."

"Me too. I can't wait until you come home. I love you."

"Love you too."

They talked for two hours straight about their dreams and plans for the pack and themselves. She realized she hadn't really thought anything about her personal future—just the pack. Eric was definitely a wonderful influence in her life.

Everyone was thrilled to learn about the mating and wanted to celebrate it in high fashion. The rest of the day she was fielding calls from both the Silver pack and her own, congratulating them on the union.

That night, Pepper fixed Eric the steaks that he'd bought and served wine, salads, and baked potatoes, while each talked about the day they'd had. Then they repeated the run, the hot tub and shower sex, and ended up in bed, tired, happy, complete. But not too tired to fool around in bed for half the night.

When they woke early the next morning, Eric started to kiss Pepper's neck as he spooned her in bed, loving that they were now mated wolves. He didn't want to think of anything else—just of her and this, enjoying the heat of her body, the feel of her softness pressed up against him, the smell of her sweet fragrance. He was just starting to kiss her again, wishing he could just take time off work, when his phone rang.

As soon as he took the call, Pepper left the bed, and he groaned at having to let her go. "Darien? Did the man talk?"

Pepper stopped in her footsteps, her naked body so beautiful that he wanted her beneath him again, to make love to her until the sun went down.

"He turned," Darien said. "You're not going to believe this. It's Ted Fairhaven, the teens' father. He's not a royal, and he knew the new moon was fast approaching. Because he'd been confined to a cage, he couldn't take it any further."

"What did he say?" Eric asked.

"He accused you of an unprovoked attack. Said he found the weed but was just curious about it. He had nothing to do with it."

"Right. And you told him we'd found that he'd been to other patches?"

"Sure did. And his scent was discovered on some of the tubing they had hidden in the brush and used to irrigate the plants. Once he knew he wasn't talking his way out of this, he implicated a member of Pepper's pack."

"Ah hell." He knew this was going to upset her.

"So you might want to discuss this with your mate."

"Who did he say was involved?" Eric asked.

"Pauline."

"He's lying." Eric wondered if Ted was just making up a story. Eric had thought Pauline seemed interested in some of the bachelor males at the gathering. Why would she be if she was involved with someone in Waldron's pack?

"He said Waldron offered her a chance to be a sub-leader if he became the pack leader. She's been seeing one of the wolves named Turbo."

Hell. Still, it could be a lie. "On the sly?"

"Must be if you haven't smelled his scent around the place at all. And Turbo is Ted's brother."

"Figures. He attacked me when we went on a run. I wonder if he knew I had taken his brother down. Or suspected it."

"Why the hell didn't you tell me?" Darien let out his breath. "I take it you're all right."

"Yeah, Pepper bit his tail though." Eric smiled at her, proud of her.

"Sounds like you have a real winner."

"I do."

"Well, it could be that he's learned his brother was taken into custody with all our wolf scents up in that area. All he'd have to do was return to the marijuana patch and smell us, and then he could have tracked where you and his brother fought."

"Right. I've got to tell Pepper the news and I need to go to work. I'd take off, but I can't do that again, not with the need they have for us at the park. I've had to take off so much already."

"I'll let you handle this then. Ted won't testify against the pack. Said we can't prove they were growing the weed. But we reminded him he's staying put and no bail. This business is too serious for our kind to get caught at. Let me know if you need our help concerning this, and watch your back at the park. In fact, I want you to call in to one of your brothers or someone in the pack on a regular basis until we catch these people."

"Agreed, Darien. I'll talk to you later." Eric felt sick about having to give Pepper the news, but he reminded himself Pauline might not have anything to do with this, and it was just Ted's word that Pepper's pack was involved too. He belatedly realized Darien was still giving him orders when Eric was now a pack leader in his own right. He smiled a little at the irony, and for the first time, it really didn't bother him, knowing his cousin only worried about him. It was hard to let go of that need to protect others.

Eric set the phone on the table and joined Pepper, her arms folded across her chest, looking like she was ready to turn into a wolf and take someone down.

"This could be bad news or all a lie," he said.

———⁓⁓⁓———

Pepper was beyond furious as she yanked on her clothes. "He's got to be lying. If he isn't, Pauline has a hell of a lot of explaining to do."

"We've been trying to uncover the culprits for weeks. I can't believe we didn't learn anything about this beforehand," Eric said, pulling on his own clothes.

"No, back it up a bit. You suspected someone in my pack at first—when you smelled someone who had come to the camp who smelled of weed. Had he been trying to see her then? Damn it anyway."

"I suspected the man was with Waldron's pack. That he had visited your camp under Waldron's orders, and I just happened to return and smell the scent, which was the same as one of the wolves who had visited several of the marijuana patches. I didn't think he was seeing any of your people. And I knew he wasn't one of your people. We've been trying to catch the wolves at this. Not one of your wolves' scents was found up there. Even if Pauline was seeing the guy, I don't believe she would be a turncoat."

"You've got to get to work. You'll be late." Pepper ground her teeth.

Eric pulled her into his embrace and held her tight.

Pepper was really upset over this whole business, but she had to keep reminding herself Ted might have lied about his brother seeing Pauline. Yet Pepper couldn't ignore that it might be true.

"Pepper…" Eric let his breath out on a heavy sigh. "If I had suspected any of your people were involved, I would have told you."

"You had no idea. What am I saying? *I* had no idea!" She relaxed a little. None of this was Eric's fault.

"I love you," he said, stroking her back with one hand, his other wrapped around her waist, keeping her close and not allowing her to pull away. "However you think we need to handle the business with Pauline is up to you. It could all be a lie. She's completely innocent in my view unless we learn something that says otherwise. I need to grab a bite to eat and head on in before I'm late to work."

"What if they go after you again? At the park?"

Eric was at risk every time he was in the park alone because of Waldron and his wolves.

Her phone howled and she pulled away from Eric to get it. When she saw it was Susan, she immediately worried that her cousin had somehow learned about Pauline and this mess. "Susan?"

"The Fairhaven boys are missing," Susan quickly said.

Had they learned of their dad's disappearance? Gone to see him? "No word to Richard? They just took off in their truck?"

"Yes. He said he got up early like usual and went to rouse them from bed and—"

A truck's engine rumbled in Pepper's driveway. "Wait, someone just pulled up out front. I've got to finish getting dressed. I'll call you back in a bit."

"You just got out of bed? You're not sick, are you?"

"No, I'm not sick." Well, not in that way, but sick of what Pauline might be involved in? Yes.

"I'll check it out while you finish getting dressed," Eric said, waiting a heartbeat before proceeding.

"All right. I'll be right there."

He nodded and stalked out of the bedroom.

"We've got some other pressing issues to discuss," Pepper said to her cousin.

"Now what?"

"Tell you and Richard in a bit. Got to go." Pepper finished dressing and heard Eric inviting the Fairhaven boys into the house.

"You had Richard worried," Eric scolded them.

"We had to come right away," Jonathan said.

Pepper joined them in the living room.

"I'm going to have them fix their own breakfast and we can discuss what's going on, if that works for you," Eric said.

"Won't you be late for work?"

"Not if we make something quickly and I drive a little faster than normal."

"All right. I'll call Richard and tell him the boys are here."

Eric took them into the kitchen and offered them bowls of cereal and fruit while Pepper called her sub-leader. "The Fairhaven boys just arrived at my house. Eric's having them fix breakfast for themselves. I'll let you know what's going on with them in a bit. And we have more to discuss."

After she ended the call, she checked to see what Eric had prepared for breakfast. "I'm glad you went grocery shopping." She poured herself a cup of coffee. All three of the "boys" had cups of coffee already. "Okay, so what's this all about?" She began slicing up the honeydew melon, and for a moment, she felt like she had a ready-made family in the nearly grown boys and Eric. But she suspected they knew something about their father and were concerned for him.

"Our mom and dad changed their minds about us being fostered with your pack," Jonathan said, scowling. He and his brother didn't look happy about it. Jonathan dumped tablespoons of brown sugar on his cereal. "We want to stay. But we're not adults so we can't do what we want."

"What? Why did your parents change their minds?" Pepper asked.

"Waldron said if they didn't get us to return, he would fire my dad as a sub-leader."

"Why does he want you to return if you're such troublemakers?" Eric asked.

"Because we're not," Jonathan said, glowering in his direction, though she didn't think he was mad at Eric, just angry with Waldron.

"You have a home with us, if we can get your parents to agree. And that's the sticking point," Pepper said.

"Yeah, but Richard got Mom and Dad's agreement that we would stay with you and work for you and make enough money to continue to make payments on our trucks and our car insurance. They gave us up," Jonathan said.

"Because they thought you could spy on me," Pepper said.

"Yeah. Only we like it here and we had no intention of spying on you. Well, we did at first, because we thought you'd treat us mean. But you haven't. No one has. Waldron would never have had us over for dinner and treated us like adults. We like the other kids our age, both in the Silver Town pack and yours. Richard makes us work, but he's really teaching us a job. And since Waldron lost out on mating you and taking over your pack, that means we'll be moving again. We'd like to ski this winter and even work at the resort with the other kids if Darien will let us."

Leroy nodded.

Eric fixed a thermos of coffee to go. "So why did he want you back? Because you wouldn't spy for him?"

Jonathan shoved his hands in his pockets. "Yeah. He's mad so he figures he'll show us we still have to do what he says."

Leroy finished his cereal. "He'll make us pay if we have to return to them."

"Finish your breakfast, and then I'm calling your mother—and Richard." Pepper wanted to get this resolved pronto for the boys' sakes. She had thought they knew their dad was incarcerated in Silver Town.

While they ate, they talked about other things, though she knew everyone was concerned about what would happen next. When they finished, Eric had them help clean up, and she got on the phone to Richard first. "You got a written agreement from the parents that they wanted you to take care of the boys—provide them with employment and a place to stay?"

"Yeah, I did just in case we had any repercussions from Waldron." Richard sent a picture of the agreement to her email.

"All right. I'm calling the boys' mother, and I'll tell them that if they need to go somewhere, they have to let you know. None of this running off. I'll let you know what happens next."

"Thanks. They're really good kids. They just need some proper guidance, which they haven't been getting in Waldron's pack."

Next, Pepper called the Fairhavens' home. "Mrs. Fairhaven, the boys want to stay with us." At least she hoped they still would after learning that their father had been involved in growing pot. If they found out that the Silver pack had jailed him, they might not be willing to stay with her pack any longer. "You agreed. They're happy here. You can either join our pack or the Silvers'." She hoped the mom hadn't been involved in the drug business too. Though she could very well have been.

"It's not that we want to change anything," the mom said.

"I understand. It's Waldron's doing."

Silence.

"Okay, what is going on with Waldron and your husband? It can't be that Ted wants the sub-leader position that badly. And just so you know, and you can tell Waldron I said so, I'm a mated wolf now, so he's not mating me or taking over the pack or my land."

"Do...do you know where he is? My Ted? He's gone missing."

Pepper looked at Eric. She couldn't tell the woman her husband was in jail unless the Silver pack gave permission. "Do you know where he's been working?"

"He's getting his real estate license."

"So no real job at the moment?"

Eric raised his brows.

Pepper didn't want to talk about this in front of the boys.

The mother said, "He's still working on getting his real estate license."

"Okay, hold on a minute." Pepper said to Eric, "Could you drop the boys off at Richard's on your way to work? They're grounded from driving their truck for not getting permission to leave Richard's place. If you don't have time—"

Eric looked half growly, half pleading with the desire to resolve things between them. "We need to talk."

"Yes, but I need to speak with…" She paused.

"Okay." Eric appeared to realize the dilemma she was in. "I'll call you in a while."

"Thanks. We'll be fine, Eric," she said, wanting him to know she wasn't really upset with him.

Eric took the phone from her, set it down on the table, and pulled her into a hug, kissing her soundly. "I love you."

She hadn't expected that and kissed him back. "Love you too. Be careful."

"Will do." Then he left with the boys.

Jonathan said on the way out, "See, that's what we need to find. A she-wolf we can mate."

Pepper smiled a little at the comment. He was way too young to find a mate.

She lifted her phone off the table and said to their mom, "Your husband has been involved in the growing of marijuana in the national park. The Silver pack arrested him, which is good for all our sakes, so he's safe. I don't know how much you know of any of this, but last night his brother attacked Eric, my mate, who's a law-enforcement park ranger. If you're involved in all of this, we'll deal with it. But if you're not or you don't want your sons to be, then at least do right by them. Let them stay with my pack."

"I…didn't know that's what Ted was doing." She

sounded shocked, then she said, "All right. I'll join your pack. The devil take him."

"He'll be in jail for a while."

"I mean Waldron."

Pepper sighed. "Everyone works in my pack."

"I'm a hard worker. Waldron made so many promises to those following him, but he hasn't kept any."

"Like?"

"He promised he was mating you, providing us with a new home, that Ted would be a sub-leader, and everyone's income would quadruple with his plan to grow some really hot-selling crops. I had no idea what they were. He said they were medicinal, good for cancer… I should have known it was too good to be true. I was furious when our sons got into trouble for stalking you. My husband blamed it all on Waldron and said we had to do what he told us or we'd lose everything."

"How many are in the pack?"

"Six of us now. Two others died, but Waldron wouldn't say how."

Pepper was dumbfounded. Waldron had told her he had thirty pack members! "Does that include the boys?"

"No, adults only. Waldron, my husband, and me, Ted's brother, Turbo, and two other men, besides the two that died. Turbo is so arrogant that he bragged he'd been seeing one of your pack members, and if Waldron didn't hurry, Turbo would be mated to her and part of your pack before Waldron was. That angered Waldron."

Hoping beyond hope that Mrs. Fairhaven wasn't right, Pepper asked, "Who was the woman?"

"I don't remember her name, but she had two little

kids and Turbo wasn't really interested in raising someone else's kids."

Pauline. "Okay, here's what I'll do. Richard, my subleader, has taken the boys in. He has a separate house behind his for when his parents were getting older. They've passed away and the house is vacant. The boys have been staying with him in the main house so he can keep an eye on them. But if you'd like, you can move into the smaller house with your boys. They're doing really well and they seem to be happy."

"All right. I'll take care of my affairs here and then get in touch with you. Can I…see my husband?"

"Talk with Darien Silver in Silver Town. I'm sure he can arrange for you to visit with him."

"Did…did you tell the boys?"

"No. I'll leave that up to you. Are you going to be all right?"

"This is a real shock, I must confess. I still can't believe it. But I want to thank you for taking in the boys and now me too. I couldn't have returned to Waldron's brother's pack. Not after all that happened there."

"Okay. I've got to call some other folks, Richard included, so he knows you'll be staying with him."

"Thank you."

Pepper felt bad that she hadn't sent Eric off to work with more of a hug and a kiss. She prayed they could incarcerate Waldron and the rest of his men before Eric had to deal with any of them further.

She called Richard to let the boys know their mother was coming to stay there. Then she called Pauline and asked her to come to her house as soon as she could. Knowing it would concern Pauline, but not wanting the distraction, Pepper asked her to find someone to look after her boys while they had the talk. Pepper had to know if Pauline knew what Waldron and the rest of his men had been up to. She was surprised Pauline had seemed to be looking at the Silver pack for a prospective mate. Maybe she realized how bad Waldron and his people would be for the pack and had stopped seeing Turbo. When had she been seeing him? When others in the pack took care of her kids? He must not have been visiting her at her place. Too risky. And there hadn't been any scent of him around her place.

Wishing Eric could be here while she dealt with all of this, which signaled another change in how she looked at running her pack, Pepper prayed he would be all right on the job. She decided she would join him there, once she resolved some of the issues with Pauline and had a talk with her sub-leaders and the pack.

Chapter 21

Eric wanted to know what Pauline had to say and how Pepper resolved the issue of the boys staying with Richard. But only because he cared about her and her pack. Not because he felt the need to make any decisions concerning either situation.

The day started out stormy, which seemed par for the course with the way his blissful morning had turned into a muddled mess. Except for helping three different families get their trucks unstuck from mud, things had been relatively quiet. He was at the ranger station, while waves of lightning rolled across the sky, forks of lightning intermittently spearing the forest floor. He hoped everyone remained safe. Despite warnings issued to hikers, some still risked life and limb to make the hike during thunderstorms.

Not only was injury to people a concern, but fires started by lightning strikes could be too.

He was about to make a sandwich for lunch and call Pepper to see how she was faring when he got a call from her.

"What's wrong?" He was ready to call the Silver troops to come to her aid.

"I wish we could have stayed in bed together for the rest of the day," she said, sounding sexy and alluring.

"My shift won't end quickly enough." He'd never watched the minutes go by as much as he had today, wanting nothing more than to return to bed with her on this perfectly stormy afternoon.

"I'm sorry for being so perturbed this morning."

"You had every reason to be upset. What's happening with the kids?"

"They're staying. Darien's arranged a time for their mother and the boys to visit their father in jail. Ted still won't spill the beans on the others in the pack. Darien's fine with that for now. He said they'll catch the others as soon as they're able to."

"Good about the boys."

"And their mother's moving to our pack too. So good news all around. When the dad gets out, not sure. But for now, the mom and kids are with our pack."

Eric smiled, realizing how much he liked hearing her say it was their pack. "And Pauline?"

"She *was* seeing Turbo. I hate to say this, but she's so unreadable that I don't know if she's telling the truth about the marijuana business or not. She said she knew nothing about it, and she quit seeing him, which makes me believe she knew something was wrong. But when I asked her why she quit seeing him, she said she didn't think he was good for the pack. That since he was Waldron's man, she felt there could be trouble. And she was getting interested in one of the men in your pack.

"She didn't want to say who because it was too early to tell about him—particularly since she already has a couple of sons, and she wanted to ensure a new mate would be as good with them as he is with her. That was another reason she said she called it off with Turbo. She said he faked being friendly with the kids. She could tell he really wasn't interested in them."

"Gut instinct about her knowledge of the drug issue?" Eric knew it had to be hard for Pepper to deal with this. He wished he could be there to help out, but it was best that Pepper had talked to Pauline right away and tried to learn what had happened.

"You never want to play against her in cards. She truly is a master at keeping her feelings masked. I really don't know."

"Okay. I had hoped she could testify against Waldron and the others, if she knew something."

"If she decides to change her mind and tell me, I'll let you know. But I'm coming to join you for the rest of your shift."

"Hell, it's nasty out there."

"You know what I do. I'll drag you around the tree farms when you have some time off from your job. I need to see what you do for the day."

"Can't you wait for a nice sunshiny day?"

"Nope. I'm nearly to your location. Just wanted to make sure you were still at the ranger station."

"I can't believe you want to do this today of all days. But of course I'm thrilled you're coming."

"I want to see you."

"All right. I'd ask if we have a vacancy at any of the cabins and rent a room for a quick nap, but I'm afraid the staff might get suspicious."

She laughed. "Great minds think alike. I already rented one. I figured as law-abiding as you are, we couldn't use it while you're on duty, but we'll have it after your shift ends. I can't wait until we get home tonight."

"You're my kind of wolf. Did you know that?"

"Yeah, well, you better remember that."

Eric didn't plan to make love to Pepper while he was on duty. He was dedicated to his job, and some of that meant ensuring everyone remained safe under his watch. But after his shift ended? He loved the idea as much as both he and Pepper enjoyed the woods. The cabin seemed the perfect way to be with his mate.

"When will you get here?" He hoped he didn't get called out before she arrived.

"Just parking now."

"Want a tuna fish sandwich?"

"Yes. And pickles and potato chips," she said, walking down the hall to the staff kitchen.

He opened the door and smiled at her, both of them still holding their phones to their ears. She smiled back at him, and he wondered how he'd gotten so lucky to have met her that first day in the park.

He introduced her to the staff there as his fiancée and she looked so pleased. Even though they were officially "married" in the *lupus garou* way, he thought a wedding would be nice to make it more official. Maybe even in the park. He made a mental note to bring that idea up with Pepper later.

They had barely finished eating lunch when he got a call that a couple with their sixteen-month-old baby had been hiking on a trail that led up to one of the higher-elevation lakes and had been caught out in the open during the thunderstorm. Eric and Pepper took off in his truck to rescue them.

When they reached the couple, they took them down to the ranger station, and Eric got a call about an off-road vehicle driving in an area of the park where driving was not allowed. The truck was stuck in a creek. Oil and other harmful chemicals could poison the water, just because someone wanted to drive somewhere that wasn't allowed and unsafe to cross. Eric couldn't help but be angered at the thoughtlessness of some people.

He ticketed the driver and hoped he'd receive a hefty fine, while Pepper told the man all the ramifications of what he'd done—the way he'd destroyed the plants his tires had trampled, the chemicals his truck left in the water, and how that ruined the river and that area for the wildlife and the visitors who came to enjoy the natural beauty of the park. She told him three times that he should be ashamed of himself.

Eric had to fight smiling at her, glad she was wearing her uniform so she looked official and could say what she had a mind to say.

The man opened his mouth to speak once, but Eric said, "The lady is talking." Ranting, but tough if the driver of the vehicle didn't like it. Everything she said was true.

Eric felt the same as she did. Helping people when their vehicles got stuck in mud on regular roads because of the rain was an entirely different story. It would be a good one on the lawbreaker if his truck was unsalvageable. A maximum penalty could result in the man getting a fine of $5,000 or six months in prison, or both, which would suit Eric fine. Before he could mention the federal law that covered destruction to National Park Service property and personal liability, Pepper was quoting it.

Eric loved his mate and was glad she had come with him for the rest of the afternoon. They spent a couple of hours checking out campsites and helping folks move their tents where water runoff had flooded the area they had been set up in.

They'd both been wearing rain gear, but when they had to help rescue a couple of canoeists from a capsized canoe in one of the rivers, Eric removed his coat and tied himself to a tree while he waded out to reach them. Pepper took care of the first of the men, shivering and hypothermic, wrapping her own raincoat around him to warm him.

Once they'd helped haul the men and their boat to safety and gotten medical help for them, it was time to quit work for the day.

Now the real fun would begin.

As soon as he and Pepper parked at the cabin and got out, Eric scooped his soaking-wet mate into his arms and set her on the covered porch. She pulled out the key and unlocked the door, then he whisked her into the room, shut the door, and they began kissing.

Her shirt was plastered against her breasts, her pants clinging to her legs, her curly hair dripping.

"I like this new look on you," he said, growling a little, his hand molding around her cold breast.

"Fire first?" she asked, kissing him back while she slid her hand around his arousal, his pants molding to his body just as much.

"Fire already started."

She smiled against his lips and rubbed her wet body against his, kissing him with enthusiasm, her hands sweeping over his buttocks.

This was the way he wanted to always end his work-day. Maybe not soaking wet at a cabin in the park, but with Pepper, kissing, touching, breathing in their heated scents, and loving every bit of it.

As she started to unbutton his shirt, he began working on hers, but he had to keep stopping to rub his hands over her wet shirt, feeling her breasts, the nipples peaking, her breath nearly ceasing at his touch.

She struggled to remove his shirt and then was pulling it off his shoulders and kissing his chest. He loved her passion and matched it, sliding his hands up her shirt and cupping her lace-covered breasts.

His thumbs stroked her nipples through the fabric. Though the cabin was cool, he was burning up as she licked the rainwater off his cheek and then began to kiss his mouth again.

Her mouth fused with his, their tongues sliding against each other, her body stroking against him. The friction against his cock had him working again on her shirt buttons. After unfastening her shirt, he pulled it off her shoulders and dropped it to the floor.

He removed her bra next, wanting to feast his eyes and then his mouth on each of her breasts. Beautiful. She pulled away and leaned down to take off her boots, and he quickly did the same with his. Wet socks went flying, then their pants, and he pulled her in for more hugging, kissing, and touching.

It wasn't enough. He wanted her in bed, on top or underneath him, her choice. But he wanted to fill her with his love. He slipped her panties down her legs, kissing her from her breasts down her abdomen, while he pulled them down. Then she did the same with him, only she licked his cock on the way down. He felt his whole body become rigid with tension, before he swept his wet mate up into his arms and carried her into the bathroom for a quick shower. Then they dried off and headed for the first of the bedrooms.

She eagerly climbed onto the bed and pulled at his

arms to join her. The kissing renewed, and he stroked her feminine nub, bringing her quickly to the top. She cried out, but just as quickly, he joined her, sliding into her, claiming her. He began thrusting, loving every bit of her—the way she wrapped her legs around his body, the way she arched to meet his thrusts, the way she stroked his back and legs with her soft fingertips. He soon followed her into that sweet state of bliss. If he'd ever had any doubts about her being his mate, their lovemaking confirmed she was perfect for him.

She was his wolf goddess.

"Where have you been all my life?" Pepper asked as they curled up together in bed.

He chuckled. "I could ask you the same thing." He loved this time with her, getting to know her intimately, but he loved too that she'd come to see him on his job and had helped him out in every situation. "Do you think the man whose truck got stuck in the creek felt ashamed of himself?"

Pepper frowned at Eric. "He ought to get ten years in jail. I know most people don't think anything of it. Sometimes it's a lark. Sometimes it's the thrill of doing what no one has done. And sometimes, the asses do it because they think they can get away with it. But I was at Cape Hatteras National Seashore in North Carolina when some jerk ran over a female loggerhead turtle attempting to make a nest. The off-road vehicle dragged her for some time before he could get rid of the dead animal beneath his truck. The turtles are threatened. But that's the thing of it. To some, it's no big deal."

Eric was opening his mouth to agree with her when he thought he heard the handle turn on the front door. He couldn't remember if he'd even locked the door, because he'd been so wrapped up in wanting to make love to his mate when they first entered the cabin. His clothes and gun and their phones were in the living room. Nothing for protection here in the bedroom.

Pepper was already slipping out of bed and shifting into her wolf form.

Eric couldn't, in case the offender was human. But she would be good protection for backup. On the other hand, he didn't want her to get shot if the person breaking in was armed with a gun. He opened the bedroom window and pushed out the screen. Before Eric could tell her his plan, she jumped out the window. Hell.

Heart pounding, he sprang into action, shifted, and followed after her.

She ran into the woods and came around to see who was breaking into their cabin. Eric agreed her plan was a good one. Then they saw one man guarding a vehicle, and two men in the cabin.

"Hell," one of those men said and hurried back toward the door of the cabin. "They've run out the back way."

Eric recognized the man's voice. Waldron. He wondered if one of the other men was Ted's brother, Turbo.

When they saw a fourth man leave the building, Eric knew they were outnumbered. Even two could be a problem if Pepper had to take care of one of the male wolves. Eric sure wished he could howl for backup, but none of his pack would hear him this far away.

"What do we do?" one of the men asked.

"Run 'em down. Hunt them. Like wolves hunt their prey."

Eric nudged at Pepper to follow his lead. He would

ensure that once they reached a creek, their paw scents would be washed away. He thought they'd have a fire when they woke after making love. But he hadn't expected to go swimming to try to save his mate and his life. It was too reminiscent of losing his first mate.

Except he half suspected these wolves wouldn't take her back with them because she knew too much. Eric had been at all the sites where their marijuana had been growing. Pepper was his mate. And, he'd been the one to take Turbo's brother down. So Eric knew if they caught up to him, he'd be a dead wolf.

The only advantage they had was that he'd been coming to these woods since November—both as a park ranger and a wolf. He had ventured over miles and miles of acreage. He just had to get her closer to the edge of the forest and Silver Town. If they could reach his pack, like he'd tried so fervently to do the last time he'd lost his mate, he and his pack could take Waldron and his men down permanently.

He had to ensure that he kept Pepper and himself out of Waldron and his men's range. Wolves could run after their quarry for long distances over even the roughest terrain. They could easily travel over fifty miles a day in search of food. So he and Pepper could continue to run. But they had to do more than that. They had to truly evade Waldron and his men until Pepper and he could howl for help. Even so, in the woods, their howl couldn't travel as far as it could over an open plain where it could be heard for ten miles. The other problem was that if they howled here, the killer wolves on their tails could also pinpoint their location.

Thankfully, creeks crisscrossed all over the mountains,

so whenever forks in the creek appeared, Eric led Pepper in a new direction. Sometimes that meant leading them both away from their destination for a half a mile or so, but only so they could lose the wolves tracking them.

They were going to have to rest for a while in just a little bit. He wished now he'd let everyone know where he and Pepper were going to be. Not that anyone would bother them if they thought they were having a "wedding night" of sorts. He didn't think anyone would be checking up on them unless the Park Service called his brother and told him Eric's vehicle was at the cabin Pepper had rented, and their clothes and ID were there, but both of them had disappeared. Then, everyone would be searching for them. But by then it could be too late.

Instead of sitting out on dry land, Pepper found a pool of water that had warmed during the day, much like the one that she and her she-wolves had been playing in the day that Susan had been injured.

For fifteen minutes, they rested, nuzzling each other every once in a while to show their affection, but listening for any sounds that could indicate wolves had tracked them here.

Then Pepper indicated she was ready to run again. Eric moved with her until he saw the wolf targeting them. The same wolf who had bitten him in the shoulder. Waldron. They couldn't outrun him now and lose the tail. Eric wanted Pepper to run off and hide, but he didn't want the other wolves to catch her. He saw no sign of the other wolves and thought they'd split up to search for Pepper and him. Before Waldron could howl and let his pack know he'd caught his prey, Eric lunged for him.

The wolf would never have a chance to tell his friends his location. He would never bite Eric without his retaliation. And he would never threaten Pepper or her pack again.

What Eric hadn't expected—and Waldron hadn't either, apparently—was to have Pepper dash in to bite his back leg, while Eric concentrated on going for his throat. The wolf wasn't going down easily, but Eric suspected Pepper was worried the others would show up, so he and Pepper had to take Waldron down quickly.

All three of them snarled and growled, and Eric hoped none of Waldron's pack members were close by and could hear them. The moving water and the trees hugging the bank of the creek would help to muffle the sounds. If the others had taken off on other forks, they could be miles away, still searching for Pepper and Eric.

Killing Waldron here could create problems though. Not that they could worry about that now.

He and Waldron kept tackling each other head on. Pepper kept aiming for Waldron's back leg. And then she managed to get it, and with a chomp, she bit down hard. Eric heard the telltale crack of a bone just as Waldron yelped, then swung around to tackle her. His move left him open to Eric's lunge and fatal bite. Eric tore into the wolf, taking him down and mortally wounding him before he could touch Pepper.

Eric grabbed the wolf's body by the neck before Waldron expired and pulled him out of the water, then hid him in some brush. He or some of the Silver pack would have to come here and retrieve the body and bury it. No roads or trails existed anywhere nearby.

Even so, they couldn't leave a human body here in case it was discovered.

Pepper was watching for any further wolf attacks, and then she waded into the water, as if to say she was ready to continue on their way. They still had a long way to go. But if Waldron's men hadn't come across them yet, they had to be a long distance off, making Eric feel as though they might make it out of the park and get some much-needed help.

Chapter 22

PEPPER ASSUMED ERIC WAS TRYING TO GET CLOSER TO HIS pack's territory so they could get help if the other wolves continued to follow them. At least at night they could remain undetected by humans. They certainly didn't need that additional trouble.

She wasn't sure how Eric felt about her helping tackle Waldron, but she couldn't let her mate do all the work. She had to help him take the wolf down, and quickly, in case the other wolves suddenly showed up. Tackling one wolf at a time was about all they could manage. She didn't know about the other wolves, but Turbo was a fast runner, and she could envision him going the wrong way, then turning and starting in a different direction, and still not be too far behind.

Pepper had hoped they'd lost the wolves, but on the other hand, she had been glad to end this tonight with Waldron. It had stopped raining about an hour ago, so her coat had dried.

She wasn't certain where they were going exactly or how close they were to Silver Town. Eric led her across a road to a river, and they ran in the shallow water at the river's edge. Then Eric woofed at her and she stopped to see what he wanted of her. She was dead tired, but she would forge on until they were safe.

Eric nuzzled her, then lifted his chin and howled. She frowned at him and then smelled the air. She didn't think they were in his pack territory yet. He nudged her and they kept running.

Again, he stopped and howled. She turned to look at him. They had to be within hearing distance. Ohmigod, this must be the pack leader's land. Or close to it. Darien and Lelandi lived quite a ways out of town so they could have pack gatherings without anyone getting curious about all the wolves!

But then they saw a wolf race out of the woods, and she recognized him at once. Turbo. She growled a warning before he went after Eric, a bigger wolf than Pepper and infinitely more dangerous.

Eric whipped around and did a frontal assault. Pepper did her maneuver like before, rushing around to Turbo's backside, ducking down, and biting at his leg.

Turbo growled at her, but she didn't get a good enough grip and tried again. He was jumping around so much, trying to avoid Eric's lethal canines and attempting to bite him with his own, that she was having a devil of a time grabbing hold of him. Just as she clamped her teeth down on his left rear leg, she heard another wolf racing to join them. She ignored him and bit Turbo hard.

He snarled at her from a sitting position and then a wolf howled. And another. Then a whole chorus of wolves' sweet symphony filled the air.

The other wolf stopped and hesitated, unsure whether to stay and fight or tuck tail and save his hide. He looked like it killed him to run off, but he did. Several wolves she didn't know by sight rushed off to take down the departing wolf. By the scent, they were Darien and two others.

Turbo looked resigned to paying the consequences

for his actions. He would end up in jail with his brother, no doubt. Both of them with broken legs. Served them right. At least they weren't dead wolves, but they'd pay their time for the dangerous illegal business they'd been in. Hopefully, Darien and the rest of the men could track down the remainder of the pack and end this now.

—～⁓～—

Eric and Pepper stayed at Darien and Lelandi's house, showered, and borrowed some of their clothes, then Sarandon drove them to Eric's home at their request. Pepper and Eric planned to stay at his home for the rest of the night. Thank heavens he didn't have to go into work until the late shift. All that was left to take care of after the fire damage was painting, so Eric's home was perfectly livable for the night. A hint of smoke could still be smelled in the den. Pepper was glad they could be alone but in pack territory.

Darien and several members of the pack had left to deal with the rest of this business—retrieving Waldron's body, setting and casting Turbo's leg, and locking him in a cell near his brother. They'd caught the other wolf without a fight and learned the location of the last wolf. CJ and Trevor were on their way to arrest him. Tom and Brett had taken care of the cabin, bringing Eric and Pepper's still-wet clothes, Eric's gun, their phones, her vehicle, and the ranger truck to Eric's home so they'd have them when they needed to leave. Pepper had updated Richard and Susan about everything that had happened and where they would be before she and Eric retired for what was left of the night.

"Can we try this again?" Eric asked, carrying her across the threshold to his bedroom.

She smiled up at him. "Anywhere and anyplace."

Eric quickly dispensed with his clothes and hers, and like a wolf on the prowl, he joined her on the bed, covering her body with his and plying her lips with kisses. His kisses were different from before, more possessive, cherishing her just as much as she cherished him. She thought it was because they had been running for their lives. She realized then that this could have been very much like the time he had lost his first mate. Her heart reached out to him, and she pulled him closer, devouring his lips, trying to prove that she was real, that they were safe.

He smiled a little at her passionate response and then poked his tongue into her mouth right before he began to stroke her nub. When he touched her like that, he was her master and she was his to command. She couldn't love him enough.

Her fingers swept over his skin, her hips moving with his strokes, her body screaming for more.

"Hurry," she said, wanting to have him inside her and to hold him as close as she could. She was so relieved they could enjoy a moment together like this now.

He rubbed her until she was arching her back, feeling the climax so close to coming. She felt herself being drawn up, hitting the peak and falling, loving the way he could make her somersault to the moon and back.

Without hesitation, he drove into her, pulling her legs around his hips and seating himself deep inside her. Nothing could be better than this.

He was kissing her, running his hand over her skin, pumping into her with love and affection. And she was burning up. She breathed in his masculine wolf scent and soaked up the feel of his mouth on hers and his body rubbing against hers. She could never get enough of him. Never.

He loved the way Pepper arched up to meet his thrusts, her body undulating with a sweet, soft rhythm. Every time he made love to her, he knew he'd want to again. She was a drug to his senses. A balm to his concerns.

He felt the end coming, held on, and felt the surge of need hitting him just as he plunged into her and found his release. He continued to pump into her until he felt her trying to reach that pinnacle again, and he helped her to the top. Then she swore in a loving way and he smiled. He captured her mouth in one long, last kiss before he pulled her against his body and re-situated the sheets over them.

"Silk," she murmured as her body rested against his, the top sheet caressing her back.

"As soft and luxurious as you."

"Hmm, you know all the right words…and all the right moves."

—⁓—

Two weeks later, Pepper was overwhelmed with the way her pack and the Silvers' had gone all out for the wedding celebration of the century. Instead of wearing a flouncy wedding gown, she wore what Eric had wanted her to wear—a simple white dress, reminiscent of the pale-blue one she'd worn in the creek when he first saw her. She knew then that he hadn't been teasing about how much she had caught his eye. Her "hand-maidens," as he continued to call them, all wore pastel colors. Pepper had asked the unmated MacTyre sisters from the Silver pack to join the wedding party, and Eric had asked his brothers and cousins to be groomsmen. Richard gave her away, and when Eric kissed her, heart and soul, she was his forevermore.

She loved that he wasn't afraid to show his love for her and that she wasn't afraid of showing it back. What really impressed her was the way the others treated this wedding. This was a joining of two packs in brotherhood. Eric was no longer just one of the followers, but a pack leader in his own right. It suited him. He deserved it. She knew they'd have differences of opinion about how to manage things, but she looked forward to the challenge.

The Fairhaven boys were showing their interest in one of the Silver teens, but she already had two suitors, so Pepper hoped that wouldn't cause trouble. Pauline was visiting with one of the ski instructors. Pepper was glad to observe it.

She was also glad Pauline had only seen Turbo twice before she realized she really hadn't liked him. They'd met for lunch at a couple of restaurants, so she had never gone any further than that with him. She hadn't known about their drug operation. Pepper was glad to learn that from Turbo and grateful to him for telling the truth.

Most of all, Pepper was glad she'd opened her heart to Eric and let him in. Though Susan, who was smiling brightly at Sarandon, probably would never quit saying she told her so.

Eric watched as Richard danced with Pepper and thought he'd never seen such a beautiful she-wolf.

"And she's all yours," Lelandi said, joining him. "Good thing you had no interest in mating a she-wolf."

He chuckled and looked down at his mischievous cousin by marriage. "I suppose you want credit for making this happen."

Lelandi patted him on the chest. "Only you and she could have made it happen."

Then Darien came to take Lelandi for a dance. "You can still take advice from me, you know," he said to Eric.

Eric smiled at him. "Hell yeah, and I can still give you advice."

They both laughed and Darien led Lelandi away to dance.

Brett and CJ joined Eric and just stood there, arms folded across their chests as they watched Pepper dance with Richard.

Neither said a word. No one had to. The family was back home where they belonged, except now they had two packs and Eric had two families that loved him and that he loved back.

Richard returned Pepper to Eric like a proud papa wolf. Eric knew he should allow his brothers a dance. Instead, he only smiled and held her in his arms the rest of the night—his mate, the wolf goddess of his dreams, his lover for all time.

Acknowledgments

Thanks so much to Donna Fournier and Loretta Melvin for all their help with the book! I couldn't do it without you! And thanks to Deb Werksman, the wonderful book artists and their creations, Susie Benton for helping to keep schedules straight, and Amelia Narigon for creating all the PR plans!

About the Author

Bestselling and award-winning author Terry Spear has written over sixty paranormal romance novels and four medieval Highland historical romances. Her first werewolf romance, *Heart of the Wolf*, was named a 2008 *Publishers Weekly* Best Book of the Year, and her subsequent titles have garnered high praise and hit the *USA Today* bestseller list. A retired officer of the U.S. Army Reserves, Terry lives in Crawford, Texas, where she is working on her next werewolf romance, continuing her new series about shapeshifting jaguars, having fun with her young adult novels, and playing with her two Havanese puppies, Max and Tanner. For more information, please visit www.terryspear.com or follow her on Twitter @TerrySpear. She is also on Facebook at www .facebook.com/terry.spear. And on Wordpress at Terry Spear's Shifters: www.terryspear.wordpress.com.

Billionaire in Wolf's Clothing

by Terry Spear

USA Today Bestselling Author

He wants answers...

Real estate mogul werewolf Rafe Denali didn't get where he is in life by being a pushover. When sexy she-wolf Jade Ashton nearly drowns in the surf outside his beach house, he knows better than to bring her into his home and his heart. But there's something about her that brings out his strongest instincts.

Rafe has good reason to be suspicious. Jade Ashton and her baby son are pawns in an evil wolf's fatal plan. How can Jade betray the gorgeous man who rescued her? But if she doesn't, her baby will die, and her own life hangs in the balance.

To get to the truth, Rafe is going to have to gain Jade's trust. If he can do that, he just might be her last—and best—hope...

Praise for Terry Spear:

"Terry Spear has a gift for bringing her *lupus garous* to life and winning the hearts of readers." —*Paranormal Haven*

"Spear has created a fascinating and interesting world that I enjoy visiting every chance I get." —*For the Love of Bookends*

For more Terry Spear, visit:

www.sourcebooks.com